THE
HAUNTING
SEASON

THE
HAUNTING
SEASON

EIGHT GHOSTLY TALES FOR LONG WINTER NIGHTS

Bridget Collins

Natasha Pulley

Kiran Millwood Hargrave

Elizabeth Macneal

Laura Purcell

Andrew Michael Hurley

Jess Kidd

Imogen Hermes Gowar

PEGASUS CRIME

NEW YORK LONDON

THE HAUNTING SEASON

Pegasus Crime is an imprint of
Pegasus Books, Ltd.
148 West 37th Street, 13th Floor
New York, NY 10018

First Pegasus Books cloth edition October 2021

ISBN: 978-1-64313-797-1

10 9 8 7 6 5 4 3 2 1

Printed in the United States of America
Distributed by Simon & Schuster
www.pegasusbooks.com

CONTENTS

A STUDY IN
BLACK AND WHITE

Bridget Collins

Perhaps if Morton had not stopped to mop his brow in that precise spot, he might never have noticed the black-and-white house. As it was, he had just replaced his cap and swung his foot over the crossbar of his bicycle when he caught sight of the wrought-iron gate in the wall, and, beyond, a fleeting impression of light and dark: so brief that he hardly knew what he'd seen, only that it prompted him to manoeuvre sideways, half perched on the saddle, and peer between the metal bars. Through the clouds of his breath he saw a house of a familiar type, ancient and half-timbered, surrounded by a sparse formal garden. It was like a pen-and-ink sketch: the narrow timbers of the house, the wintry drive white with hoar frost, the clipped symmetry of the yews and their long shadows ... But the other, similar, houses he'd seen were ramshackle, their gables leaning sideways or tipped forward, sagging with the weight of centuries; this one was upright, its lines straight and its angles true. And yet it was not, to all appearances, a new house.

Morton regarded it at length. He enjoyed order, rules and discipline; this house, with its refusal to compromise, its apparent mastery over the forces of gravity and time, met with his approval. He stood for a long time, staring through the bars of the gate. It was peculiarly quiet. The place reminded him of something, but it wasn't until he had – at last – wrenched himself away and pedalled a little way down the road that he realised what it was, and only then because in glancing back he saw the house from another direction, where more rows of topiary stood on either side of a wide lawn. These trees were cut into elaborate, familiar shapes: rooks, knights, bishops, king and queen, and in front of them the long ranks of pawns. On a summer day the effect might have been playful; as it was, in the cold stillness, it was sombre, arresting. Morton and his bicycle wobbled, and he fought to regain his balance as he rounded the corner. Yes, that was it. The house had put him in mind of a chess set: a box of pieces, a flat board, the monochrome pattern of frost and shadow. It was a coincidence that he had thought so before he saw the topiary – unless the owner of the house had had the same fancy, and designed the garden accordingly – or, no, Morton thought, he must have caught a subconscious glimpse of the trees through a gap in the wall, and made the association without realising. No doubt that was it.

He bent over his handlebars and pedalled harder, resisting the impulse to turn back. At first he seemed to feel the house recede into the distance, as though every turn of the wheels took an extra effort, but after a few minutes he encountered a most demanding hill and the exertion required drove everything else out of his head. The sun rose higher, flashing into his eyes above the trees. He grew pleasantly warm, and then hungry. His itinerary brought him round in a figure-of-eight, back towards the village where he had planned to stop for lunch at a famous old inn; but the road by which he returned was a different one, and when he finally dismounted at the Swan he was thinking of nothing but a pint of local beer and a plate of rabbit stew or devilled kidneys. He walked into the bar, divested himself of his cap and gloves, and sat down in front of the fire.

It was only then, as he felt a pleasant lassitude creep over him, that the house came back into his mind's eye. He saw again the clipped yews in their ranks, facing one another across the pale lawn, and in his imagination he gave a little push to the queen's pawn, moving it forward. He had a fondness for chess; he had happy memories of triumphs over his cousins and his sister – who had once, in tears, thrown the board across the room, and refused to play ever since. There were few things so satisfying as announcing checkmate, or watching an opponent's resentful finger tip over the king to concede defeat. He still felt the interior glow of his victory in a House match: he'd been playing the captain of the Chess Club, who had given him a limp, hateful handshake before slinking away in humiliation. Morton had enjoyed that.

A woman's voice said, 'What'll you have, sir?'

Morton blinked and ordered a pint of ale and – after some deliberation – a plate of mutton chops. The food, when it came, was surprisingly good, and half an hour later he was still sitting in his armchair, feeling as satiated and content as he had for some time – since, indeed, he had left his previous address somewhat precipitously, after a certain little unpleasantness had come to light. It was fifteen miles or so back to his boarding house in Ipswich, but he sank deeper into his chair and asked for another pint of beer. When the maid put it in front of him, he said, watching the firelight play in the amber liquid, 'Do you happen to know the house just east of here, with the chess pieces of topiary?'

She hesitated. Surprised, he raised his eyes, just in time to catch a flicker of wariness in her expression. She said, 'The black-and-white house, sir?'

'That's the one,' he said. Somehow, although surely that description could be applied to hundreds of houses, he was certain that she knew which one he meant.

'Yes,' she said. There was a silence, and she turned away.

This was impertinence. 'Who owns it?' Morton said, reaching out – not that he would actually take hold of her, naturally, but his outstretched hand was enough to make her flinch and halt mid-step.

'No one local,' she said. 'The old man was the last.'

'But someone must own it, a place like that.' She shrugged. 'Then who lives there?'

'No one, at the moment.' She bent to wipe the table next to him, avoiding his gaze.

An odd spark leapt in Morton's breast. He said, 'It's empty, then?'

She didn't answer, and he took a deep breath, repressing his irritation. They were perhaps unused to educated men in these parts; presumably they catered more for peasants and farmers. He said, more loudly, 'I should very much like to see the garden. To visit, I mean.'

'The gates'll be locked, I expect.'

'Yes, I'm quite aware of that. I simply wondered whether ... oh, never mind.' He threw himself back in his chair and flapped his hand to dismiss her. She left, with neither an apology nor a backward glance.

'It's for rent.'

Morton gave a start. The voice – a wheedling, desiccated one – had come from a dim corner of the room, which until now he had assumed to be empty; but now he saw that there was a figure at a little table there. 'I beg your pardon?' he said, leaning forward.

'The black-and-white house,' the man said, without moving, so his face remained in darkness. Until that moment Morton had not realised that the winter sun no longer reached into the room, and the afternoon was drawing in. 'Forgive me,' he went on, 'but I couldn't help overhearing. It is a handsome property, isn't it?'

'It is certainly very striking,' Morton said.

'If you want to look around, I imagine the agent will be able to show it to you. Letterman, on the Square.' The man gestured; he had a jerky, awkward manner, as though he was held together with string. 'Up by the Guildhall. You had better hurry, he closes early in winter.'

'Yes. Yes, I see.' Morton found himself on his feet, although only a moment ago he had been too full and drowsy to move, and most of his beer still stood in its glass. He was glad of this new information, of course, and eager to make enquiries at the letting office; his haste had nothing to do with the man's glinting eyes, or the way the shadows huddled and plotted on the wall behind him. 'Thank you,' he said.

'Not at all.'

'Good afternoon.' Morton fumbled for his cap and gloves, knocking one to the floor; as he bent to retrieve it he saw that the man was sitting in front of a chessboard. 'Ah,' he said, conscious that his hurry to get away was unseemly, 'a fellow enthusiast.'

'Ye-es,' the man said, and smiled. 'You might say that.'

There was a short silence. Morton might, under other circumstances, have lingered for a while longer to indulge in a little learned chatter regarding, say, the relative merits of king's pawn and queen's pawn openings. Instead he said, 'Well, thank you,' and hurried outside, glad to feel the door shut behind him and cold air on his face.

The letting agent – a little man with spectacles and a threadbare collar – couldn't conceal his surprise at Morton's query, but after the first widening of his eyes he said, 'Yes, yes, indeed, yes,' and produced a key with great enthusiasm. 'The black-and-white house,' he said, 'my goodness, yes. A very reasonable rent. Very reasonable. Have you looked at other properties in the area?'

Morton explained that he had taken a room in a lodging-house in Ipswich, and that until that day he had not wanted – it had not even occurred to him – to rent a house. He expected further questions, since after all it was hardly a rational position, but after a single twitch of his eyebrows the agent said, 'Ah, yes, yes, indeed,' and reached for his hat. 'I expect you want to view it.'

It was closer than Morton had realised, just on the out-skirts of the village, but by the time the agent unlocked the gate the sun had sunk below the trees and the garden was in shadow. In the gathering twilight the topiary seemed massive and solid, like black stone. He paused, turning slowly to look at the ranks on either side of him. Black against black, he thought, and the back of his neck prickled. 'Mr Morton?' the agent said, from the doorway. 'Shall we?'

Morton shook himself. 'Excuse me,' he said, and hurried forward to lean his bicycle against the wall.

'As you see, it's fully furnished,' the agent said. 'I under-stand the current owner takes no interest, so the house is exactly as it was when the old man— yes, well. A little old-fashioned, perhaps, but you could move in immediately. This evening, if you wanted!' He gave a little braying laugh. 'This way, please . . .'

It was dark inside; the ceilings were low and the furni-ture – which was more than a little old-fashioned – took up so much space that Morton had to weave his way around it as he followed the agent. The rooms were long, with wide mullioned windows that glowed bluish in the dusk. They went through into a narrow passage, and then up the stairs; the agent said, 'Here are the bedrooms,' but now he was moving quickly, not giving Morton time to look properly.

'It's getting late,' he said, 'and it's rather gloomy in here. I don't want to rush you, but ...'

'Is there gas?'

'No – lamps, still, I'm afraid. Or candles, of course. But it would spoil the charm to have gas, don't you think?' His tone belied the words; he turned, manoeuvred past Morton and went briskly down the stairs. 'Have you seen enough?'

Morton hesitated, staring through the open door into the bedroom, where there was a bed with hangings, a looking-glass, a table with twisted barley-sugar legs, a candelabra with wax-shrouded, half-burnt candles. But his attention was caught by the view outside, the massed rows of chess pieces waiting on the lawn. It was hard to wrench his gaze away. 'Yes,' he said. 'Quite enough.'

'Oh. Well, then, shall we ... ?' The agent gestured, with a limp arm. 'It wouldn't suit everyone. I can see that. These historic places can be oppressive in the winter.'

'I'll take it.'

'And of course—' He stopped. 'Pardon me?'

'I'll take it,' Morton repeated. Why were the local people so slow to understand the simplest utterance? 'I shall have my things brought over tomorrow. Should we go back to your office? I suppose there's something I should sign.'

'Oh – no, no, plenty of time, whenever you've settled in,' the agent said, stammering. 'That's – well – I'm pleased it suits. We'll sort out the details of the lease at your convenience.'

Morton nodded. There was a brief silence; then, with a

faint incredulity, he realised that the agent was waiting for him, so that they could leave together. 'I'll stay here,' he said. 'It's late to cycle back to my lodgings. I imagine I can dine at the Swan?'

'Certainly, but—'

'You did say I might move in this evening, if I chose.'

'I did, yes.' The agent cleared his throat. 'It's up to you, naturally. If you're anxious to take possession.' He held out the key. 'Tomorrow morning, then. You know where to find me. And . . .' He shifted from foot to foot; then he added, 'If you change your mind overnight – we'll say no more about it.'

'I'm sure I'll manage,' Morton said. 'I can get a good fire going in the parlour.'

'Yes. Well, goodnight, then.' The agent gave him a nod and disappeared. Morton heard his footsteps accelerate along the passage, and the heavy closing of the front door. He waited until he thought the agent would have had time to make his way along the drive and out into the road. Then he heaved a deep, gratified breath, and strode along the passage, feeling the thrill of possession. How unexpected, how miraculous! He could almost laugh at the memory – had it only been this morning? – of seeing the house from the road; now it was his, to explore, to conquer . . .

In the last few moments night had nearly fallen, so he picked up the candelabra from the table in the bedroom and lit the candles. Then he lifted the candelabra and went from room to room, skirting around clawed-foot chairs and dusty hangings to pick books from shelves, and open cabinets and drawers. The agent had called the house 'furnished', but it was more than that; it gave the impression of having been left untouched, of being abandoned between one chime of the clock and the next. Only one room was in perfect order: a child's bedroom, at the back of the house, with a neat shelf of toys, a miniature cricket bat propped in a corner and, in the window seat, a child-sized chessboard and a pile of books. Morton paused in the doorway; then he shut the door with more force than he needed, and moved on.

In every other room there were traces of the old man: nothing so obvious as food left uneaten, or a half-smoked pipe left on a side-table – but the candles, the soap left on the washstand, the towel hung upon a rail . . . He found a copy of the *Chess Player's Chronicle* in the parlour, splayed across the arm of the couch, as though the reader had wanted to mark his place. In front of it – in the corner of the room, where the shadows gathered – was a chess set, arranged for the beginning of a game. It was made of stone – or was it jet and ivory? Morton picked up a pawn, feeling the oil-smooth weight of it, and then replaced it neatly in front of the queen. Later, perhaps, he would find a chess problem in the *Chronicle* and study it until he was sleepy enough to retire to bed; he always found them easier when he could contemplate the pieces on a real board. He straightened the pawn with the tip of his finger, ensuring that it was exactly in the middle of its square, and then turned away. As he left the room he had the sudden, irrational sense that he had forgotten something – or made some mistake, like leaving a glass where a careless sleeve would almost certainly catch it, or a window unlatched before a storm. But it was only when he was in the kitchen, taking stock of the dried goods that still remained in the cupboards, that he realised, with a wry smile at his own whimsy: he should, like any polite player, have murmured *J'adoube.*[*]

It was freezing. The first thing to do was to dull the biting edge of the cold; and as he stared at the enormous unlit range, Morton had to concede that it was not, in fact, the most convenient place to stay the night. But he seemed to remember that on the way here the agent had mentioned a charwoman – no doubt that accounted for the absence of dust and cobwebs – and tomorrow he could make proper arrangements for her to look after him; in the meantime there was something rather exciting about being here alone, searching in the cupboards for everything he needed. Once, as a child – after some misdemeanour or other – he had hidden for hours, listening with growing pleasure to his mother's voice as she grew worried and then, finally, afraid. He had let her call for a long time before he finally emerged, savouring his power. He didn't know why that came into his head now, but he felt a sort of dry, uncharacteristic grin on his face as he rummaged for old newspapers and kindling, and then knelt to build a fire in the great drawing-room hearth. Once he had got the fire going, he sat back on his knees and drew a deep

---

[*]   In chess, there is a rule that if you touch a piece you must make a move with it, unless you say 'J'adoube' (literally 'I adjust') first.

satisfied breath. He had meant to go to the inn for dinner, but he wasn't hungry, and now that the fire was lit he had no inclination to venture out into the bitter night. He stood up, brushed ash from the knees of his trousers, and crossed to the window to draw the curtains. As he drew them across he paused, struck by the sight of the garden. The moon had risen, tinting the lawn silver, the trees and their shadows a dense black; under its wintry glare the whole world was transformed into pearl and ebony. It was otherworldly, alien, and Morton thought he had never seen anything so lovely.

But he was not the sort of man to be seduced by anything so intangible as beauty. He closed the curtains with such a decisive jerk that a cloud of dust made him cough, and turned back into the room. His eye was caught by a decanter of brandy on the sideboard. He sniffed at it – first gingerly, and then exultantly – and poured a generous measure into one of the glasses that sat beside it. Then he settled beside the hearth, leant back on the couch and presented the soles of his shoes to the fire. He congratulated himself: a house like this, for a minimal rent . . . The brandy was excellent, the fire was taking the chill out of the air and after the morning's exercise and the afternoon's unexpected events he felt almost light-headed. He could feel the heat lapping around his ankles, spreading out into the rest of the room; the crackles of the flames were accompanied by the roar of air in the chimney and the groans of old walls settling. The joists overhead murmured a little as the warm air reached them. As Morton's eyes began to close he heard a long chain of thuds along the floor, approaching him, and he jolted upright, his heart in his mouth, half expecting to see someone there. His eyes took a moment to focus, and for an instant he thought he saw a dark blur pass and dissolve into nothing before he could blink. His heart skipped a beat. But of course there was no one. It must have been the wood shifting in the joints between the boards; he'd heard other old houses make noises that were uncannily like voices or footsteps. He relaxed, tried to chuckle, and let his head fall back against the corner of the couch. At the same time the leather armchair opposite him, across from the chessboard, gave a little sigh, as though someone had settled into it.

It was easily explained – even more easily than the floor-boards: the air inside the cushion must have expanded and contracted, according to some eddy of fire-warmed air. But he couldn't help staring at the chair with narrowed eyes and a foolishly hammering heart. Nothing moved. The leather held the shape of a body – a man, he thought, bony and narrow-hipped, with the habit of leaning his elbows on the padded arms – and for a fraction of a second Morton almost saw him there, among the dipping fire-shadows. He blinked the image away and took another sip of brandy. The fierce sweetness of it calmed the shiver at the back of his neck. He took a bigger mouthful for luck, and shifted his buttocks, trying to find the comfort of a few moments ago. His gaze drifted to the chessboard.

The white pawn was out of place.

Morton froze. Instead of waiting neatly in line, the pawn had advanced, and was standing clear of the others: the queen's pawn opening. It was impossible. He had replaced it – hadn't he said to himself, *J'adoube?*

But – no. He must have moved it. He had picked it up to feel the weight of it, and put it down again. He must have mis-remembered its position, that was all. It was the most natural thing in the world, to set that pawn down in a new position – to begin a game, automatically – so automatically it had hardly registered – and then forget – so that now, absurdly, staring down at it, he felt stuck, short of breath . . . He reached out, but his hand stopped above the board as though he had encountered a pane of glass. He didn't want to touch it. He remembered the heft of it in his palm, and the faint greasiness that had made him wonder if it was ivory, not stone.

He drew back. Some instinct made him raise his eyes again to the armchair in the shadows: but it was empty, and the contours of the leather were impersonal, after all, just the shape of an old chair, imprinted by years of use. The electricity that had tingled in Morton's spine died, leaving only weariness. This was the effect of exertion and excite-ment and – he glanced at his glass, noting that he had drunk nearly all of his brandy – intemperance. He swallowed the last drops and set the goblet down beside the chessboard. It was time for bed.

He slept uneasily. The bedroom was icy, and he had been too squeamish to crawl under the blankets, choosing instead to lie fully dressed on the eiderdown and cover himself with his overcoat; so perhaps it was unsurprising that in his dreams he was back in his dormitory at boarding school, part-remembering, part-reinventing the endless mischiefs and tricks that he had inflicted on other boys. When he awoke – as soon as he understood where he was, for the vivid aftermath of his dream hung like fog in front of his eyes for a few moments – he thought of coffee, hot shaving-water, and the merry fire in the breakfast-room of his lodging-house. He cursed. What had possessed him to stay here – worse, to have agreed to rent the place? He swung himself stiffly off the bed and hobbled into the passage and down the stairs, groaning aloud.

But when he passed the window at the head of the stair-case his spirits lifted. The day was as clear as a diamond; the garden was silvery green in the dawn, the topiary a miracle of symmetry. It would, after all, take very little to make this place habitable. Good fires, clean sheets, a delivery of groceries and the services of some respectable biddy, and then he would be – Morton smiled – the master of all he surveyed ... He hurried down the stairs and out into the bright, bracing air; a minute later he was sailing down the drive on his bicycle, in and out of the shadows of the trees, and then out onto the road that led to the village.

And he had a most satisfactory morning. If the agent was taken aback that Morton was still as eager as ever to rent the black-and-white house, he concealed it admirably, and dealt so briskly with the papers that Morton left his office within a quarter of an hour. He even gave Morton the address of the charwoman who was in the habit of dusting the rooms every week or so; and she, with the glint of avarice in her eyes, agreed to provide food for Morton to heat up, and to manage his washing and ironing and any other domestic details that might prove necessary. Morton left her cottage and rode along the High Street with a light heart, whistling. He had only foreseen a temporary sojourn here – a few months at most, until that unfortunate entanglement at home had blown over – but he might stay here longer, even permanently . . . He stopped at the post office, to send instructions to his lodging-house to have his things delivered; then he went to break his fast at the inn. This time he sat deliberately on the other side of the room, feeling a mysterious reluctance to encounter the gentleman who had spoken to him previously; but, it being market day, the room was packed with farmers and traders, and when the crowds parted enough for Morton to glimpse the shadowy corner opposite he saw that it was empty, and even the chair and chessboard had been removed, presumably to allow a greater crush of people.

He took a long detour on his journey back to the house, enjoying the exercise and the clean breeze in his face, and arrived back to find that, as agreed, the charwoman's son had left a meat pie and a pot of some sweetish-smelling pudding on the doorstep. Morton put them in the kitchen and – after a long battle – lit the range, hissing with triumph when the sooty old beast finally bent to his will. A little while later he had hot water. He performed his overdue ablutions as best he could – although he used a half-petrified bar of old soap, he stopped short at using another man's razor – and then, with a pleasing sense that he had done all his chores, he took himself into the library, lit another fire there and began to peruse the bookshelves. Clearly the previous inhabitant had not been much of a reader, for Morton took down book after book – all handsome editions of the classics – only to discover that their pages were uncut. He put them back and moved on, until he came across a little cloth-bound volume on local history, more a pamphlet than a book. He flipped through the pages, which were dotted with neat line-sketches of notable buildings: the Guildhall, the church, and – aha! – the black-and-white house itself.

> Built in the late seventeenth century by Sir Jeremiah Hope, of whom we know little except that he was known by his neighbours, in a play on his surname, as 'Abandon' ... More recently, the house has become notable for its formal garden and elaborate topiary, created by the current inhabitant, Mr E. E. Hope, M.A. (Cantab.) in memory of his son, who inherited his father's passion for chess, becoming a prodigy before his tragic death at the tender age of ...

Morton yawned and flicked forward, but there was very little more on the house, and nothing of interest. He settled himself on a chaise longue and let the book slide to the floor. After his broken night, his bicycle ride, and the day's achievements, he was drowsy; he slept, and dozed, and slept again. Finally he surfaced, with a clear head and an appetite for dinner. As he got up, his mind running ahead to the meat pie, he hardly noticed the pamphlet underfoot; going out into the passage he shut the library door, and forgot it entirely.

After dinner – which was substantial if not especially enjoyable – he retired to the parlour. He cleaned out the grate, clumsily, getting ash on his trousers, and resolved to tell the charwoman, when she came, to make up every fire in the house; then he poured himself another brandy, lit the candles against the gathering dusk and sat down in the place he'd sat the evening before. It was then that he remembered the little book, and wondered whether he could be bothered to brave the draughty passage to go and get it; but no, there was the *Chess Player's Chronicle*, and the board set ready. Perhaps, if he was going to stay here for a long time, he should prepare a programme of reading or correspondence to while away the solitary hours. In the meantime, there would be several meaty problems in the *Chronicle* to pass the time until he felt tired enough for bed. He took up the journal. By chance it fell open on a page of problems, with their neat little hieroglyphs and chequered tiles. *By R. B. Wormald, B.A., London. White to play and mate in three moves.* At first glance he could see a promising first attack – the bishop to take the rook – but there was a tempting pawn on the last rank of the board, which would take only one move to transform into a queen. He pulled the chessboard towards him, to set it out. His heart stuttered.

Another piece had been moved.

Morton noted, automatically, that it was the Dutch Defence: the bishop's pawn had advanced two squares, unbalancing the board, an aggressive but dangerous move, weakening the king ... But that was by-the-by. There was no possibility that he had moved the black pawn himself. Last night he could blame forgetfulness or even drunkenness; but now he was sure – icily, sickly sure – that he had not touched the black piece. And yet it was there. The two pawns faced each other across the ranks. A riposte. As though an unseen opponent had—

He raised his eyes to the chair. His neck and head muscles were rigid, as if he were bracing himself for a shock: but the chair was empty. Of course the chair was empty. There was only the old leather, with its cracks and valleys, the memory of limbs and fingers. Absence. He stared at it, reluctant to blink. The firelight flickered and played, and the shadows slid over the walls; the wood gleamed, smooth as water, dustless ...

Morton exhaled, sharply. The charwoman must have been here. It must have been she who moved the black piece – or her son, perhaps, when he came to drop off the food. Yes, more likely to be the son – the charwoman was old and igno-rant, hardly the type to play chess – but whichever of them it was, it was a cheek, a damned cheek, Morton thought. He wondered fleetingly if the woman might have knocked the pawn with a duster. But the move was considered – a true reply to his opening – and it could hardly be a coincidence. It was definitely intentional, and definitely the son. He must have some rudiments of education. Morton clenched his jaw. He didn't believe for a second that the boy wanted an honest game of chess; boys were nasty little beasts. No, it was to get a rise out of him. How dare he? Morton remembered a similar campaign at school, which had been successful – too successful. Well, he was not going to fall for it.

He considered the chessboard for another moment. Then, with a quick gesture, he pushed his king's pawn forward to the square beside its fellow. The Staunton gambit: offering a pawn as sacrifice, in order to launch an attack on the black king. That would show the little bastard that he wasn't scared. He sat back, rubbing his hands on his thighs, imagining the look of disappointment on the little boy's face when he realised that Morton had called his bluff.

But that flash of satisfaction died almost as soon as Morton felt it, and a few seconds later he got up and paced, first to the sideboard and then to the window. He pulled the curtain aside, but the garden was in darkness – clouds blotted out the moon and stars – and he saw nothing more than indistinct patches of deeper black where the trees stood against an obscure sky. Moving his own pawn would only encourage the child, the last thing he wanted to do. He tapped his fingernails against the glass, considering, but the noise rang out oddly in the quiet room and after a moment he dropped his hand. The most dignified course of action would be to set the pieces back in their places. Or – better still – to put them away, out of sight. The boy could hardly ask what had happened to them, could he? And Morton's own appetite for chess problems had lost its keenness; indeed, the presence of the board behind him made his vertebrae tingle, like a hostile gaze. He swung round to look at it. It was absurd, but he wished, heartily wished, that he had not played that counter-move.

The candles were burning low. Now the shortest one flared, licking thirstily upwards. As Morton watched, the shadows in the corner leant forward, avid; then the candle flame shrank to a tiny bubble of blue, and vanished. For a second – while his eyes adjusted – the stains on the chair seemed to grow solid, like a vessel filling with smoke, so that a casual glance might have given the impression that there was someone there. Something in Morton's insides tightened, and with a sudden resolve he strode across to the chessboard, reached for the box and threw the pieces into it higgledy-piggledy. There were two compartments for black and white, but he ignored them; he pushed and pushed at the lid until at last something gave – was it the head of a bishop, snapping off? – and it slid shut. The sound echoed off the walls. He had never stopped halfway through a game before, never begged for quarter, never admitted weakness. He felt it now, even though he was alone: a curious mixture of shame and defiance and, underneath, a creeping unease. Another candle dipped, threatening to gutter. He flinched. Somehow the thought of being left here, alone with the leaping firelight, was unbearable. He grabbed convulsively at the stem of the candelabra and went out into the passage; and although the skin between his shoulder blades crawled, he didn't allow himself to glance back.

৵

It took a very long time for Morton to fall asleep. He despised those who dwelt unnecessarily on the past, but for some reason he found memories of his school days running through his mind's eye, over and over. He could see the boy who had been so terrorised by their jokes – Simms Minor, was it, or Simmons? – and his wide eyes, the night he had asked Morton for help . . . He had been a weakling, anyway. He should have dealt with their treatment of him as Morton had dealt with the chess set: sweeping it away, disdainfully. That was the manly thing to do. And the accident— well, that was hardly Morton's fault. But nonetheless Morton felt sticky and uncomfortable, and tossed and turned on the eiderdown, wrapping himself more tightly in his overcoat.

But he must have dozed, because he awoke. There was a peculiar stillness in the air – the same stillness he had remarked when he first saw the house through the gate, as though the world itself was listening. He had the impression that some particular sound, now extinguished, had woken him: that, or a movement inside the room, like a person coming within a few feet of his bed. It was not the latter, since when he sat up he was clearly alone. Clearly, because the moon had come out from behind the clouds, and was shining in through the window-panes in squares of black and white.

He pulled his coat closer about his shoulders and swung his legs over the side of the bed. The floor was icy under his bare feet, but he got up and padded silently to the window. He stood there, waiting for the sound to repeat itself. He heard nothing, not even the call of an owl or the rattle of a draught hissing through the gaps in the window frame. Could it have been the very depth of silence that jerked him out of sleep? But no, he was sure – almost sure – that he had heard something. He tried to describe it to himself: a low grinding, a deep resonant creak, halfway between wood and stone. He stared down at the trees, feeling a kind of vertigo that was not quite fear. The unearthly light – the dark shapes against the moon-drenched sky – the clarity of outline, the density of the shadows . . . He felt the space contract, so that for a sickly second the chess pieces were both huge and small enough to fit in his hand. He shut his eyes, but it made him dizzy and he hastily opened them again. The shadows flickered against the pale glare of the moon, seeming to shift.

He clutched at the window frame. He'd thought – only for an instant, he'd seen— No. No, nothing had changed, nothing had moved. It should have been reassuring to see all the trees lined up, orderly, exactly as they should have been: but the pressure built in his ears, humming. If he saw one of the trees move forward – the pawn, say, advancing across the silver expanse of grass – then he would know he was hallucinating, he would almost be relieved. But this sense of waiting – and that weight in the air, the immobile trees, the game set out – it was unbearable, terrifying, somehow worse; and he couldn't move, he couldn't turn away.

He didn't know how long he stood there, gazing at the pieces, waiting for something that never came. At last he became conscious that the moon had dipped behind the house, a soft breeze was murmuring in the chimney and his feet were numb with cold. He hobbled back to bed; and, unexpectedly, he dropped swiftly into sleep, exhausted as though from some great struggle.

He was roused by knocking. He rolled blearily down the staircase and along the passage, rubbing his eyes, and wrenched open the front door. A small boy was standing there, with a pudding basin and a parcel in brown paper. He thrust them towards Morton.

'. . . Empties,' he mumbled.

'What?'

'My ma said to collect the empties.'

'You can have them tomorrow,' Morton said, and started to shut the door.

'You'll be snowed in tomorrow.'

Morton paused. In his half-asleep hurry to answer the door he had hardly noticed, but it was true that there was a new rawness to the wind, and the low clouds were flat and featureless. 'All right,' he said. 'Wait here.' A few moments later he returned with the empty pot and pie-dish and held them out. The boy was shifting from foot to foot as though he needed the lavatory; he grabbed at the dirty crockery, shoved it into a knapsack and turned to leave without another word. His haste – although not quite insolent – flicked Morton on the raw: he was paying the child's mother's wages, wasn't he?

'I say,' Morton said, 'not so fast. You've been messing about in the parlour, haven't you? Well, you can jolly well stop it.'

The boy stared at him. 'En't been inside,' he said, after a pause.

'Your mother, then. I'm not an idiot.' Morton glared at him, but the boy held his gaze, his expression blank. 'Tell her not to fiddle with anything. As she did yesterday. Just tell her to keep her hands off things, all right?'

'She en't been in yesterday, either,' the boy said. 'She only cleans on Sundays. Sundays there's nothing walking.'

'What?' But the boy didn't answer. He hunched his shoulders and let them drop again. Morton took a deep breath. 'The gardener, then. There is a gardener, isn't there?'

'He en't got a key to the house. Only does the trees.'

'Well – whoever it is,' Morton said, 'if I catch them at it . . .'

The boy went on staring at him, chewing his lip. Finally – as if Morton had missed some opportunity – he turned away. He walked down the drive with his eyes on the ground, and when he had cleared the last rank of trees he broke into a run.

Morton watched the boy until he had slammed the gate shut and disappeared along the road. Then he turned back into the house, shivering. Now he had time to notice, he could smell the metallic tang of snow. Perhaps, after all, it was foolishness to stay here; perhaps a room at the Swan might be more cheerful . . . But that would mean admitting defeat. He went into the parlour, slapping his arms against his body to warm himself, and knelt to see to the fire. His hands were stiff and his head was aching. He fumbled for a long time with matches and sheets of newspaper before the fire eventually took hold. Then he collapsed onto the sofa. He might be coming down with something; he was neither hungry nor thirsty, although when he consulted his watch he discovered that he had slept very late, and it was well past noon.

A single flake of snow drifted past the window, pale against the grey sky. He blinked, wondering whether it had been a trick of his eyes, but then there was another and another, until a whirling veil blotted out the low clouds. Slowly Morton relaxed. It was comforting to be inside, beside the crackling fire, while the noiseless storm swirled around the house. He sank into a kind of trance, watching the white dance of the blizzard, the almost-shapes that blew and billowed against the window-panes. This time – perhaps it was because it was colder outside than before – the groans and murmurs as the warmth spread through the room were louder and more distinct: the creaking of hinges, the pattern of knocking in the floorboards that sounded so like footsteps, the sigh of the chair ... He turned his head, reflexively, although he knew that there would be no one there.

The chess set was on the table.

The blood roared in his ears. He took in a trembling breath. Surely he was seeing things: but no, it was there, perfectly solid, one bishop splintered at the neck where he had pushed it too roughly into the box. Four pawns were out of place, two white, two black. Someone had set it out, painstakingly, and played another move. Someone who had been in the house; someone who was not the charwoman, or the gardener, or the boy.

And it had not been there when Morton knelt to make up the fire.

He sat very still. He would have liked to cry out, or run from the room, but he could do neither. For a long, horrible moment he thought he might never move again. Then, at last, a wave of anger came over him, strong enough to drive away the terror that had paralysed him. He pushed himself forward and with shaking hands swept the set into its box, ducking for a pawn that rolled to the floor. Then he shuffled to the fire on his knees, and dumped the box and its contents into the flames. The fire sank under the new weight, and, horrified, he reached for the poker; but then it flared, leaping around the box, catching at the corners and gulping at the pieces that jutted from the top. Dark crowns and towers and horse-heads were silhouetted against the red-gold dazzle. Then they were gone, enveloped in flames, and the room was full of jumping firelight. Morton felt triumph flood through him. He sat back, breathing hard. Then he glanced into the corner and the air caught in his throat.

There was a man in the chair.

A malevolent, eager, hungry old man, made of shadows and hollows: there and not there, withered and thread-thin but dreadful, a man whose only wish was to *win* . . .

How Morton got to his feet he didn't know; how he staggered to the door and into the passage, how he made his way blindly to the door and out . . . He never knew how he stumbled out into the snow, or whether he cried for help, or whether that terrible shadow-man followed him; all he felt was the consciousness of his own powerlessness, and an appalling, desperate panic. He had no time to wonder who the man was, or to care. All he knew was the awful burden of his mistakes, and the impossibility, now, of ever righting them.

§

It caused little surprise that Morton did not stay in the black-and-white house; no one ever did. Since the old man died there only a few strangers had remained more than a few hours under that roof, and all of them had left without notice and never returned. It was generally assumed that Morton, like the others, had found the atmosphere unwelcoming, and had packed his things and made his way back to wherever he came from; and the local people, who were pleased not to concern themselves with the house, were equally pleased not to concern themselves with Morton. If it had not been for the snow, no one, not even the agent, would have given him a second thought. As it was, only Robbie, the charwoman's boy, questioned what had become of him; and he told such an outlandish story that his mother instructed him sternly to hold his tongue.

It seemed that, the next morning, when the storm had blown over and the sun had risen, little Robbie had ventured out to play. The world was glittering white, the sky blue and gold with winter sunshine, and he had wandered a long way, throwing desultory snowballs and wading through drifts. When he finally turned for home his path brought him past the back gate of the black-and-white house. He paused, shivering, to look through the bars, and saw ... something. In the end his curiosity overtook his habitual wariness of the place, and he crept forward into the dazzling space to look more closely.

What he saw was the footprints of a man, emerging from the front door: blurred by the wind and more snow, but still unmistakable. He had walked – run, perhaps – in a straight line for a little while, until he was between the ranks of trees, and then ... Then, Robbie said, the tracks changed. They were jagged, zig-zagging, in broken lines, as though he had gone hither and thither like a man in a maze, and now and then he had fallen and struggled again to his feet. If he had been running from something, it had left no trace in the white snow. But the strangest thing, Robbie said, was that the tracks ended so abruptly, at the foot of one of the taller trees; as though Morton had disappeared entirely, taken by the black king.

THWAITE'S TENANT

Imogen Hermes Gowar

We arrived in the driving rain, a real rage of a storm that scared the horses. The night was black, and as water sluiced across the windows of the carriage I thought, *the flood has come to sweep us all away,* and pressed little Stanley closer to my bosom, but he was fast asleep and never noticed. *It's a judgement on me,* I thought, but did not cry because if my father noticed at all, he would only remark, 'Feeling sorry for yourself?'

We had made swift progress at first but as the rain went on the carriage slowed, lurching and slithering. With increasing regularity, my father put his head out of the window to talk to the driver, and pulled it back in with rainwater streaming over his nose and beard. The driver cursed the horses in one breath and cooed to them in the next, and I became afraid as the carriage swayed and the beasts jostled, Stanley's head rolling against my shoulder. At last we stopped where the road diverged, and did not move again.

'All well?' my father called, and the driver made a noise I didn't catch. 'Confound it,' said my father, and jumped down, the mud gulping around his boots. Water swished beneath the wheels of the carriage, road gone to river, and I sat alone but for my little boy, cradling his cheek in my hand.

When my father came back, he said, 'It's no good. We must walk from here.'

'What? How far?'

He consulted with the driver. 'Two miles. A little more.'

'We are a woman and a child,' I cried. 'Surely we cannot be expected to—'

'Idiot! The horses will slip if we go on; the carriage will overturn. I suppose you prefer to be in danger than discomfort.'

If that were so, I might have said, *I'd still be at home.* But I held my tongue, and turned my attention instead to rousing Stanley, who burrowed his face further into my cloak and knitted his fingers through mine. 'We have to walk,' I said. 'Can you do that?'

'Mama, no!'

'I'll carry him,' my father said. 'You take your overnight bag. The trunk will have to stay.' It was lashed to the roof of the carriage and I wrung my hands to think of it all – my dresses, my pins, my handkerchiefs, Stanley's toys and books – slithering from side to side, rainwater seeping through the corners and the seams of the trunk, dirtying everything that was good and pleasant.

I wrenched Stanley from my lap and set him in my father's arms: he cried out in fear, the little thing, but I could find no words to comfort him. There was no hand to help me down from the carriage, and I leapt as if into a void, stumbling as I landed in the road. It seemed to me that I was drenched almost immediately, but as the carriage faded into the rain and we set out along the diverging road – narrow, unpaved, uphill – I learned how wet a person really can become. The water swilled under my bonnet and through my hair; it ran between my shoulder blades and pooled among the bones of my corset, where air bubbles moved fleshily across my body. My skirts dragged about my legs and every step was one of anxiety, for I could not be certain that the ground would hold beneath my feet; the water rushed through my boots and I thought, *well, everything is ruined.*

Blind, deaf, mute, I followed my father's dark form as he stumbled ahead trailing Stanley's little limbs. I did weep then, not for myself but for my little boy, who had asked for none of this, who had been happy where he was, with his toys and his favourite climbing tree, his dog Dash and his nurse and even – God forgive me! – his Papa. What right had I to drag him here, when he had no part in our quarrel? Was I as selfish as my father said?

I was shivering by the time we came to the house. There was a narrow drive between high walls, and then stone steps all of different heights, so that each one confounded me, and I slipped and staggered. My father had pulled his oilskin cape around Stanley but I saw those tiny pale hands clasped about his neck, the fair head lolling on his shoulder. *Oh, what have I done?*

The old Thwaite house had acquired some notoriety between me and my sister. We had never visited the place but our father had, rather more often than we thought necessary. Sometimes he did not go for a year or more but whenever he mentioned he was engaged 'out Skipton way' or 'attending to business in Bradford', Mariana and I shared a glance, for in that direction we knew the Thwaite house also lay. He had been a handsome man in his youth – he still was – and it seemed obvious what he must do here. I had supposed it a tawdry, opulent place with dense carpets and thick curtains; cabinets full of exotic spirits; rustling gowns barely-worn, and so you may forgive me the flicker of curiosity I felt when my father unlocked the door.

It was nothing like I had imagined. A single candle burned in the narrow entry-hall whose grey-distempered walls smelt sour as if they had not been much lived in; off that was a dark parlour, sparsely furnished in an ugly, old-fashioned manner. Surely no paramour would be pleased to be brought *here*. My father laid Stanley down on the couch while I stood in the hall, dismayed. Water dripped from my bonnet, my nose, my wrists. I took off my cloak and draped it over a blackened old chair, carved in that crooked, unlovely style of two hundred years back.

'Well then, miss,' said my father. He said *miss* in a stiff, peremptory way as if I were a stranger he'd found in his favourite train compartment. 'I'll leave you be.'

'Don't go out in that weather,' I pleaded. I was deathly afraid at the prospect of being alone with Stanley in so inhospitable a place. 'Stay. Please. There must be room for you.'

'I'll rejoin the carriage at the inn, if it got that far. If not, my help will be needed.' He sighed, and the sigh said: of course *you* may rest now, Lucinda. Of course *your* day is done.

'Oh, Pa,' I said. I looked about at the stone floors, the hallway so dour and empty with no flowers put out to welcome me. There was a foxed print of 'The Raft of the Medusa' in a black frame, and that was all. 'You'd really leave us here? All alone?'

He said nothing.

'Pa,' I repeated, dissolving into tears. He never could bear to see me cry, and I knew no other way to move him. Helpless appeal was my only rhetoric. 'Can't you help me?'

'My girl,' he said, 'this *is* the help.'

৯

Stanley was shivering when I fetched him from the couch, and his hair was slick to his head, sending up a pathetic animal-cub smell that reminded me of his babyhood. He stood quite mute, with no curiosity to explore the rooms as he had at the pretty hotel in Scarborough where I first took him, calling it a holiday, or Mariana's house where we fled when my money was exhausted. I had supposed that exuberance was his natural state, that I could take him anywhere and he would be happy enough, but now all the jollity was gone from him. We ventured upstairs, and found two bedrooms. One was large but queer, with dark panelling and I thought at first no window at all, until I ascertained that a once-sizeable casement was now all but boarded up excepting a narrow chink at the very top. The other, at the head of the stairs, was smaller and more welcoming.

'This will be your room,' I said. He put his thumb in his mouth.

The water in the basin struck me cold to the bone, but there was nothing for it. I stripped Stanley and he shivered and whimpered as I sponged him down, crossing his arms over his little white chest.

'No, Mama,' he cried, batting me away, but I persisted – too roughly, perhaps, just to have it over with – and he shoved me, hard. 'No!'

'How dare you?' I cried. My eyes smarted, and so did the places on my shoulders where his palms had pressed.

'I want to go home!' His voice cracked. I could scarcely bear it. 'Why are we here?'

I seized his shoulder but he shrieked and twisted away from me. 'Behave yourself!' I said, but he screamed again, his little feet pattering on the floorboards, and stood half-crouched, with his arms and legs spread wide, glowering at me in furious defiance like a little naked white savage. Not for the first time since he was born, I asked myself *what have I bred? How has all this come about?* At least I had thought to pack his warm flannel nightgown, and it was not so damp as all that, but when I held it out to him he would not wear it, and I pursued him around the room until he screeched in pure sharp-toothed temper, and the candle went out. 'Well, then, you will sleep as you are,' I cried, and slammed the door closed. It had a bolt on the outside; I pushed it swiftly to. His fists hammered, and I stood on the landing listening to his rage turn to fear.

'Mama!' he cried, then 'Mama!' quaveringly. I could have softened, but he roared again in fury, and I walked away.

Downstairs I struggled from my dress and petticoats which collapsed into so many swampy puddles on the parlour floor: my corset I removed with care, since I had no other besides what was in my trunk, and therefore perhaps lost forever. I laid it out on the couch but underneath it my shift was soaked too. My shoes were clotted with mud, which I had tracked up and down the stairs; my skirt had bled dye into my stockings. I crouched at the hearth quaking with cold; my jaw clattered in my skull and my hands fumbled over the matches.

'Come on,' I muttered to the sparks that faded on the damp kindling, 'come on, come on,' but it was too long since the fire was last lit, and what flames I coaxed up were faint sickly things that curled and smoked and expired. I swore.

In the dark I pulled my knees to my chest. My body was unpleasing without its corset: this part too bony, that part too yielding, slack cold breasts that hung too low on my chest, their moist undersides clinging to my skin. The cold rattled through my body and the hairs stood up on my calves: I glared about the room and wondered if this was the beginning of madness or if in fact it had been encroaching for some time. Not so long ago I was an ornament to my husband's house. Not showy, no, but *polished*, and I had considered that polish an innate personal quality of mine, just as happiness was Stanley's. And yet in mere weeks I had been reduced to a gaunt, weathered itinerant! Handsome Lucinda Lisle, penniless and friendless, cursing alone in a faded little room while her son wept above.

I seized a rug from the back of a chair and tossed it about my shoulders, waiting for warmth to kindle. In my head I began to compose a letter to my sister Mariana, but every time I thought of her I saw her face as it was when I told her I had abandoned my marriage. First she looked alarmed, then suspicious – then, all of a sudden, quite blank, as if she had locked a door against me. *Why did you turn me out?* I wanted to write. *How, when you knew what I had endured?*

Thud, thud, thud.

I froze. The noise came again. *Thud thud thud.* Footsteps, upstairs! Heavy ones, a man's, crossing the landing.

Even as I knew it was not possible, I thought, *Lisle has found us. He has come here!*

Then, *thud thud thud.* I was on my feet. Oh, dear God, if it was not my husband then who could it be? Someone – *someone* – was upstairs, where my little boy was and I was not. I hurtled up the stairs with my rug over my shoulder like a Highland Scot but I knew as soon as I reached the landing that nobody was there. One knows when another body shares one's space. And I knew I stood alone.

Such dread rushed through me as I cannot describe. My scalp was a-prickle; I clasped my hands to keep them from shaking. *Well,* I thought, *that settles it. I am leaving my senses.*

No noise came from Stanley's door. Perhaps he was asleep. I drew back the bolt and said, 'Have you been running about?'

'No, Mama.' He was huddled on the floor opposite the door, his thumb in his mouth.

'I hope you would not lie to me.'

'No. I was here. I was frightened.' He reached his arms out and I went to him without hesitation. His face was hot and wet with tears, and soon so was mine. When he was a baby I used to lie all day with him in my arms, singing songs and kissing his little face. I had understood, then, that as a mother I must be all-encompassing, that he and I were a benevolent little republic of two that none might intrude upon. The distance had occurred when he had been breeched, and his pretty curls all cut off, and became – as boys must – more his father's creature.

'It's all right, I said. 'Now, into bed.'

He clung to me. 'I don't like it here.'

What would Lisle have said? *Be a man, Stanley!* There was a time when I might have said it too, but now I whispered, 'It will seem better in the morning.'

'Please, Mama. Don't go away.'

'I won't.' I was exhausted, after all, and rattled by what had happened. *I cannot go mad*, I thought. *I simply cannot.*

I put on my nightgown and helped him into his. He complied meekly now. We got into the narrow cot together, and although I hesitated to draw the clammy blankets over us, fearing what vermin they must harbour, the cold won out. First Stanley cried, then he shivered, but nestled against me he quieted and I lay listening to his breath, thinking how much less trouble a sleeping child is, and how much easier to love.

த

But sometimes sleeping children do make trouble.

I dreamed I was at Scarborough again, sitting on the terrace while Stanley raced on the sand below. The sun was low and lit the sea rose-gold to the horizon. As pretty a vision as all that was, what was conjured most powerfully was not the place but the feeling: a rosy excitement for the morrow, which I had assumed must fade naturally with girlhood and never persist beyond marriage. Most glorious to me that day in Scarborough was the sense that my future was utterly uncharted: for the first time in my life there was a blank page before me, and it was invigorating. In those first two weeks away from Lisle I believed that the worst was already over, and that now we had escaped him all our days might be Scarborough days, long and carefree, blushing into the sunset. But in this dream, I held in my hand a sheet of pink paper, and upon it I read my sister's words:

You cannot call yourself blameless.
You might have tried harder.
I wash my hands of this.

Looking up I saw the sea had turned grey, and was racing to shore. I cast about but could see Stanley nowhere, and before I could run to find him the water had reached me, swirling around my ankles with an awful dread cold, rising as I floundered and stumbled, my skirts twisted around my legs, soaked to the bone, crying out voicelessly, searching for sight of that dear blond head but knowing him already lost to me.

I woke gasping. The sheets were wet, and full of a thick, sweetish smell that went up my nose. It was still quite dark and I lay baffled a while, moving my legs with the dawning horror I remembered from childhood, feeling how the blankets clung and the eiderdown lay with a strange dead heaviness, thinking at first that I had done it myself. Then I realised it was Stanley of course, and propelled myself out of the bed. My nightgown was soaked with his urine.

'Stanley!' I shook him. 'Stanley! Wake up! Come, come, you must get out of bed.'

He woke slowly, then all at once, and cried out in dismay when he understood what had happened.

'Mama, I didn't mean to!'

'It doesn't matter.' I was too busy dragging the sheets from the bed to think much of him, and then I had the coarse wool underblanket to deal with, hoping against hope that the mess had not penetrated to the mattress. No such luck: it was ruined. 'Oh, Stanley, how did you have so much in you?' I cried, and he set up sobbing as I heaved the tick from the bedframe. It was stuffed I think with horsehair, dense and comfortless, and as it lolled in my arms I was put in mind of a picture I saw in the *Illustrated News* – 'Burial at Sea' – where sailors struggled with just such a featureless burden.

'Why did you not use the pot?' I panted as the tick thudded to the floor.

The poor child put his face in his hands, his shoulders

heaving. In the little light the moon afforded us, his legs glistened. 'I was afraid,' he sobbed.

'Come now – come now. There's no harm done,' I said. 'We'll sleep in the other room.'

'I don't want to go out there, Mama!'

'Why?' I asked sharply. Had he heard what I heard? Which was the worse? That he had, or that he had not? Poor child! Either there was an interloper outside the bedroom door or a deranged mother within it; he hardly stood a chance.

'It's dark,' he said.

'That's nothing to be afraid of. Come with me.'

I lit the candle and led him out onto the landing, although my hand faltered on the doorknob. The moments it took to cross to the other chamber were fraught: with every step I expected unseen fingers to close around my arm, or a body to jostle against mine, but I kept myself in front of Stanley and would not let him know my fear.

On second inspection I liked the room no better. The ancient panelling drained all the light from the place, its corners so dark they devilled the eye, and that narrow portion of window too high to afford any view was unsettling too. I determined at once that I would let the candle burn all night. Still, I was pleased to find in the press a stack of folded ladies' nightgowns, which although they had lain there some time were not strangers to careful laundering. They were the first trace of my father's women I had found in the house, and I felt rather sickened as I helped Stanley pull one over his head, but at least we both had something to wear.

'You see?' I whispered to Stanley once we were in bed. 'It all came out right, did it not? We are safe, and warm enough. And you are with me, so no harm can come to you.'

I said it with more conviction than I felt, but it seemed to satisfy him. I wrapped my arm around him and drew him in to me, his back to my belly, his wrist in my hand so I could feel the flicker of his pulse as he dropped back to sleep. I felt such a pang for him, then, that I had wrenched him from a home where he was happy and safe. For let me be clear, although Lisle was cruel to me, our son was never in danger. His life was one of comfort and enjoyment; he was made a pet of by all. My objection was that although the fabric of his life was pleasant, it was not *good*: he would, by and by, be contaminated by Lisle, learn to swagger and bully and berate, to mock and belittle and brutalise. And how could I object? I was only his mother; I had no right at all to dictate what manner of man he might be. For there is really only one manner of man, is there not?

Thud thud thud.

I sat bolt upright, my hands clasped to my chest. Those footsteps again! *Thud thud thud* outside the door, up and down the landing, and now perhaps the rapping of a cane along the banisters. These were the footsteps of an angry man, full of bluster, a man out to frighten me and whom I was wise to fear. I sat stock still.

Oh, what it is to realise that the only thing worse than there being *somebody there* is there being *nobody there*. And nobody *was* there, nobody of flesh and blood, nobody whose eye I could catch or whose blows I might dodge. Nobody was there, and I was certain they meant me terrible harm.

The footsteps went on with swift urgency, heavy angry boots patrolling the landing outside my door, then up and down the stairs as if searching for something, storming through the house with the air of one who wishes to be noticed, who is not afraid to make his ill mood known. In and out of the parlour they went, to the back door and the front, returning always to my chamber.

'Lisle?' I whispered stupidly when they stopped outside my door.

Thud thud thud.

'Go away,' I hissed.

Stanley's breath whistled in his nose. I'd not have woken him for anything: I laid a hand on his back and comforted myself with his peacefulness. The stamping continued, up and down, up and down. Sometimes when it retreated to the head of the stairs I dared to hope my visitor was leaving; sometimes the steps paused and I thought, *There! It is over!* But he always returned.

Lisle used to tear through the house this way. When I heard his steps turn swift and purposeful I would hide, but he'd go from room to room until he found me, his jacket billowing, his shirt half done, wrenching open doors and whisking curtains aside. He would seize me by the wrists and bring his face close to mine to spit his rage. If I flinched it would be worse for me.

So I stayed in my bed, listening to my strange new companion's circuits. How could I have fled one angry man and found another waiting for me? Was there some penance I must do, I wondered as I watched that little slot of window grow paler with the breaking dawn. Was this to be the albatross about my neck?

By and by I heard a sheep bleat on some hillside, and the valedictory shriek of an owl. Then, as if a nurse at my bedside soothed my terrors, I let my mind fill with quiet dawn scenes: white ashes raked from a grate; milk warming in a pan; a head bowed over a worn prayer-book. They belonged to the gentle, ordinary world that I trusted I might yet return to, and as the morning brightened I at last slipped into a fitful doze. By the time Stanley stirred, and wound his arms around my neck, the footsteps had fallen silent.

&

I prayed there was food in the house, for I was not fit to be seen in my borrowed nightgown, and Stanley's was far too large, with sleeves so long he had to wave his arms like a mesmerist to find his hands as we crossed the landing. My head buzzed with lack of sleep, but in daylight the house appeared hardly malevolent: it was only shabby and tired, no Gothic ruin, and the worst of its dereliction might have been remedied with a few rolls of pretty wallpaper. Descending the stairs, I looked to the little black chair in the hallway where my cloak had lain. The floorboards beneath it were dark with its run-off water, but the cloak itself was not there.

I seized Stanley's hand, as if to keep him from tripping.

'Somebody has been here,' I said, and tried to sound pleased, although my heart had quickened and the blood roared in my ears.

At the foot of the stairs I peeped into the parlour and saw again the dark patches where had lain my garments – but again the garments themselves were gone. The most peculiar sensation rushed over my whole body, a flush pursuing a chill, so I was at once both hot and cold, perspiring and yet shivering. Somebody had been here. Somebody had moved through these rooms without my knowing. An alien hand had wrung out my soaked stockings; a stranger had turned over the flannel drawers that lay so lately against my naked skin! These relics of the darkest night I ever lived, the few belongings left to me! Picked over, inspected, removed!

I had forgotten to breathe, and was almost at the point of collapse when the back door opened and a middle-aged woman entered carrying a bucket, her round face such a mask of weary disgust that I was in no doubt she was the one who had picked up what I had left. When she saw me standing there her expression did not change, although she eyed my boy with surprise.

'Good morning,' I said. I held Stanley before me by his shoulders, but she could not miss how little I wore, how unshaped my body was beneath the nightgown. She said nothing, only put down the bucket and stood looking at me expectantly as if there was something I ought to say.

Eventually she grunted, 'So *you* made this mess.'

'I am Mrs Lisle,' I persisted, smiling all the harder, 'and this is my son Stanley.'

She darted a quick shrewd look at him when she heard he had my father's name, and nodded briefly.

'Were you upstairs?' I asked.

'Aye, and found what you did *there* too.'

I tightened my grip on Stanley's shoulders. 'That'll not happen again,' I said. Lisle had told me that when he was our boy's age, and fouled the bed, he was whipped and mocked for it. I had begun to think that there were better ways to rule a child than with shame, if one sought to rule him at all.

'Well,' said she, 'I am Mrs Farrar. I char 'ere. I'll not trouble you long.'

'What?' I faltered. 'There is to be no housekeeper? No maid, no governess?'

Mrs Farrar looked as if she were about to laugh. 'Wi' all this room for them?'

I was taken aback to the point of speechlessness. Never in my life had I sunk to the services of a daily-woman! They were for the wives of clerks, poor women with rented furniture and pretensions. What could my father be thinking? Before I could help it, tears swam across my eyes, shocking in their volume. They trembled there, threating to spill, and I could not conceal the flush that rushed up from my neck, nor the muscle that twitched in my cheek as I struggled to compose myself.

'Mr Stanley sent dry clothes for you,' she said after a moment, in a gentler tone. 'There's bread-and-milk for the boy, and you may have as much tea as you like. 'E said that.'

I nodded dumbly, and the tears plummeted. One splashed onto the back of my hand by Stanley's ear, but he did not notice.

'Go on,' said Mrs Farrar. 'I've work to do. You get the lad fed.'

The kitchen was at the back of the house, another plain little rustic room, and yet in an imperceptible way so different from the others. Where the landing had bristled, the kitchen was all welcoming geniality, and I felt that same peace creep over me that had soothed me at dawn. This ought to be the domain of a solicitous friend, to whom all the pans and jars and books were beloved companions, who offered hot drinks and kind advice at the large scarred table. Stanley ate his bread-and-milk and I sat by him in silence, gazing into my teacup, trying to recall what I knew about the Thwaites. They were my grandmother's people, I thought, and there was a whiff about them – not quite impropriety but shame, that in some way they had not quite been what they ought. The memory eluded me. I went in search of Mrs Farrar.

I found her at the back of the house, stooping over the ruined tick. Her sleeves were rolled to the elbow and she was shaking out the horsehair in a series of thumping blows. A cloud had blown in to envelope the hill, so that beyond her

I could see no landscape, no houses, no sky, as if she stood before a theatre backdrop.

'I had a trunk,' I said. 'What news of it?'

'It's at the New Inn.' She stood back from the tick and pressed her hand into the small of her back. The yard was strewn with short-chopped hanks of grey hair. 'But the ford is flooded. Easy enough to walk over't tops, as I do, but a wagon won't pass.'

'How long until anything can get through?'

She squinted up at the sky, not that much could be seen of it. 'If t'weather turns fine, a few days. If it rains again, why,' – she puffed out her cheeks – 'who knows?'

That vexed me, for I was keenly in want of my toilet set, but now she rummaged in her pocket and drew out a tin no bigger than a snuff box. 'I suppose you'll be wanting these,' she said.

I reached for it without thinking. It rattled as she dropped it into my palm. 'What's this?' I asked.

She looked about furtively as if we stood on a crowded street. 'Female pills. Pennyroyal. If they don't work Mr Stanley knows a doctor. You are not yet quickening are you?'

Again, all my speech deserted me. I almost staggered, and dropped the box of pills so it clattered on the flagstones. How naïve I had been, to think my father kept this house for his seductions! There had been no abandon here, no illicit pleasure: this was a cruel, cold, lonely place to end an affair, not to start one. 'No!' I croaked. 'Mrs Farrar, you have me wrong. This isn't what I came for. I am a respectable lady in a little distress, that is all.'

'Oh, madam,' she said pityingly. 'They all say *that*.'

჻

Days passed. Stanley and I, decently clothed albeit in nasty borrowed things I should never have chosen, spent much of our time in that genial kitchen, where the fire was reliable and the teapot was full. From our brief forays to the end of the drive, I understood better where we were, and it was a remote situation indeed. The house rode on the crest of the moor, surrounded by wilderness on three sides, and sitting more often than not directly in a cloud. Eastwards, a valley unfolded, revealing – depending on the weather – a view that stretched from the chimney of a lead mine on the tops, down to a little mill in the river valley, with a village about it. The fields there were half-submerged, grey lakes blooming from the riverbank, and I appreciated how treacherous the road must be as it dipped down to the flooded fields.

I skulked in the porch while Stanley ran hither and thither on the drive or the little garden, prevailing upon me in a high plaintive voice to see what he had found, come try his new game, the compass of his play closing in upon me until we sat side-by-side on our desultory bench, watching the rain fall.

It was in the porch we found ourselves one darkening afternoon a week after our arrival, with Stanley clambering almost into my lap although I stooped my head over a book. 'Mama! Mama, what shall we do now?'

'Let's sit quietly awhile.' The novels in the house were cheap, sensational things I could not concentrate on, even if it were not for Stanley; I wondered too much about who had brought them here, and in what circumstances. Had they been as bored as I? As bored, and as afraid? Had they, too, heard those footsteps?

For each night they returned.

The thump of his cane; the stamp of his feet; the creak of the banister. I acknowledged these disturbances wearily now. I called him Mr Thwaite. Stamping and swiping, he stole all peace from me, and each night I laid down my head not with relief but dread, nursing the certain knowledge that I would have no rest. My eyes stung; my head was heavy. I was nervous, jumpy, wound too tightly to be any sort of companion to my son who now took my chin in his hands and lifted it to gaze into my face, his fingers digging into my cheeks. His eyes were bright earnest blue. His breath was on my skin.

'Let me be, Stanley,' I said.

'Play with me!' He seized the corners of my mouth and dragged them upwards into a smile.

'Stop that.' I pulled his hands away and he sprang from my lap.

'Horrible Mama!'

I rose too, exclaiming, 'I'll not have that!' and he flung back his arms and screeched pure rage in my face. I did not see a fractious little boy, but his father, whose anger might hurt me, in whom tenderness might dissolve at any moment into tyranny. My cheeks were hot. The book was still in my hand, and before I knew what I did, I had caught him by the collar and thwacked it once, twice, against the seat of his trousers. There was awful silence for a moment. Stanley and I stood quite stupefied. Then he set about crying, and I gasped, 'Stanley – Stanley! I did not mean—'

A man's voice broke in.

'Is this what your experiment has come to?'

I shrieked, and snatched Stanley bodily into my arms, casting about for the owner of the voice. Was Mr Thwaite here? Could he now pursue me beyond the bedroom?

But of course it was my father, standing at the foot of the steps, watching us from under the brim of his hat. I released my son and stood flustered and red-faced, twisting my hands in my skirts. Stanley stopped crying too: he wiped his nose on his sleeve and I saw him rub the toe of his shoe against his calf.

Shame struck me quite dumb as my father mounted the steps. He took the book from where it lay splayed on the dirt, and handed it to Stanley. 'Go inside and return this to its shelf, young man. Stay with Mrs Farrar. Lucinda, come walk with me.'

To see my boy vanish into the house was painful. It was all wrong to send him away miserable: I wanted to gather him up again, but instead turned away, and followed my father down the drive. He must have news – a plan for how he would next help us.

The road was thick with mud and jagged here and there with rocks, never a comfortable surface for a carriage. Better by far to do as we did, passing through a gate and onto the path that traced the edge of the moor, its limestone slabs laid by heroic, lonely effort, where the wind blundered about the fringe of my bonnet like a trapped fly. I pulled my shawl around myself and quickened my step to match my father's.

'I never strike him,' I babbled when we had gone a fair distance. 'That was the only time.'

'You're too fond of him,' he said.

I did not reply. A cloud was gusting in, thick as damp wool, but its drops were sharp cold needle-points against my face.

'Too jealously attached,' my father continued. 'What sort of a man can Stanley hope to become, with you clinging to him so?'

'A better sort than his father.'

He studied me gravely. 'I forgive you that, for you are upset. But it serves to illustrate how unfit you are — how unfit any woman is — to guide a boy into manhood. You are emotional, you are impulsive, you are childish. Think of how I found you today.'

'I was never all alone with him before! He is bored here, and unhappy. I will learn — I am learning. I will do better . . .'

'No, Lucinda. His place is with Lisle, and so is yours.'

'I'll not have that man near my child.'

'*His* child. You cannot treat the covenant of marriage as a mere caprice: this is not how I raised you.'

My father spoke these words in sight of the very house in which he concealed his own indiscretions. Disgust rose in me but I suppressed it and said quietly, 'Lisle broke the covenant. *He* was the adulterer; he the profligate; he the . . . ' This last word I could not say. My heart fought just to think of it; I felt sick. I seized my father's gloved hand and gathered myself. 'He misused me,' I hissed. 'He *did* things . . . '

My father looked at my hand on his, and then at me. 'As was his right,' he said coolly.

The tears rushed to my eyes, and I stood again blinded as I had before Mrs Farrar, shame burning in my cheeks. My father walked on as if he had not marked me at all. I thought *perhaps I will stand here forever*, still as Lot's wife, still as Myrrha when the roots sprang from her toes and delved into the soil, and shame and grief coarsened her skin and stiffened her limbs until they groaned in the breeze. It would be pleasant to give up. I could stand there on the moor until the wind blew all that was human out of me, and remain unfeeling as a stump forever.

'I gave you respite,' my father said over his shoulder. 'Now you must return home.'

That galvanised me. 'I want a divorce,' I said boldly, pursuing him into the wind. 'It *can* be done. His adultery is well known.'

He shook his head. 'That's not enough.'

'Then I will say what he does to me.'

'All men do that to their wives! You'd drag your family to the High Court because *you* cannot tolerate what other women endure tenfold? You are fed, are you not? If he beats you it is not sustained, if he is adulterous it's hardly to your detriment, since you do not welcome his attentions. You enjoy leisure, fun, fine clothes.' He shook his head pityingly. 'You haven't a leg to stand on.'

'But I—'

'And do you realise you have already forfeited all? You *might* have kept Stanley until he was seven, but after this performance . . . ' He stopped to pinch the bridge of his nose and screw his eyes shut. When he opened them again they were sorrowful. 'This is kidnap, Lucinda. No court could find you a fit mother.'

I felt like a drunk, tottering and histrionic, my terror spinning around me. I groped for facts, for rationality, but knew myself capable of nothing beyond an inchoate burst of feeling which would only be grist to his mill. I slumped, and held my tongue.

'The floods are receding,' my father said. 'It is safe to travel home, and this sorry episode need never be spoken of. You extended your Scarborough visit, that is all.'

The light was dimming, and our path, which had swung a wide loop behind the house, now approached it once more. I cast my eyes to the windows, hoping to spy Stanley there, but my gaze was drawn to that upper casement, boarded from the inside. Something was irregular. I could not at first make out what, but then I saw it: a white hand, pressed palm and fingers against the glass.

Cold rushed through me but I did not let my step falter; I

walked on, staring, hardly believing what I saw. Who was in my room? And how was it possible? It was *not* possible: there was no reaching the window-pane. Not even a person of Stanley's size could fit between boards and glass. And yet there it was still, one pale hand, fingers splayed against the pane as if in appeal. My father talked on – Mariana would not breathe a word; Lisle had already forgiven my silliness – and I said nothing. Insane to speak of ghosts and superstition, as much of divorce and mother-love. My eyes ached: I pressed my cold fingers against their sockets to dispel the pain. It had been so long since I slept.

'Pa,' I said, 'how do you come to own this place?'

'The Thwaites were my mother's people. Emily Thwaite – the last Mrs Thwaite – was her eldest sister. *She* left her husband.'

Ah. There it was. 'She may have had good reason,' I said.

'She abandoned her children,' he rejoined, 'and they were sent away; their father could hardly raise them alone. He did not achieve old age and nor, I'm afraid, did they. Perhaps you imagine wives are insignificant, but a house of cards may be toppled as easily by a pip as an ace.'

'But what of *her*?' I demanded.

'Who can say? Paris, perhaps, or London – the sort of place these unfortunates end up. Flat on her back under the Adelphi arches, I wouldn't wonder.'

We reached the high garden wall, and entered through a wicket-gate. I looked once again to that window, but no hand was there, and where it had been I saw distinctly the battened panels, black as ever.

'I know what happens here,' I said quietly. 'Those women.'

He stood still and looked at me for a long time. 'And?'

'If it were to come out . . . '

He laughed. 'Don't embarrass yourself. There is a differ-ence between secrets and knowledge nobody wants: if you make a scene about this it will end worse for you than for me.'

The dusk was stealthy that afternoon. There were no long shadows or golden sunbeams, just a smothering of the light, and the dark seeping in like damp. When we reached the porch, my father pressed my hand. 'I know you are a good girl. I will come for you and Stanley tomorrow.'

ⵦ

That night, as every night, Stanley fell asleep on the couch while I read. There was no possibility of his sleeping alone upstairs: the thought of some ghastly entity barring my way to him was intolerable. For myself, I sat sick with sorrow. I had thought my father was protecting me by bringing us here, but I understood now that his loyalty lay with Lisle. The divorce I had wildly snatched for was impossible, and even if my father had allowed me to stay here, Mr Thwaite would give me no peace. I gazed upon Stanley, slumped on the couch beside me, and knew that if he must go back to Lisle then I must go with him. Even if it meant his witnessing my misery; even if he came to scorn me; even if he grew into a man I feared. My place was with him.

I rose quietly and went about collecting our few posses-
sions to pack. Then I took him into my arms. He was heavy,
and stirred as I lifted him, but when he knew it was me he
laid his head on my shoulder and his limbs relaxed once
more. I could have held him there forever, breathing the
warmth behind his ear, and the perfect trust expressed by
his half-curled fingers. Instead I carried him upstairs to bed.

Mr Thwaite came late in the night, making the candle
gutter. I sat up in bed, my patience quite gone: now I was
resolved to leave, his bullying strides got my blood up. 'Let
me alone,' I said. 'Let me be!'

He set about a furious rushing up and down the landing,
banisters thrumming, floorboards creaking. I heard a crack
and the sound of breaking glass – a picture falling off the
wall, no doubt.

'You have your wish,' I said. 'I am going back. Now let
me sleep, I beg of you.'

Downstairs another crash: 'The Raft of the Medusa',
hitting the floor. I had never known him so feverish in his
movements. His footsteps vibrated through the floorboards:
the bed curtains shivered, and the water-glasses on the
dresser clinked together.

I rose from the bed and went to crouch by the door, with
the candle at my feet. I thought I felt him there on the other
side, a crackling, blackening presence, impatient with me. I
thought, *Tomorrow, wherever I am, I will sleep,* and felt a bleak
and silly joy. 'Mr Thwaite,' I said.

A grunt, of sorts.

'Your trouble is not with me. I am not your wife. Mrs Thwaite is gone, and you must go too.'

A silence. A long silence. All I heard was the pull and release of Stanley's breath from the bed, like the tide on a quiet evening: gentle, imperturbable, enduring. I had not been a good mother, but I would be a better one. I accepted now that I could not break us free in the way I had imagined: if there were no Lisle there would be other men, for they were all for one and one for all, a hydra I could not defeat. Why, even dead men did their part! Kneeling, I pressed my forehead against the door. The relief I felt at the prospect of physical comfort, of rest, of sleep after such a sojourn was tempered by grief for that brief and rosy hope that had blossomed in me in Scarborough, watching Stanley run across the sand. But the hope was gone. I could not win. I gave up.

And then, as if in confirmation, I heard the bolt slide to.

What! I sat up on my haunches, tested the door once lightly, then more frantically. It was locked, that was certain: locked from the outside. I rose and rattled the handle, but dared apply no more force while Stanley slept on. Ghastly as my situation was, how much more ghastly it would be if my boy knew anything of it!

'There's no way out,' came a deep and creaking voice. My candle went out as if it had been pinched between finger and thumb: I half-stifled my cry. One still burned on the dresser, but in a moment that too was extinguished. The room was dark as the grave, so devoid of light that my eyes sought to invent it, and blots of red and green swelled and dispersed before my vision. I tried the door again, fruitlessly. I felt my way along the panelled walls to the window, hand over hand, stumbling on objects no longer familiar. I had hoped to let in a little moonlight, if moonlight there was, but I could not slip my fingers under the boards to get purchase, and besides they were nailed true. My heart was pattering: I rested on the edge of the bed and clasped my hands in my lap, twisting and retwisting my fingers.

More noises below – the kitchen now – jars shattering on the stone flags, pans crashing. 'You won't leave!'

He continued, pacing back and forth along the landing as if caged, his steps punctuated every now and then with another burst of activity downstairs. Books thudded off their shelves, wooden chairs tapped from foot to foot. This was no longer a campaign to menace me, but a victory lap. He was the sportsman who, seeing his opponent prostrate, took the opportunity to beat them all the harder, for it was not enough to best me. He must break me.

I lay down next to Stanley, on top of the bedclothes, and let Mr Thwaite's rage agitate the air around my head once more. A tear rolled down the side of my face and into my hair, hot then cold in the folds of my ear. I wiped my eyes but the tears still came. I thought how I must go back to Lisle, and how much crueller he would be now that I had tried, and failed. Before, I had at least been beyond reproach; it would not have been right to use me *so* badly. But now – well, he had provocation. This trip of mine would justify anything he did to me.

Something tugged at my attention. Something gentle and

tentative, nothing like Mr Thwaite and yet equally undeniable. I can't say that I saw something, or heard it, or if I was physically touched. But I was alert at once to another presence in the room.

Emily.

There was no speech. I thought the air simply greeted me.

Emily, Emily, such insubstantiality!

She stood at the blinded window that admitted no moonlight, by the candle whose flame had been extinguished. And yet I saw her, moth-coloured, smudged, wavering as the darkness swam. She wore a pale dress in the style of sixty years ago, stained upon stains, and its hem and those of its petticoats hung at all different lengths where pieces had been ripped for what variety of purposes I dared not guess. Her hair was long and ragged, and she was thin, thin in the way of someone too far gone, so her joints were bulbous, and her diminished lips strained to meet over her teeth, and her eyes sat heavily in deep hollows.

Outside Mr Thwaite was still storming, muttering, 'Never leave! Never leave! *She'll* never leave.'

I pressed my hand to my mouth. Mrs Thwaite had not run away. Perhaps she had threatened it – perhaps she had tried – but she had not succeeded. Here she had huddled listening to the raging of her husband, and the muffled voices of her children departing, and then the silence that they left. She must have watched the light in her chink of window change colour, felt the hour and the season stretch and shrink, waited here helplessly. And nobody came for her, but Death.

She turned her head on its plucked-fowl neck and looked at me.

I reeled back, but something stayed me. Despite her awful appearance, she emanated sweetness. And although she did not move, it seemed she came to sit by me, as Mariana might have done in times gone by, as any dear friend would, to bear with me my unhappiness. I had not felt such solidarity in a long time, and I wept the harder. She had sat like this in the dark with the other women my father brought here while they waited for their dose to take hold, or after the doctor had been paid off. Perhaps one or two had been here a long time, heavy with a child they could not mother. She had borne with them. And she had been here with me all this time, putting warmth into the kitchen and suffusing my thoughts with safety and gentleness while her husband kept me from sleep.

Stanley sighed and rolled over. I put my hand on his shoulder to feel his beloved warmth, his flesh, his bones, rising and falling. And a quiet intimation reached me:

You can leave.

I hesitated.

You must *leave.*

'My father takes me home tomorrow,' I said.

Emily Thwaite shook her head. *No! No! Don't go with him.* With effort she left the window and walked to the centre of the room, limbs too stiff and sinews too slack, so she lurched and bowed like a marionette. I felt the breeze from her garments as she passed me by. Her hair was in wads; her nails long and yellow. She pointed to the door.

Thwaite is your warning, she told me. *I am your warning.*

I saw Scarborough. The pink light, and the gold gloss on the sand. My son's hands red with cold, and his eyes screwed up with joy. When darkness fell, we would climb the hill together counting the steps, and I would not complain that he was holding us up, but instead turn my face to the stars and wish it never had to end.

∽

I awoke to the rattling of the door. I was too mazy to understand, at first, whether I dreamed or woke, and I cried out when the bolt shot back and the door opened. Grey daylight from the landing crept in, not much but enough to show my father standing there.

'What's this?' He asked, perplexed. 'What has happened downstairs? How were you locked in?'

I rubbed my eyes. I lay atop the covers still, fully clothed as I had been the night before, with Stanley curled like a dormouse in the bedclothes beside me. My last memory was of Mrs Thwaite, her pinched face, her outstretched hand.

'How did this happen?' my father persisted. 'Who did this?'

'Stanley must have slammed the door,' I said. 'I have often noticed that bolt is unreliable.' My heart was still thudding: if he had studied me he would have seen its pulse disturbing the pintucks on my bosom, and stirring my cuffs. I stood, smoothing my skirts, and crossed to the dressing table. 'Fortunate you were here,' I remarked lightly.

'At least you are dressed and ready,' he said, entering the room with uncharacteristic hesitancy. I watched him in the mirror but did not catch his eye, and he preferred to turn away and muse upon Stanley in the bed. He did so studiedly while I brushed and parted my hair, then went to the window where Emily Thwaite had stood the night before and inspected its fortifications.

'I've not much liked being shut up here,' I said, smoothing my hair. In the mirror's image I saw another figure join him, pale and angular, a smudge on the glass or a beam of light refracted. *You can leave,* she told me.

I faltered. I pressed my hands onto the table to calm their shaking, but they would not stop, and my elbows knocked against the drawer-handles. 'Is Mrs Farrar here?' I asked. 'I must say goodbye.'

'I told her she needn't come today. But I see she will have a deal to clear up on Tuesday.'

I nodded. I pinned the last of my hair into place and cast my eye to the bed, where Stanley sat up and looked about himself. 'You're awake! Come, sweet boy. Are you ready to go on an adventure?'

He shook his head and lay back down. 'Mama, no.'

'This will be the last time,' I said. 'No more dashing about the country after this.' I went to him and gathered him up in my arms, rocking him on my lap and pressing my nose into the nape of his neck without shame although I knew how my father watched me. Emily Thwaite watched *him*, and while reproach and sorrow commingled in her expression, I picked out another emotion too: determination. I dressed Stanley swiftly while he clung to me in a hot-cheeked daze, and Mrs Thwaite's voice came to me again: *you can leave. You can leave. You* must *leave.*

She kept close to the wall, moving in a low slow crouch with her eyes fixed on my father, like a captive panther which, though faded and emaciated, still burns with instinct. I began to feel afraid.

I will be his warning, Emily Thwaite whispered. *He will know what he has done.* My father browsed the books on the window-sill, tawdry novels that made him curl his lip.

'We are to ride in Grandpapa's carriage,' I told Stanley cheerfully.

'I didn't like it the last time,' he said, hiding his face in my skirt.

'It won't be like that.'

There was an atmosphere in the room that spread like a perfume: it was of sweet and patient grief. Emily Thwaite sat in the corner, pressing her brow to her clasped hands and I thought for a moment that my father saw her, for he lingered at the mirror for some time, squinting at the room in its reflection. But there were many things he might have seen, and many things that might have troubled him. 'Are you coming?' I asked him, taking up my bag and sweeping Stanley from the room before me.

He looked pensive, as if something was settling over him that never had before. 'Presently,' he said.

Stanley was already clattering down the stairs. I waited

until my father's back was turned before I closed the bedroom door. Slowly, silently, I slid the bolt across.

The hall was strewn with broken glass and spreadeagled books, the kitchen ransacked. My father's greatcoat was laid over the hall chair and I rummaged through its pockets until I found a purse of money, and then in the lining a wad of notes enough to keep us for some time.

Stanley stood watching me, knitting his brow.

'It's all right,' I said. 'Grandpapa will join us later. Put your hat on.'

I took his hand and we stepped outside. Down the steps the carriage waited, the horses tossing their heads, and when the sun came out the vista across the valley was at last revealed, mother-of-pearl mist; glints on the windows of farms and cottages; the mill chimney rising as if from a mirage. The fields, the becks, the crooked walls and the hawthorn hedges were all suffused in a pink haze. I wrapped my arms around Stanley and squeezed him tightly. After I had helped him into the carriage, I turned to look back at the house. The windows were blank.

'Drive on,' I said. 'Take us to Scarborough.'

THE EEL SINGERS

Natasha Pulley

Keita Mori could remember the future, and if he was being honest, which he wasn't often, he did not enjoy it.

Fortunately, he was a bad actor, so there was no special need for honesty. Thaniel had rented the spare room from him for long enough now to know when he was unhappy.

Tonight, they were walking through the Christmas market of the Japanese village in Knightsbridge. When Thaniel had first come to live in Knightsbridge a couple of years before, the village had been a smallish affair, set up in one broad showroom; but it had proven so popular that after it burned down the owners rebuilt it much improved, with beautiful bridges outside, pagodas and bright shrines with prayer bells. The people who lived there, artisans all, had brought everything outside for the season. There were stalls and lights everywhere, gleaming on enamelled jewellery, parasols, bolts of kimono silk. The lady who owned the teashop had hired extra staff to walk around with trays of hot matcha tea, which was so brilliantly green that it made Thaniel think of that gorgeous moss that grew in only the richest woods. You could buy it cut with sake or whisky, and along with everyone's pipe smoke, the steam coiled sweet and hot into the night air, tinted orange by the lamps. The murmur of the crowd was a mix of English and Japanese. The air had a happy fizz that felt like holding your fingertips above a freshly poured glass of champagne.

Mori seemed so brittle that the children's voices around them might shatter him soon.

'Something on your mind?' Thaniel hazarded, turning up the collar of his coat against the cold.

Just ahead of them, Six was negotiating with the firework-maker, who looked worried that he might be getting out of his depth.

'We should rescue him,' Mori said, nodding that way. 'Before she tells him any more statistics.'

'Anything else?' said Thaniel, who was used to diversionary tactics.

'I – no, I'm fine,' Mori said, but they were coming up to the firework-maker's stall, where the cracking glow of the sparklers lit him starkly. It made his hair and his eyes look like black glass. He flinched, and held his hand flat under a boy's matcha-and-whisky tray a second before the boy dropped it, having been bumped by a passing dog. Mori gave it back.

Thaniel wondered guiltily about the tray. Probably it wasn't very honourable to think of it, but Mori was from one of the oldest samurai houses in Japan, one which had spent a thousand years breeding delicate ladies of below five feet tall, and crystalline knights. One cup would get Mori drunk and honest pretty quick.

Mori's eyes slipped away and down just before Six rushed back to them with a paper packet full of what were probably a lot more fireworks than the firework-maker would usually have sold to an eight-year-old. Like always, she wouldn't take anyone's hand. Instead, she stole Mori's pocket watch, then Thaniel's, so that she could walk between them at the short length of the chains.*

Thaniel nudged her. 'Why all the fireworks, petal?'

'So we can have a firework display on Christmas Day, so it feels more like New Year for Mori and less like a heathen festival about housebreaking and a worrying pervert,' she explained.

'Right,' Thaniel said. 'Right; for the fourteenth time, *both of you*, the nativity story is *not* about housebreaking and a worrying pervert. The Angel Gabriel appears unto the Virgin Mary to tell her the good news about the coming of the Holy Spirit, that's all!'

'But do me a favour,' Mori murmured, 'and run away if some demented stranger tries to come unto you with his holy spirit.'

Thaniel made a fist at him.

They had been making their way out, and Thaniel nearly didn't notice that Mori had stopped dead on the edge of the pavement. They were about to cross the road, which thrummed with cabs and horses, and people

---

* They were an accidental sort of family. She had used to work for Mori, hired out by the local workhouse, but one day he just hadn't taken her back there and now she lived in their attic. She had said she was happy to adopt them both permanently, if they remained polite and quiet.

crossing from and for the market. An omnibus with an advertisement for Lipton's tea on the side skidded on the ice and went onto two wheels for a moment before banging back down onto the cobbles. Some girls gave the driver a round of applause.

'Kei?' Thaniel said.

Mori smiled a bit. 'Sorry,' he said. 'It's busy, isn't it?'

It took Thaniel a moment to understand. When he did, he felt annoyed with himself for not having thought of it before. Of course, if you were a clairvoyant, then a busy icy road must have been a jumble of horrible potential memories of being crushed under wheels or hooves.*

You couldn't ask Mori if he wanted to stop for a minute until he felt better; he took concern in the way most people took being sworn at.

'Six,' Thaniel said instead, 'shall we buy some hot choco-late from that stall there?' There was a queue, and it would give the crowd on the road time to die down.

Six looked, not with instant enthusiasm. A hot chocolate stall was not on the schedule for the usual walk home, and

---

* What Mori remembered were *possible* futures. At first, Thaniel had thought that must have been reassuring, because the very fact of possible futures meant that nothing was set in stone. If Mori remembered being hit by a brougham, it didn't mean he would certainly be; just that there was a vivid chance of it. But Mori's perspective was that if you had to go through life remembering what it felt like to have just that instant fallen down the stairs, been murdered, or otherwise severely inconvenienced, it would be a miracle if you weren't a nervous wreck by the end of a week. Mori was not prone to being wrecked, and usually, it was impossible to tell if anything terrible had just smashed into his memory; he had one of those ironclad souls that had much more in common with an unsinkable luxury ocean liner than the fragile schooners most people were stuck with, but he said darkly that even so, there were always icebergs.

sudden variation was not something she encouraged. If she could have put them on train tracks with clear timetables and no request stops, she would have.

Thaniel squeezed her shoulder, trying to communicate that he hadn't asked just to be irritating. He saw her study Mori. 'I think,' she said gravely, 'that would be superb.'

❧

At the house on Filigree Street, Mori's workshop was closed for Christmas. When they let themselves in, Thaniel had a guilty wave of relief. He loved the workshop and all the sheening clockwork there, but it was good to know that no one was about to come in and ring the bell on the desk now. Until New Year, the house was just theirs, with fires in every grate and lightbulbs glowing in among the holly twined down the banister of the stairs. Mori made the lights himself, and inside each bulb the filaments were coiled into different shapes: trees, stars, a Japanese castle. The light was honey-coloured, and full of home.

When Thaniel fell into bed around midnight, after Mori had given Six some mulled wine, he was asleep almost straightaway. His ribs ached from laughing. Six was a quiet person usually, but slightly drunk, she had given him a piece of her mind about why it was so upsetting when he unexpectedly wore a different coat, and would he mind *awfully* pencilling it in on the Significant Things That Might Happen Today chart in the kitchen.*

He wasn't sure what time it was when something woke him up. He sat up in bed, listening. Dimly, he had a feeling it had been a bang, but the memory was fogged from sleep. It made him jump when someone knocked on the door.

'Six, are you all right?' he said into the dark. He must have heard the ladder drop down from the attic. 'It's unlocked, petal.'

'It's me,' Mori's brandy voice said. He sounded shaken. 'Can I . . . ?'

'Yes,' Thaniel croaked.

They had lived together for three years and never once had Mori knocked on Thaniel's door. It was always the other way around, and Thaniel agonised before he did. He was never sure he was welcome. Mori let him in, always, but Mori was Mori; he wasn't English, wasn't a Christian, had grown up in a place where a knock on the door between friends was unremarkable. It didn't mean he was in love, only that he was being polite. Thaniel didn't dare ask him which it was. It was cowardly, but if he didn't know, he could live hoping.

---

*   The Significant Things chart was one of the advantages of living with a clairvoyant. Mori noted things down as he remembered them — a possible suicide on the Underground tomorrow morning, pouring rain. There was a separate column for Six-only concerns. Tuesday: Mistress Jenkins might announce a spontaneous school trip to the vivarium.

    Six had thought Mistress Jenkins ought to be killed for the spontaneous trip. It had taken a while for Mori to negotiate her down to a revenge prank with some icing sugar. Thaniel should probably have intervened and pointed out that primitive bomb-making wasn't something normal people taught their children, but he had enjoyed the experiments in the garden too much.

Mori let himself in quietly, closed the door again, and then folded into the space on the near side of the bed, his back to the wall and his arms around his knees. 'Thank you. Sorry. Vivid nightmares.'

'About the road?' Thaniel asked softly. He moved the blanket so they could share it more evenly. Moonlight and cold came from the window beside them, which cast diamond-hatched shadows across the bed.

Mori nodded. 'It's just the time of year. Everywhere's heaving. I can never settle properly.' He pushed his hands through his hair. 'It gets worse every year. I don't even want to go outside. I just – I endlessly remember being run over or falling, or Six going under a cab, or you, and then hospital and funerals and . . . '

'Don't go out then. That's what I'm for,' said Thaniel, who was grateful when he could be *for* anything. He wasn't, generally. He was a clerk at the Foreign Office. 'I can do groceries and that.'

Mori gave him a rueful look. 'But that would be giving in.'

'Shut up. If I kept doing something that was hurting me, you'd be the first one to give me a slap and tell me to sit down.'

Mori laughed. 'True.'

Tentatively, Thaniel put one arm around him and pulled him near. He had a stupid overjoyed thrill when Mori let him. 'Is there anything that would help? Somewhere we can go that's quieter?'

'We can't take Six on an unexpected holiday, she'd explode.'

'She has to live in the world, though,' Thaniel said. 'And – call me a bastard, but I don't think people should sacrifice their health to their children. You end up hating them.'

Mori was quiet for a few seconds. When he spoke again, he did it carefully, as though he were testing ice on the edge of a lake. 'There's a place where it doesn't work.'

'Doesn't work?'

'All this,' Mori said. He touched his own temple. 'I don't know why.'

'How do you know it doesn't work there?' Thaniel said, struggling with the whole idea.

'Because I can remember our going there, and then nothing else.' Mori hesitated. 'I can't remember anything about it. Usually I'd know everything. It's like . . . a gap in the weave of everything.'

'Where?'

'The Fens. Towards . . . Peterborough.'

'I thought you were going to say Mongolia,' Thaniel said incredulously. 'Peterborough's only a few hours on the train. Why aren't we there already? I'll persuade Six.'

Mori gave him a look that was gladness and shame mixed up, one that made Thaniel feel happy to have done something useful, but excruciatingly young and pointless too.

❧

The fen stretched grey and glittering in every direction. The sky was dusking, and the biggest Thaniel had ever seen it, mauve and pewter from horizon to horizon above the rippling silhouettes of the reeds. This station had no name; it was just a wooden platform, with no office and no guard, only a path that led away from one end, into the marsh.

Thaniel didn't care. He was just grateful to get off the train.

The platform was the tallest thing for what must have been miles around. He couldn't see a single building, except maybe something half-ruined in the distance. It had to be the wrong place. There couldn't have been people here for a thousand years.

'No, this is it,' Mori said. He looked like he was listening.

The caretaker of the guest house had been meant to meet them, but there was no sign of anyone. Thaniel was about to ask Mori what they should do now when he saw a lamp, half-hidden among reeds much taller than he'd thought, and behind it, a woman and a man wrapped up in scarves and hats. They waved.

'Evening!' they both called.

'Evening,' Thaniel called back gratefully.

Never one for new people, Six took Mori's watch and looped the chain once around her hand so he couldn't stray further than six inches away. Thaniel hurried down the steps first to make sure the people didn't think they were being rude. He had to blink twice, because they were much nearer than he'd thought. Something about the endless flatness was making it hard to tell how near or far anything was.

'Hello – is one of you the caretaker?'

'That's right,' the woman said. 'And you'll be Mr Steepleton and Mr Mori? It's this way.'

'This way,' the man echoed cheerfully. 'Anything to carry?'

'No, it's all right,' said Thaniel, who had been in service. He hated people who handed over all their bags at the drop of a pin.

'It's a bit of a way,' the man warned him.

'Bit of a way,' the caretaker joined in at the end.

'We're all right,' Mori said. 'We need some exercise. It's five hours from London.'

They both looked at him with a sudden, intense attention that made Thaniel uneasy. Nobody in a place this isolated could be used to foreigners. But then they were both smiling. 'Welcome to the hreodwater!'

'What does that mean?' Thaniel asked, curious and relieved. He was from Lincolnshire, not even that far from here, but the Fens was its own place and people were different there. They even looked different, with watery dark hair and watery blue eyes. Nobody could have moved far from home since the Danelaw. The marsh kept them hemmed in. It must have hemmed in the language too.

'Oh . . .' They looked at each other, and then laughed. They must have known each other for years, because they did it at exactly the same time, and in the same way. 'Just this place!'

Thaniel looked instinctively at Mori, who was a walking international dictionary. But Mori was shaking his head. Thaniel had never seen him look so happy. Looking at him now, with no context, Thaniel would have thought he was seeing a man who had had a migraine for years, and just this instant felt it vanish.

'I have no idea,' Mori said. He started to laugh, and the caretaker and her husband joined in. Thaniel smiled too, glad it was working. Six, though, was looking at all of them strangely. Without a word, she pulled the paper tab on one of Mr Tanaka's Self Lighting Long Life Sparklers, and went on down the tiny path ahead of them all, her shadow vaulting.

For a quarter mile, they saw nothing but mires and reeds. After London, the air tasted sweet – Thaniel had always thought it was just a thing people said, but it was true, and blindfolded he would have said someone had just shaken icing sugar about. Sweet and earthy and cold. Sometimes, he saw bright white dots in the marsh, and he couldn't make out what they were until one lifted a long neck. Swans, dozens of them. His sense of perspective swung. He'd thought they were a lot smaller and a lot nearer. It was an uncanny feeling, but it came with a thrill too.

And then the balance between the water and the land changed. The path stopped, and became a wooden causeway, the struts sunken into a stretch of black water.

There was one island, and on that island, sudden and stark, was the house. Its lights looked disembodied from here, in a way that made Thaniel think of alchemy. He glanced at Mori and grinned. He'd never seen anywhere like this before, much less stayed. He found himself quite hoping for a ghost.

The caretaker led the way onto the causeway. The fen was

playing more tricks, and the way was much, much longer than it had looked at first. Their steps echoed deep under the wood, which was so old that the surface had a kind of spongy give to it. Moss grew along the rail posts. The dark had thickened now, and the caretaker's lamp cut light a short way ahead, flinging black lines along the hem of her skirt.

The fen must have flooded sometimes, because a tall flight of wooden steps led up to the front door of the house. On either side there was a garden laid out for vegetables and herbs, but mostly waterlogged and reed-choked for now. Even by the warmth of the lamplight, the house was a bleak place of high sheer walls and sharp points, and slit windows. But when the caretaker pushed open the front door, heat rolled out. Inside, on the generous kitchen table, was a basket of food and instructions on how to use the oven (gentlemen don't always know). The stove was already lit, and all the lamps.

'The basket should do you well, but the village is two miles over there,' the caretaker said. In proper light, she was so watery she looked like she might evaporate at any moment. She and her husband both pointed through the fireplace at the same time, still strangely in sync. 'Maps on the side.'

'On the side,' her husband joined in.

'Well,' she said, and once again they both beamed at Mori. 'We'll leave you to it!'

Thaniel thanked them and saw them off. Six was still in the garden, writing her name in the air with the sparkler.

The caretaker and her husband were soon nothing but the orb of their lamp fading back to the jetty. Once they were at the boat, they started to sing; it was a weird, eerie song, and they started exactly together. Something deep in him recognised the language, though he didn't understand. It sounded ancient.

Thaniel glanced at Mori. 'They were kind. In a ... probably-been-kept-in-a-cellar-for-years way.'

Mori laughed, and Thaniel's heart hurt, because Mori didn't normally laugh so easily. 'Cheery though.'

Thaniel went to bring Six inside, because the cold was deepening and an ashy snow was beginning to fall. When he brought her back into the kitchen, he found Mori standing by the open stove, watching the flames play over the coal as if he were in a trance.

'All right?' Thaniel asked, anxious.

'Watch me not have hysterics, look.' He put his hand close to the fire. 'Maybe it sparks, maybe it doesn't, do I care? Not a bit. This is why people play chicken with the sea, isn't it? You can't remember drowning if it all goes wrong. Christ, you'd actually have to touch this to feel it, wouldn't you – do you feel immortal *all the time?*'

Thaniel laughed and put the kettle on. 'Can you tell why it doesn't work here?' he said.

'No. It feels like ... ' Mori inclined his head. 'It's like this place is insulated. There are others like it. They're always small, just a few square miles here and there. There's one in Russia. A few up in the Himalayas. I don't know why.'

Thaniel glanced back, charmed, because without any future memory, Mori had an accent. Obviously; he had only been in England for a few years and you could not learn English fluently from Japanese and vice versa in much less than ten. Thaniel knew that painfully thoroughly. He always thought he was getting pretty good, but then someone told him about politics and all his brain would come up with was that he liked octopuses.

Six had been looking into the fireplace. Because the stove was so hot, the grate was unlit. Already, snow was coming down the chimney and settling on the grate. 'There's a dead cat in here,' she reported. 'Can I poke it?'

Thaniel expected something horrifying, but it was just a skeleton curled among the ashes in the fire-pit. 'Ah, don't disturb it, petal. That's been put there for a reason. People round here used to do this to keep away witches.'

'A couple of weeks ago, used to?' Six said.

'No, no, hundreds of years ago.'

'The heat would have warped it by now if it had been here hundreds of years.'

She was right. He thought of the caretaker, with her ancient-sounding song. Perhaps other ancient things were still alive here too. 'Maybe it's just the polite thing to do.'

෧

The snow kept up all night. Thaniel knew that because he jolted awake at two o' clock in the morning in the garden.

He was standing at the gate, facing out towards the black lake, barefoot in the snow.

It must have been the cold that shocked him awake. He wasn't wearing a coat, just his night things, and the wind that hissed through the reeds was bitter. He stared down at the ground, his own hands, the glint of the water, trying to tell if this was an especially realistic dream or if it was really happening. He slapped his own wrist, hard.

It hurt. Awake.

In the few seconds it had taken to see that he really was outside, that he must have been sleepwalking, that the house was just there behind him, something under his heart had coiled tighter and tighter, and now it unwound all at once into panic, and he was shaking.

He ran back to the house and pushed the door open hard, remembered everyone else was asleep and closed it much more softly. He had to stand with his forehead against it, trying to work out why he was so spooked. Sleepwalking didn't mean anything horrible was wrong with you; only that you were unsettled.

After the snow, the slate floor felt hot.

'Are you all right?' Mori was on the stairs. He took the thick blanket folded over the banister and held it out, puzzled. He had a black kimono sashed with white over his night things. It made him look as if he had taken holy orders.

Thaniel meant to laugh and say, yes, fine; a funny thing just happened. He said, 'No, I just woke up by the gate and now I feel like I'm having a heart attack.'

Mori came down to him and put one hand flat to his chest, and waited. 'You're not. This used to happen to me when my brothers went to war. You'll be all right.' He rubbed Thaniel's arm. 'Sleepwalking; that's new, I think?'

'It's never happened to me before.'

'We should have a glass of wine,' Mori said, glimmering. 'If you're having sleep trouble, then you must be grown up now. Finally. This is momentous.'

'Oh, you're old and bitter,' Thaniel said, weak with gratitude.

'And now you are too. Come on. Wine.' Mori towed him to the kitchen, where he put Thaniel into a chair near the stove. He took the coal shovel and scraped some of the still-glowing coals into a cup, which he gave to Thaniel to hold, then a glass of red wine from the caretaker's basket. When he had, he studied him quietly. 'You look half a shade better. Are you?'

Thaniel nodded. 'Thank you,' he said softly. He held the cup of coals against his heart. Blood needled through his fingers.

Mori kissed his forehead. Thaniel bumped forward against his chest and felt safe again, but ashamed too. It had been the sort of kiss you might give to a child that had got itself flustered about a spider.

ço

In the morning, everything was white. Six burst down the stairs already in her coat and boots, and stood vibrating until Mori opened the door for her.

Thaniel had grown up too cold all the time, so he had been sitting close to the stove with a cup of tea, feeling grateful he was *inside,* with no intention of going out, but Mori was looking out at it all as if it were magic.

It occurred to Thaniel that he might win a snowball fight if Mori didn't know when the snowballs would be arriving. 'Shame not to go for a walk too,' he said brightly.

The fen was different in the daylight. It stretched forever, muted beneath a gauze of mist.

The lake was so clear that you could see all the way down. At the bottom was a strange impression of waving that might have been fields of dark weed. But there were other things too, gleaming around the causeway's struts. Coins, and bigger shapes that could have been knives or jewellery, and bones. He could even make out the teeth on what he was nearly certain was the mandible of a horse.

Instantly, he hated it. He didn't even like walking above it on the causeway. Mori was telling Six that sometimes, in ancient places, people left offerings in the water – everyone had forgotten to what, but they had – but Thaniel barely heard what they were saying. For all it was beautiful, the water looked dead. His whole skeleton ached to get away from it. Which was idiotic. He had never just *decided* in his soul that a place was bad before; until today he would have said that the sort of person who decided things like that was probably also prone to spangly costumes and spelling contests with The Other Side. It must have been the disturbed night.

As soon as they were ashore, Six shot away by herself, but it was easy to see her; her coat was bright red. There were no trees, no hedges, nothing; just the grass and the snow-bowed reeds, the black pools, and rags of mist caught in the spiky marsh grass. Thaniel had thought he would feel better to get off the water, but he didn't. He was the tallest thing here. It was exposure like nothing else.

The snow was pristine, and it creaked under their boots. Thaniel kept glancing over at Six, and soon found he couldn't tell how far away she was. Unease knotted itself in his stomach again. He called over to be careful, that not all the solid-looking patches *were* solid, but she had already found a stick to test the way with. She pole-vaulted over a pool.

Mori touched his arm, gave him an innocent look, slung a snowball at him, and ran away. Heart lifting again, Thaniel chased him, which was a lot more difficult than he'd imagined, because Mori was fox-fleet and unscrupulous when it came to laying ambushes behind reed banks.

They slowed down when they heard the singing.

There was a fishing station, grey in the mist.

The station was a few boats and a few people set up on a wooden jetty, hung about with old cartwheels wrapped up in wadding to cushion the boats as they bumped their moorings. There were high wooden frames inside a half-covered shed, where they were smoking or salting the fish or both, and a row of younger boys and girls slicing up the new catch. The knives made a slick noise. It was the children who were singing; the same song as the caretaker and her husband.

They all noticed Thaniel and Mori at the same time, and all looked at once. Thaniel felt that panic-pressure from the night lean against his ribcage again. He had twice been there when people snapped at Mori in the street. It never seemed to bother Mori,* but it corkscrewed into Thaniel's sternum.

Everyone beamed.

'Morning!' It was a perfect chorus.

'You'll be staying at the guest house?' someone said.

'Just for the week,' Thaniel said, shocked with himself, because for the first time he understood Mori's mistrust of people who were too nice. He felt as though they wanted something. He ordered himself to get a grip. 'Merry Christmas.'

'Merry Christmas,' they all agreed together. It might have been the mist, but like the caretaker, their colours were all faded. They had black hair, but it was a diluted black, nothing like Mori's.

Six appeared at his elbow. Slightly in front of him, he noticed. He held her shoulder to try and promise it was all right.

'Come and try our famous water,' one of the women said, still smiling. When she came up nearer, there was something hungry about the smile. 'Good for your health.'

'I am ... absolutely not going to do that,' Six said, and walked away back the way she had come.

Thaniel winced. 'Six, don't be rude, come back,' he said,

---

* Who arranged the offender's future in such a way that it involved falling immediately into the Thames.

entirely for show. Six wasn't offended by the same things other people were, she pointed out, so without that frame of reference it was a guessing game, and personally she didn't feel it ought to be the main business of her life trying to work it out. Thaniel agreed.

The lady only laughed.

'We'd like to though,' Mori said, and again, everyone looked rapt.

As the lady led them across to the jetty, Mori studied the barrels of salt and fish, looking as fascinated by them all as he had by the snow. Knives flashed as the others started work again. They were all left-handed. Thaniel swallowed. The snick of the knives was beginning to make the roots of his teeth sting, and so was the wet click of the new offal as it hit the piles in the buckets. And the way they were all looking at Mori — it was starving.

They weren't just catching fish, he saw now. The nets writhed with eels. One wound its way right up a girl's arm.

The lady sank a pitcher into the water, and poured out two chipped teacups.

'There you are, lads. Cheers to your stay.'

Thaniel's whole body reacted as though she'd handed him a cup of maggots. He wasn't expecting it, and it must have been visible, because Mori gave him an inquisitive look. He shook his head. Amazing what one night of bad sleep could do.

The water was icy and bitter. There was nothing bad about it, but Thaniel nearly choked as he felt it slide down.

They both promised it was excellent, thanked the lady, and excused themselves in case they lost Six.

Thaniel took Mori's arm once they were well into the mist, wanting to be near to someone who wasn't wearing that hungry look. 'There's something odd about them. The way they all . . . they were all left-handed, did you see that?'

Mori nodded. 'Maybe it runs in families. A place like this, everyone will be related.'

Thaniel tried to excavate why he had felt – still felt – so skittish. He wanted to tell Mori that he didn't like the fen, that it felt dead, or sick, but he had nothing to explain why he felt that way, and even if he had, Mori would take it as a request to go home. And then whatever Thaniel tried to say, they would be back on the train by tomorrow. He was not going to let Mori go back to London just because of a feeling.

He had been quiet for too long. Mori was watching him.

He snatched at the first thought to present itself. 'Or perhaps I'm not used to being grinned at quite that manically.'

'I'm glad you said that,' Mori said. 'I didn't like to say anything; all white people look a bit lunatic-albino-trollish, so it's hard to tell when that's particularly the case.'

Thaniel shoved him, aware that Mori was teasing him to take his mind off things, and glad of it, because it was working. Around them, the snow feathered down.

∽

He woke on the island shore in the middle of the night.

When he looked back, the garden gate was about fifty yards behind him, and again, he was nearly sure it was the cold that had woken him. The snow was thick and the dark was deep; he could barely see the boat right next to him. In London, there was always light; the street lamps, the electric lights along Knightsbridge, lanterns and candles in windows, and on those strange dense days that came before the fog season, the whole city cast the underside of the clouds orange at night. None of that here. It felt wild, here. The stars were huge and bright, clearer than he'd ever seen; as clear as those coins and bones in the water.

He had no coat, but he was wearing shoes this time. He managed to laugh. At least his subconscious, or whatever it was that wanted to go for midnight walks, had got itself some common sense. He pressed one fist against his heart and pushed hard as he started back to the house, trying to persuade that panic-tightness to ease.

It wouldn't.

He found himself wondering where he would have ended up, if his sleeping mind had had its way. Maybe he had been trying to leave.

He pushed his hand over his face. He had to wonder if all this wasn't just years of steady unease breaking through now that he'd relaxed. He loved home, loved Filigree Street, London, but always there was that rotting voice in his head that rasped to be careful, never to touch Mori when anyone might see, never to look at him too long or speak too gently.

He had never seen the inside of an asylum, and he never wanted to, but the asylum waited at the end of this road, iron gates open.

And now for the first time in years, despite all this vast open space, there was nobody to watch.

All this, the sleepwalking and the stupid anxiety about the lake, it was just like getting a headache once you came home from a trying day at work.

Out on the fen somewhere, someone was singing the same song the caretaker had.

ॐ

The next day was Christmas Eve. There was a piano in the living room, so Thaniel set up there in the morning and played carols while Mori and Six made a little Christmas cake. They were talking about whether or not humans really ought to ingest currency (he had asked her if she wanted to stir in the sixpence). Thaniel was in a new, half-meditative state of mind wherein he could listen to them and play the music at the same time. Between those two things, his thoughts felt as though they were finally balancing out. He hadn't told Mori about sleepwalking again, and he was glad now. He spent enough time as it was panicking uselessly at Mori, who must have been feeling more like his father than his friend.

There was a pause. Then, 'Dad,' Six said, her voice flat and odd.

'I'm listening, petal,' Thaniel promised.

'What's that you're playing now?'

'It's a carol.'

'No, it's not.'

He didn't understand, but then, like he was waking up, he heard it; he was playing the song the caretaker had sung, and the forager in the night. In his head, the words were playing too. They were about a girl whose sister had turned into an eel. He couldn't tell how he knew that. The language was too different to guess at. 'I must have picked it up,' he said, but that was a lie. He couldn't have picked it up that well.

Six looked at him for a long time, blank, then left without an explanation. Mori leaned to the side to see where she was going. The front door opened and shut.

'Have I upset her?' Thaniel asked helplessly.

'I think she didn't want the song stuck in her head,' Mori said. He smiled a little. 'She has to be careful what she puts in it, doesn't she. Everything turns so loud, once it's there.'

Having decided that Six would come back when she wanted to see them again, they went to put the cake in the oven, and to wash up. Mori held his hand under the tap as the hot water began to come through from the stove, waiting to feel the difference, as though that were a sort of magic. Of course he would just know when it was hot, usually. Thaniel watched him and thought, again, how much happier he looked, and how much less brittle.

He was even humming. It was the caretaker's song again.

'What does it mean, do you think?' Thaniel said after a while. 'I want to say it's about a girl and an eel but I don't know why I think that.'

'Hm?'

'The words to the song.'

'What song?'

'You were singing it just now.'

Mori looked unsettled. 'I didn't . . . know I was. Sorry.' He blinked twice at the soapy water, then stood back from the sink, the bones in his shoulders sharpening. Then he was his normal self, the glass-brittle one. 'How long have you been standing there?'

Thaniel stared down at him for too long and caught himself too late. 'A while. Are you . . . ?'

'Sorry. I'm sorry. I'm just . . . hazy.' Mori pulled his sleeve over his eyes as though there were gauze over them. 'It must be standing here in the warm, it's turning me into a vegetable.'

Prickles were still nettling down Thaniel's back. 'Well, let's go outside for a minute.'

Mori must have seen that he was unsettled because, awfully, he sealed away his own unease and sparkled. Thaniel had never known he was such a good liar. 'Time to build a snowman, I think.'

៚

They did build one, just by the vegetable patch where the snow was heaped up high against the garden wall. Beyond it, Six's bootprints led towards the causeway. Mori saw him looking that way and brushed his shoulder.

'She's all right.'

'I know,' Thaniel said. He shook his head. He wanted, again, to say that the lake felt wrong, that he didn't want to let Six play anywhere near it, and again, he knew Mori would just take him straight home, and he would feel embarrassed and stupid. 'I, um . . . I didn't sleep, I ended up outside again.'

Mori nodded slightly. It wasn't anything as sickly as pity, just acknowledgement. He let the quiet stay open. He was resting one shoulder companionably against the snowman.

'I think I'm more of a house mouse than I thought,' Thaniel said, doing his best to laugh. 'I seem to have gone into profound psychic shock now we've gone away from home. Embarrassing.' He put another handful of snow onto the snowman to smooth out a dent.

Mori kicked his ankle, very lightly. 'Thaniel. Something strange must be here, we know that. I have no idea what it is. All I know is that it switches off the top half of my brain. Perhaps it's doing something to you as well. A serious enough something to make you sleepwalk. If that's the case, then sod all this. Do you want to go back to London?'

'No! No, don't you bloody dare. I'm just jittering. Anyway, there'll be no more trains. It's Christmas Day tomorrow.'

'Six is back,' Mori said, past the snowman.

Like a puppy, her natural pace was a quick jog. Instead of

opening the low gate, she vaulted it, and then stopped when she saw them.

'Good jump,' said Thaniel, in case she was worried they would disapprove.[*]

'Why did you make that?' she asked. She was looking past them, at the snowman.

'People ... make snowmen, petal.' Had he really never made one with her?

'Yes,' she agreed, 'but that isn't a man.'

Thaniel looked back.

She was right. It wasn't a man. It was something he had never seen before. A great spider leaned over them, a shape he didn't know but did, too, in the same part of his mind that knew the caretaker's song.

He wasn't a coward, he knew that. But he had never once seen a thing he couldn't understand at all, and terror like he had never felt before snaked around all his organs and squeezed harder than he had known it could.

Mori sliced one arm through its nearest leg, and it collapsed. But parts of it still held that awful shape. The snow made a whickering noise as it settled, clicking and alive.

Six pulled them both inside.

---

[*] Mistress Jenkins at school seemed to believe any sort of physical fitness was unladylike. This baffled Mori, whose grandmother had ridden into battle with her sisters and beheaded one of them rather than let her be taken by the enemy. Thaniel suspected that Mori would have been secretly proud if Six had beheaded Mistress Jenkins.

He found a pamphlet of train timetables in the study, but there was only one train a day, and it had gone at nine o'clock that morning. Certain he did not want to spend another night here, he found the map and hunted for the next house. How big had Mori said the effect of this place was? A few square miles – they wouldn't have to go far to get away from it.

A village was marked on, just beyond where they had found the fishing station, but that was very definitely *inside* the few square miles.

The only other house on the map was a tiny place away in the marsh; a hunter's house, or a charcoal burner's. But it was six miles away, in the deepening snow, and there were no roads, and no landmarks. The map didn't mark the marshy pools. They must not have been permanent enough.

Slowly, he became aware that someone was humming; and then that it was him. It was the eel song again. He knew which word meant eel now, which word meant woods, even though he had never even heard the language until they came here. He knew what the language was too. It was English as it had been when the Vikings came.

He took the map down to the kitchen, where Mori and Six were near the open stove.

'I think we should try,' he said once he'd shown them the house on the map. 'It's far, but there's still daylight.'

Mori was shaking his head. 'In the snow, through the marsh, with no road; how are we going to find it? I won't remember how to get there until we're well away from here.'

'But something is wrong. *Really* wrong.'

'I agree. But nothing here has hurt us. Even if we don't get lost, six miles in this weather won't be safe. I don't know how far Six can go, and if we overshoot that house . . . it gets dark before four now. It's already one o'clock. I think it would be safer to stay here for the night and then go in the morning. That gives us a lot longer with the light.' He looked up at Thaniel. 'Unless you think . . . ?'

Thaniel sank down in a chair. 'No. No, you're right. Nothing has hurt us here.'

୭

They all stayed in the same room that night. They played cards well into the evening, the lamps burning and a fire lit, all of them sitting on Thaniel's bed, Six wrapped up in a blanket. She loved it; they couldn't normally play card games with Mori, because he always knew which cards were coming so he was bored to extinction. Thaniel found himself relaxing into it too. Mori was right; nothing dangerous had happened, and despite those lapses, the song, the snow-spider, it was still good to see him laugh over the cards and lose to a triumphant Six.

He fell asleep with one hand closed over Mori's. The night had been quiet, and all of them had set their watches to ring at seven in the morning. As he sank away from normal thinking, a sharp part of him demanded to know why he wasn't tying his wrist to something to keep from sleepwalking, but dream logic had already taken over, and he couldn't remember why he was worried about sleepwalking.

৵

He woke up with the frozen lake water up to his shoulders.

It was so cold that it burned, the air above the water seemed sauna hot, and every atom in him went rigid with shock. The surface was frozen an inch deep; he was in a jagged pool. He caught the edges and dragged himself out, which was far harder than he had thought because the strength in his arms had died. He had to lie flat on the ice and try to breathe. Somehow the ice felt warm. When he pulled himself onto all fours, his heart was sledgehammering.

It was trying to drown him. Whatever it was – he had been six inches from going under.

He got up and stumbled, and had to stop, because the ice creaked. It took a long time to get to the shore, and longer again to get back to the house in the dark. His clothes started to freeze on the way, the creases turning solid over his elbows.

The front door was ajar.

He ran in and almost thunked straight into Mori, who was quick even when he couldn't remember ahead, and stepped sharp to one side. His lamp swung.

'Thaniel! We were just about to look for you,' he said, slouching. 'Christ, you're soaked – what—?'

'The lake, I woke up in the bloody— hello,' Thaniel added

stiffly, because the caretaker had just come from the kitchen, with another lamp.

'She came to check we were all right,' Mori said. 'Opportunely.'

'In the middle of the night?' Thaniel asked, hearing his own voice turn to steam.

'It's when the sleepwalking can get to you a bit,' she said gently. 'I'd have come yesterday, but I clean forgot. You ought to get warm.'

☙

Thaniel came down to them once he had washed and changed his clothes. He was still frozen, but he wanted to know what she had to say more than he wanted to get warm. Mori, though, had hung up a blanket by the stove, and handed it over when Thaniel took the spare chair at the table.

'It's always the way,' the caretaker said, not as though it bothered her at all. She was holding a cup of tea. Mori put one in Thaniel's hands too. 'This place takes people strangely. I should have left a note, but I didn't want to frighten you. It's nothing to worry about. Something in the water, you know?'

Thaniel looked down into his tea. 'It isn't just sleep-walking,' he said. 'We, ah . . . ' He looked at Mori, not sure how to go on.

'We seem to be forgetting a lot,' Mori provided.

'Oh, yes. But is that not why you came?' she said. 'People come here to forget.' Her water-blue eyes slid across to Thaniel. 'You didn't, though, did you? It's better not to come here if you don't want to give a few memories to the place.' She sounded severe.

He couldn't tell what he was meant to say.

'But all the memories from this one! What a feast.' She smiled at Mori. 'There is a *lot* more of the future than the past. A miracle it all fits in one head. We haven't seen one of you, in— oh, a thousand years.' She was still smiling, and it was the same hungry smile as the eel lady had aimed at them. Not them; Mori. 'Since the saint came.'

Thaniel stood up fast, and stalled when he saw that Mori hadn't. Mori was still sitting still, just watching her as if she were speaking normally.

'We think,' the caretaker said to Thaniel, 'that you should go back to sleep, and stop trying to take him away.' She tilted her head at him. 'We think you should go back to sleep and drown in the lake.'

Thaniel took a breath to say that she was mad, but whatever she was, whatever all this was, the words had weight. He *was* sleepy. He was desperately tired, and now that she had said so, sleep felt like a wonderful idea.

There was a thudding that was Six coming down the stairs.

The caretaker smiled at her.

'We think you should stay with us too, little one. You remember everything very well, don't you? All loud and sharp. Those are memories to cut a man with.'

The voice sounded wrong, and in gradual stages, like egg yolk sliding down his spine, Thaniel realised it was because she was speaking in perfect tandem with Mori now. They were both watching Six.

Six stared at them all. Thaniel was paralysed and some-where deep in his soul, he could tell that he needed to move and run and get Mori and Six away *now*, but he couldn't. An immense weight was dragging at his whole mind. He could feel he was about to fall down asleep right here in the kitchen, and then, God, after that – after that, this thing would walk him back to the lake.

'No, we're not doing that. Put your coat on,' Six said to Thaniel. 'And bring Mori.'

'No,' the caretaker and Mori said. 'You should stay with us.'

'No,' Six said solemnly. 'They're mine and you can't have them, so bugger off.'

Thaniel felt whatever it was that was tugging at him waver. It was just enough to give himself a shake and hold his hand against the side of the kettle. The burn rocketed him awake, and as he hissed at the pain, the caretaker yelped and clenched her hand too.

Mori came back. Thaniel saw it happen. He came back into his own eyes.

Six pushed Thaniel's coat into his hands and pulled Mori to the door. The caretaker only sat and watched them, humming.

☙

They had been right before; it was hard to walk in the snow, even as heavily dressed as they could be. The snow dragged at them, and so did the thing from the lake. The caretaker didn't follow them out; she didn't need to. Whatever it was, it was in the snow, and in the water. Thaniel felt like he was trying to think through treacle. He surfaced from it and couldn't remember what he was doing out here in the dark. Six put a lit sparkler in his hand.

'Concentrate or it'll burn you,' she told him.

He stared at the cracking flame. 'Six, how come you're not . . . ' he asked, and even to himself, he sounded groggy.

'I'm wired wrongly,' she said. It was the oldest she had ever sounded, and it wasn't proud, only sad. Part of his heart broke away. 'I went wrong, at the workhouse.'

'Six, you seem exactly right to me,' Mori told her. He was shivering.

'If we don't get somewhere warm soon . . . ' Thaniel whispered. He couldn't feel his hands. A mote of hot ash from the sparkler settled on his wrist, and again, the tiny scald jolted him more awake.

'As soon as I can remember properly again, we'll be fine,' Mori said, but he sounded scared, and neither of them said aloud that for all they could tell, they were walking in circles. Here and there in the fen now, other people were singing, all perfectly in time. Some were very close.

∾

Thaniel didn't know how far they went in the end. They came out onto a road, two feet deep in snow, and he felt as though he couldn't walk any further – had felt like that for what seemed like hours – when Mori remembered where to go. There was a cottage down the next lane. They would never have seen it from the road, because there were no lights, and no one was there. Mori picked the lock and hurried Thaniel and Six in, and within a minute, the fires were burning and two kettles were set to boil.

'I've never felt so bloody stupid,' Mori said once they were all sitting with their hands in hot water.

'Will they follow us?'

'They can't,' Mori said, with an acidic laugh. 'If they leave, they'll realise their memories are all gone. They'll run away. No more food for that thing.'

'It's like a honey trap,' Thaniel said quietly. The feeling was burning back into his hands, and common sense was burning back into his head. 'The forgetting. For ... people like you. Why couldn't you remember this, before? When you could still ... ?'

'I don't know. I'm so sorry.' Mori looked at Six. 'Thank you,' he said to her. 'You were spectacular.'

She swung her legs and kicked her heels against the bar of her chair, and shrugged happily. Mori gave her his watch. She hugged it, glowing.

࿔

Home was entirely itself. The holly was still there, light-bulbs, and pinned to the front door was an irate note from Mrs Haverly, saying that Mori's pet octopus had been through her cat flap again and stolen all the teaspoons. Feeling as though he never wanted to leave the house again, Thaniel stayed in until New Year, and then, reluctantly, had to go back to work. After the companionable leaning of the medieval timbers at home, Whitehall was grim and cold.

'Good Christmas?' the section chief smiled as he came in.

Thaniel had to pause. He had been about to say, *eventful,* but now he was thinking of it, he couldn't remember why he had wanted to say that. It had been the opposite. In fact he couldn't pin down any particular memory of Christmas at all. The days at home had run together into a general glow of mulled wine and firelight. He had strange echo-memory of a train and a long journey, but he must have been confusing it with some other Christmas. 'Lovely,' he said. 'We didn't do anything.'

LILY WILT

Jess Kidd

Young Walter Pemble, the finest memorial photographer currently employed by Sturge & Sons (Photographic Studio, First-class Portraits Taken in All Weathers, Postcards, Cabinets, Plain or Coloured in the Highest Form of Art. All Pictures Permanent and Guaranteed to Last the Test of Time, Theatrical Groups, Invalids, The Recently Expired, Children, Residences, Equestrian, etc., Masters of All Known and Unknown Advancements in Fashion and Method), presents himself at a townhouse in Hanover Square at the appointed hour.

He is brought before the master of the house.

Mr Wilt scowls up from his desk. Pemble bows and smiles winningly. Mr Wilt fixes Pemble with a cold look.

'No funny business,' says Mr Wilt. 'No touching, leering or rubbing yourself up against the casket. Mrs Wilt may believe that our dear departed daughter is an object of chaste veneration but I know the effect my darling Lily has on people. Game bucks like yourself most of all.'

Pemble is horrified. He blushes to the roots of his beard.

Mr Wilt is satisfied. 'And take a few of the visiting crowds, for posterity.'

'Visiting crowds, sir?'

'We open at nine. Chop, chop.'

ॐ

In a gilded frame, on an easel, outside the entrance to the drawing room, Pemble views the page from last night's paper bearing Lily Wilt's obituary. It is penned by a pre-eminent author and frequent dinner guest of Mr and Mrs Rumold Wilt. The pre-eminent author imparts, in evocative language, the transports of wonder he experienced while gazing upon the deceased. In life, Miss Lily Wilt had been a poppet. In death, she is nothing short of a miracle. Her beauty grave and sublime. Her expression enigmatic. Her mortal shell exquisite and untarnished by natural processes.

The pre-eminent author declares the late Miss Wilt to be an inspiration – perfection, even in death, is possible! The printed poem likens Lily to a nodding snowdrop, a nestled dove, a dreaming lamb.

A sight worth seeing indeed.

ॐ

The moment he sees her, Pemble cries. Pemble has never cried before, not even as a baby, not even a birth cry.

It isn't sadness that elicits the young man's tears, nor fear, nor even pity. Pemble has seen his share of corpses. Little ones in lace-dressed coffins. Venerable ancients in neat repose. Stiff and proper pillars of the community. Buffed and nestled, the dead are like best spoons put away until Sunday.

No, Pemble sheds his tears in wonder.

His vision blurs so that the apparition before him swims, glows, even. Pemble adjusts some complicated mechanism on his camera and peers again. It takes him a moment or two to realise that the equipment isn't at fault; it is himself.

Now he regards his subject not through the lens but with his naked eye.

Her halo of gold-spun hair, her narrow-flanked, white-gowned, body. Her palms pressed together, like a martyr's. Her face – a saint in repose! Although, not quite a saint. For her mouth wears the ghost of a knowing smile and has a certain plump-lipped voluptuousness (holy souls usually being thin of lip with a tendency towards turned-down mouths).

Nan Hooley, housemaid, watches from the window. She is waiting for the photographer to finish, so that she can release the velvet drapes (deep scarlet, tasselled, eight times the weight of her) and return the room to its state of all-day-night. Then she must roll back the carpet and take her position and bow her head as the nut-crunching public drift past to gawp in the casket. She must call the footman if anyone becomes *overwhelmed*. Then she must tend the fires, set the table for the servants' luncheon, listen to the carol singers and have a drop of something and a bite of figgy pudding, what with Christmas approaching and all that.

Pemble takes his handkerchief from his pocket and wipes his face. He is sweating, although it is cold in the room.

Arctic. Despite the honeyed slant of winter sun in through the panes of the undressed window and the conflagration of a hundred tapering white candles.

The air is solid and sickly with the scent of lilies. Legions of them. They arrive swaddled, by the armful, at the cellar door every morning, from hothouses up and down the country. Lilies in the depth of winter! With frost on the ground and ice at the windows! Her namesake flowers work the same pure intoxicating magic as the late Lily, the only daughter of Mr Rumold and Mrs Guinevere Wilt, residents of a top-notch townhouse in Hanover Square, London. A house sunk in mourning. The mirrors are covered and the pendulums stopped. The windows are shuttered and the doorknocker tied about with crepe. The family speak in whispers and the servants talk in eye-rolls.

Pemble dips and twiddles at his camera, steps forwards and back, stops to gaze. And gaze. And gaze.

The housemaid gives a polite cough. Pemble blinks and resumes his work.

Nan has never seen anything like it, Mr Pemble's strange dance with his contraption. He touches it with wary fingers, as if it might bite or run skittering from the drawing room. With an apologetic air, he rummages about its skirts, some-times disappearing underneath. Reappearing to frown, or move a bloom, or an occasional table. She's not to know that Mr Pemble is an artist and an alchemist. This young man is capable of capturing the essence of the deceased. The very cut of their jib as they sail off on their last adventure. Here is a young man who grapples daily with glass plates and dwindling light, chemistry and dust. To create miraculous images in which the dead live again, reposing with a fine glow of health, captured in a state of freshness, fullness, in their exact prime of life (whatever age they were) for all eternity. Pemble could capture the soul's last flutter and preserve it for posterity.

Only not today.

Today Pemble's hands shake and his head spins and his breaths are taken in gulps.

'Would you be so kind,' he says to the housemaid hanging on to the curtains, 'as to fetch me a glass of water?'

Even with the housemaid gone and the room perfectly empty he feels it: the unnerving sense that someone is watching him.

༄

Nan Hooley traverses the drawing-room floor on her hands and knees, sweeping up spent tealeaves. These things happen: a picture frame tips over, the candleflames gutter, a wintry breeze whisks about her knees. Nan sits back on her haunches, brush in hand. She frowns up at the casket, swagged about with black crepe. The polished wood fogs, as if with breath. Letters appear, as if traced by a finger.

L. I. L. Y.

Nan stands and casts a stern eye over the corpse. Luminous, hands pressed together, oh, saintly like. Only, Miss Wilt was never a saint, not with that mouth – the filth that came out of it. Nan detects a sly look under the closed lids.

'Now, just you stay put, miss,' she says firmly. 'Don't you go gallivanting.'

෴

Outside the light is making a big point of its dying. Tattooed rooftops against a smoky orange sky. The streets are a glorious festive muddle, hot chestnuts, orange sellers, shops lit by gaslight, the endless traffic of hansom and omnibus, cart and barrow.

Mrs Peach's Guest House, however, is as joyless as ever.

A tall, thin, tired house with frowning gables and draughty windows. The entrance hall is in darkness and a few degrees colder than the outside.

Pemble takes the staircase at a bolt, his equipment strapped to his back for ease of ascent. He intends to avoid Mrs Peach tonight.

The door to her room is sprung, her feet patter into the hallway.

'Mr Pemble, a word—'

Pemble breaks into a gallop, achieves his rooms, locks the door behind him.

He has a burning question on his mind. It ignited the

moment he left the dead young woman's side and has roared into quite the inferno.

How can he hope to do her justice? With his egg whites and his silver-nitrate baths.

Can he capture Lily Wilt's supernatural beauty?

Pemble's two-room attic domain is haunted by the scent of tripe and onions and afflicted by erratic slopings of the ceiling. At home he adopts a stoop for he bangs his head often, never quite getting used to the tip and slant of the rafters nor the seasick nature of the floorboards. The smaller of the two rooms is his darkroom.

It is here he labours.

The paper fogs. The chemicals cloud.

Finally, as dawn breaks, a likeness!

Pemble peers at the photograph. The lilies arch in their vases. The candles taper. The lovely corpse reposes—

But wait!

Pemble grabs a magnifying glass, turns up the gaslight, scrutinises the image.

Leant against the mantelpiece, looking dead at the camera with a twisted grin, stands . . .

A trick of the light surely? A strange accident of chemistry?

But it is her. The perfect little upturned nose, the full lips, the halo of fair hair!

Lily Wilt.

And not quite Lily Wilt.

Pemble takes a slow breath. The magnifying glass trembles in his hand. He sees a beautiful face. He sees a graceful body. He also sees an ormolu clock and a vase full of flowers *through* that face and body.

∾

Pemble returns to the townhouse in Hanover Square. He fights through the gathering crowds and gains access to the front steps where he admits to the butler that due to the intricacies and challenges of the photographic process he has been unable to capture a satisfying likeness of Miss Wilt.

Pemble is brought before the master of the house.

Pemble bows and smiles weakly. Mr Wilt glares up from his desk. He hears Pemble's excuses. Such is the reputation of Sturge & Sons (*By Appointment to Nobility Various & Persons of High Quality*) that another session is granted.

'This is your last chance, Pemble. I won't have the viewings interrupted. People, illustrious types, are coming from far and wide to lay eyes on our dear dead Lily.'

Pemble thanks Mr Wilt profusely.

Mr Wilt, with a snarl, turns back to his reckonings.

∾

How Lily's fame has grown!

A steady file of people moves past the little casket. Nan stands ready to nudge the mourners along if they get overly rapturous.

Even Nan, in all her down-to-earth wisdom, will concede

that Miss Wilt certainly seems miraculous. Miraculous in the way that none of the natural processes you would expect to take place with a cadaver have taken place. The changes to pallor, the tempestuous collection and release of bodily gases, the popping of the eyes, the pushing out of the tongue and all the attendant horrors the grim reaper brings.

An old woman lingers before the casket. 'God bless her! Why, she's a little saint!'

Behind her people jostle, craning their heads to see.

The old woman lunges forward with pinking shears to snip herself off a relic. Nan calls for the footman.

෨

The drawing room is empty. The public have been ushered out for the purposes of Pemble's final portrait. Nan has changed the candles and rearranged the flowers and straightened the tassels on the Turkey rug. Mr Pemble sets up his contraption. Nan takes her position by the curtains.

Pemble clears his throat. 'Would you be kind enough to fetch me a glass of water?'

Pemble waits. His gaze riveted to the fireplace. But no spectral vision of Lily Wilt appears. He takes a few steps to the casket and looks inside. He touches the edge of her coverlet, then her hands, palm to palm in prayer, like a child's. They are ice. He bends and kisses her forehead, bewitched by her polar beauty. His lips tremble on contact.

These things happen: a picture frame cracks on the

occasional table, the candles burn blue, laughter as cold and bright as early spring fills the room.

And a honeyed voice at his ear. 'Look through your contraption.'

Pemble takes his position at his camera, tangling in the skirts, fumbling with the focus, near to fainting with fear and yearning.

Pemble cannot stop to consider the ifs and the whys and the wherefores – not with such an adorable spectre manifesting before his lens.

Oh, how she manifests!

This time she's not by the fireplace, she's leaning rakishly over the edge of the casket, blowing him a kiss, like a girl in a soap commercial. Only Lily Wilt is perfectly translucent, perfectly beautiful.

Pemble races to make image after image.

The ghost of Lily Wilt draped diaphanously over a love seat.

The ghost of Lily Wilt looking radiant by the parlour palm.

The ghost of Lily Wilt, close enough to steam the camera lens, if she had breath.

The ghost of Lily Wilt, in the close dark, behind the lens, standing right beside him. A freezing mineral blast, he shivers deliciously.

'You seem to know your way around this contraption,' she whispers. 'You must be a man of science and learning.'

Pemble is flattered. 'Photography is an art too, Miss Wilt.

The very word photography is derived from the Greek terms for light and representation by means of—'

'Yes, yes. Look, I've a proposition for you. If you can put my spirit back in my body, I'm yours.'

Pemble groans in the dark. 'Lily, darling!'

'I'm tired of being a spectacle.' A small catch in the voice. 'There's so much I never got to do.' The voice grows coy. 'Like being a wife.'

Pemble's eyes well with tears, this time of joy.

But then the enormity of her request strikes him. 'But how?'

'Some trick with lightning, trips to cemeteries, that sort of thing, you can figure it out. Promise me you'll save me, dear, erm . . .'

'Walter.'

'Dear, Walter.'

Pemble nods. 'I promise.'

∽

It has started to snow. Great fat flakes lit by gaslight, dancing and turning. Snow brushes against the window-panes. Snow alights on the rooftops. Snow settles on the eyelashes and noses of happy children. Pemble turns his face to the sky and is blessed with soft frosty kisses – as if from the lips of his dear dead beloved! He steps lightly through the jostle of London's streets. Like all young lovers he feels blissful and damned, thrilled and terrified. He delights in the windows decorated with bauble and bough. He delights in the excitement of the street urchins thieving hot pies. He delights in the arboreous procession of pine trees being barrowed through the heaving streets. He delights in the people that pass by, laden with packages and parcels.

Christmas is but a week away.

Christmas with Lily Wilt.

Strolling, talking, sharing an orange, riding an omnibus, tumbling like puppies in the bed (how Pemble blushes at this thought!).

He just has the small, and possibly profane, matter of reuniting Lily's spirit with her body.

✎

He starts early the next morning at Mudie's lending library. Driven by his passion to save his beloved, he is barely intimidated by the hallowed main hall, or the library clerks with their raised eyebrows and uppity glances. He boils at every tick of the clock. He is irritated by every dithering spinster. Murderous towards each leisurely footman ferrying reservations to waiting carriages.

Finally, the book is in his hands.

How to Resurrect the Dead.

In a nearby alleyway Pemble tears off the brown paper wrapping and is dismayed. This is not a helpful guide, it is a story about a returning sea captain and a plucky-yet-lonely widow, set largely around Portsmouth.

Pemble could weep with frustration. Then . . . revelation! He heads to Seven Dials.

Pemble purchases a hot toddy from a leering barmaid, nods nervously to the regulars and makes his way to a booth. It is said that at this pub (which shall remain nameless) anything in the world can be obtained at a price. Anything.

Presently, a sly and somewhat dirty character slithers into the seat opposite him and touches his cap.

In a low voice Pemble gives a sense of his unnatural endeavour. He is directed to Camden Town.

In a dark lane, down a dark passageway, in a dark recess, is the façade of a gloomy bookshop. The sign above the door reads:

NARCISSUS P. THOOMS

BOOKSELLER

SCIENTIFIC AND ESOTERIC

TAXONOMY AND TAXIDERMY

Pemble hesitates a moment, screws closed his eyes and conjures the adorable shape of Lily Wilt. Fortified, he steps inside.

The shop bell rings. Dust motes dance in the sudden inrush of air.

At first glance the shop seems empty of a proprietor. Piles of ancient, cobwebbed books cover every available surface. Shelves ascend dustily from floor to ceiling. Behind the desk sits a stuffed screech owl wearing a monocle.

Pemble clears his throat several times.

Movement in a shadowy corner, and from a veritable mountain of books arises a naked man with an impressive beard.

'Your clothes, sir!' exclaims Pemble.

'I'm absorbing knowledge,' says the man serenely. 'Are you looking for something in particular?'

Pemble relays his unenviable quest. Mr Thooms listens with an unwholesome glint in his dark eyes. Clad now in a silk kimono, he abstractedly scratches the animal pelt of his chest. From time to time, he nods encouragingly.

When Pemble concludes Mr Thooms shakes his hand with a punishing grip.

'My dear boy!' he effuses. 'You have strayed off the well-lit path into a world of thieves and costermongers, whores and labourers, artists, visionaries and gin palaces. Rich with stink, even in the deep winter. Rich with clamour, all hours, what with the calling and jibing, fighting and loving.'

'To Camden, yes.'

'You have come in the pursuit of knowledge. Wishing to probe the very secrets of nature, finger the mysteries of life and death, verily, to assume the role of God. You want to get your quivering hands upon tomes ancient and occult!'

'If it's not too much trouble.'

Thooms looks to be deep in thought. His voice, when it comes, is grave. 'There is a way. A profoundly wicked and dangerous way. Which is against every law of decency, morality and nature.'

Pemble thrills.

'A way which,' continues Thooms, 'when combined with a bit of surgical trickery, will have that lovely little cadaver breathing and sighing and blushing and playing the pianoforte to your heart's delight.'

'Is it really possible?' ventures Pemble.

'It's fully possible, my dear boy, to bring Lily Wilt back to life.'

⁓

While Mr Thooms searches for the exact edition of the book with the secrets of life and death in it, he shares with Pemble his own tragic history.

Once upon a time Mr Thooms had a very different career ahead of him.

His great-uncle Thaddeus 'Red' Thooms could take a leg off in less than two minutes; his father, Theodore, could liberate a tumour in one. Such was the talent of this illustrious medical family that if you gave Thooms's granny a butter knife she'd have your gallstones out before the tea was served. Thooms' promising surgical career was cut short by a tragic affair of the heart.

He fell in love over the dissection table.

Thooms pauses in his recollections and throws a harrowed glance at Pemble. Such is the misery and horror and wretchedness at play on Thooms' face that Pemble cannot help but shiver.

'The corpse was a rare beauty. I was a brave and bold

young man.' Thooms' eyes fill with tears. 'Some sights you cannot unsee, Pemble. Some acts you cannot undo.'

When the tome in question is found the men share a decanter of decent claret. Thooms wraps in black paper the leather-bound book of monumental proportions and delivers it into Pemble's hands.

He waives the money that Pemble counts out for him.

'I have but one final question before you leave.' Thooms tightens the belt of his kimono and looks Pemble in the eye. 'What you are about to do is not for the fainthearted, you must be certain. Is she the one you want?'

Pemble cradles in his arms the monstrously heavy book containing all the secrets of life and death.

Lily Wilt. Lily Wilt. Lily Wilt.

The sorcery in her name and in all of her!

Lily Wilt is captivating.

Pemble conjures before him her body lying in sweet repose. Her golden hair, the upturned button of her nose, the slim breast under white lace. Her downy arms and heavy lashes and pearly little nails.

He conjures her voice, sweet and honeyed and girlish.

He conjures her spirit, shimmering and blithe.

Pemble is suddenly struck with the indescribable feeling that he has always loved Lily Wilt, always worshiped her! She was fashioned for him and him for her.

'Yes,' Pemble replies. 'Lily is the only one.'

໖

The work is long and hard. The ancient tome lies open on his desk; Pemble pursues dreadful secrets through its yellowed pages. The insights he seeks are inky nymphs, they flutter away, just as he is near to grasping them.

Pemble does not leave his rooms for days, failing even to keep his photographic appointments. When he sleeps, he is plagued by the same dream.

It is not a good dream.

He is in a crowded place amid the press of a mob of shabby young fellows. There is a din of shouting and jeering and ribbing. There is the smell of stale alcohol, spent tobacco and cheap hair oil. Dimly Pemble begins to understand what he is witnessing; the men that surround him are medical students, this is a dissection theatre.

Silence falls.

Double doors are thrown open and a body is stretchered into the theatre by two burly dressers. On the stretcher lies Lily Wilt. Bare legs, naked feet, her trunk covered with a sheet, her face hollow and her hair matted as after a long illness.

A surgeon, head bowed, the brim of his top hat pulled low, follows the stretcher, stepping in time. The medical students hum a requiem.

Lily is manoeuvred onto the table, one white arm drops, her golden hair spills. All the shabby young gentlemen in the room simultaneously sigh and lean forward.

The surgeon nods to his assistant, who steps forward and rolls up the gentleman's sleeves. A butcher's apron, stiff with gore and terrible to see, is solemnly presented and tied about.

The surgeon divests himself of his top hat. Narcissus P. Thooms, smiling benignly, surveys the collected audience.

He turns to inspect the table laid with instruments, tiptoeing his fingers along them, he selects a long, brutal-toothed saw. With a salacious wink Mr Thooms wanders to the operating table and lays a hand on Lily's cheek.

Her eyes open—

It is night in the townhouse in Hanover Square. Mr Wilt is fast asleep, his grand moustache flutters with each fruity snore. Mrs Wilt nests nicely in nightcap, wittering through her dreams of pug dogs and silver teapots. Downstairs Saint Lily lies in state in the drawing room, cosseted in gauze and lace and silk, her hands placed in eternal prayer. The cook, the butler, the footman, the mice in the larder, the dogs in the kennel – all are slumbering. Only Nan Hooley is awake. She lights a candle and walks through the quiet house.

She closes the door to the drawing room softly and fires up the gaslights. The air is cool in the room yet and the casket polished bright, but there is a smell of sweet decay in the air. The lilies are turning, their trumpets droop, their petals curl.

Nan pulls up a chair beside the casket. Lily's face looks the same as it did on the morning of her death. Nan narrows her eyes and looks closely. After a while she sees that Lily has, in

fact, changed. Her beauty has faltered. There is a thinning of
the full lips and the suggestion of a squint around the eyes so
that the cadaver has a sour, peevish, kind of look to it. The
skin has a greenish pallor and there's a looseness to the hair
around the temples.

Lily may be working some unnatural magic on the
world – but no one can trick death.

'What are you up to, miss?' Nan whispers.

These things happen: the picture frame hops on the table,
the stopped clock on the mantelpiece starts ticking, the tassels on the Turkey rug ruffle.

Nan waits. The polished wood on the side of the casket
fogs, letters appear.

L. I. L. Y. L. I. V. E. S.

'Don't you be getting ideas,' Nan scolds. 'What you need,
miss, is a nice peaceful burial. It's not seemly to be paraded
about and gawked at by half of London. It's not natural!'

Nan fancies she sees a shadow of irritation cross Lily's fine,
still features.

She ponders for a while, her eyes on the sleeping face of
Lily Wilt. By degrees she resolves to seek the advice of a
particular pre-eminent author and regular dinner guest of
Mr and Mrs Rumold Wilt. After all, his obituary started all
this. Nan is confident that she will obtain an audience with
the illustrious gentleman, for hasn't he sketched a likeness
of her in one of his popular stories?

'I shall be having words with Mr D_____, you see if I don't. He'll talk sense into your dear mama and papa.'

These things happen: the gaslights flare, the lilies shrivel in their vases and an arctic wind howls about Nan's ears.

Nan, uncowed, closes the lid of the casket with an air of good riddance.

๛

Pemble wakes to a persistent tapping at the door. He opens his eyes. The pages of the book of life and death lie rumpled beneath his cheek.

The tapping stops and is replaced by a determined knocking. He sits up at his desk.

The door handle is tried. Rattled. A voice calls out; an insidious nasal whine.

'Mr Pemble, would you happen to be within?'

Pemble closes the book, hides it and manages to put on his trousers before Mrs Peach is in through the door, making light work of the lock. Pemble's landlady stands before him, a fright of a woman, thin as string, all elbows and clavicles and a startling head of raven hair (not her own).

'Do excuse my intrusion, Mr Pemble.' She gives him a bitter smile. 'I haven't seen you all week and what with it being rent day.' She glances around the room, at the bed that hasn't been slept in, at the debris of half-eaten repasts.

'You're intent on summoning rats to my guest house, Mr Pemble?'

'Sorry, no.'

'I run a clean establishment, Mr Pemble.'

'I'll bring the money down directly,' offers Pemble with all the politeness he can muster.

Mrs Peach crosses the floor. She lifts the curtain to Pemble's darkroom and looks inside. 'Mr Pemble, I thought we'd agreed that this is supposed to be your bedchamber?'

'Sorry, yes.'

Mrs Peach turns her attention to the prints that hang around the room.

Pemble feels a rush of anger at the sight of Mrs Peach peering and prying at the glorious likenesses of the corpse of Lily Wilt.

'Dead, is it?'

'Sadly.'

'Poor little popsy, twelve?'

'Seventeen.'

'Consumption, was it? That great scourge of lovely young women.'

'No. Not consumption.'

She squints at the picture. 'An accident then? A funny shape to the head, a bit of a dent to the temple there.'

'Her head is perfect. Lily Wilt passed away in her sleep.'

'This is Lily Wilt?'

'Yes.'

'The *famous* Lily Wilt?'

Pemble acquiesces.

'"The Perpetually Sleeping Beauty!" The papers call her "London's Top Festive Spectacle!"' Mrs Peach casts him an arch look. 'Only not for long.'

Pemble has a bad feeling. 'What do you mean?'

'She's been sold to a showman. Lily Wilt is to be shipped abroad, America no less.'

Pemble startles.

'Imagine!' rattles Mrs Peach. 'That little slip of a thing has a soap named after her!'

Pemble grabs his hat and greatcoat and rushes for the door.

'Mr Pemble, the rent if you please!'

Pemble makes haste to the townhouse of the Wilt family in Hanover Square. At the doorstep the butler takes note of these things: a dishevelled appearance, a wildness of the eyes, a significant trembling of the hands and lips. The butler informs Pemble that in his absence his esteemed employers, Sturge & Sons, dispatched their second-finest memorial photographer, Mr Stickles. Mr Stickles visited promptly, conducted the session discreetly and supplied Mr and Mrs Wilt with a selection of likenesses they are entirely enchanted with.

'Could I just? . . . Please, one moment with Miss Wilt—'

'I'm afraid not, sir.' The butler closes the door, firmly.

Pemble walks on. He hardly knows it is Christmas Eve. The merry crowds and dancing snow, the glad urchins and orange sellers, the hot chestnuts and bedecked shop windows – all are lost on him. But then, oh, a shaft of light shines through the gloom. He is struck by a remembrance of his beloved. In his mind's eye he invokes her jaunty spectre, her sublime saint-like body.

He hears her cherished voice again.

'Get your finger out, Walter, dear. I'm waiting.'

With renewed vigour Pemble turns towards Seven Dials.

Pemble purchases a hot toddy from a surly barmaid, nods knowingly to the regulars and makes his way to a booth. Presently, the sly and somewhat dirty character slithers into the seat opposite and touches his cap.

In a low voice Pemble gives a sense of his criminal requirements.

Dirty Character sucks air in through his remaining teeth. 'It'll cost. Double-time. Christmas Eve and all that.'

'Just make sure she's handled with care.' Pemble remembers the rules of dealing with undesirables. 'A bonus for safe delivery.'

Dirty Character grins and tips his cap. 'We'll treat her like a snowflake.'

❧

Midnight. A bundle is carefully hauled up the stairs of Mrs Peach's Guest House and into Pemble's attic rooms. The delivery is without incident, the landlady being insensible on spiked gin.

Pemble has the bundle taken into the darkroom. The place he has prepared for the reunion of Lily Wilt's body and spirit.

He is breathless with excitement waiting for the masked men to leave. He locks the door behind them.

Pemble's hands shake as he unwraps the package. He is awestruck, hardly daring to look at the physical form of his beloved in its entirety. Instead, he takes in little sips. Her delicate toes, lovely shins, the beautiful arch of her eyebrow, her dear stony cheek—

'Walter, dear,' says a waspish voice, 'I've had quite enough of being spectated at. How about you get on with bringing me back to life?'

৭

Pemble consults Thooms' tome on life and death. He checks off the needful equipment and runs through the procedure again in his mind. He tries to still his beating heart.

The spirit of Lily Wilt drifts about the room, shimmering in her form-fitting shroud, inspecting the images of herself. 'I do take rather a good photograph, don't I?'

Pemble wipes his forehead. 'Yes, dearest.' He hesitates. 'We could just keep things as they are. I don't mind if you're a bit, you know, incorporeal.'

Lily's glare is icy. 'Well, I do mind. You made me a promise, Walter. I want to eat bonbons and go out dancing.' A lascivious note creeps into her voice. 'I want to taste the physical aspects of life again.'

Walter blushes and looks away. 'I'll see what I can do, dearest.'

The mortal remains of Lily Wilt lie on a sturdy bench.

Around the body lanterns are lit. Next to the bench there is a table – Pemble shudders to look at it – laid out with surgical instruments. Under the bench there is a tin bath and several glass demijohns. Sawdust is scattered over the floor. In the corner of the room is a washstand holding a mysterious array of objects. Among them, a linnet's wing, a mirror, a dish of chalk and a chalice.

Hours pass. The church bells ring out. It is Christmas Day.

Lily Wilt, spirit and body reunited, sits in a chair by the window. She has a teacup full of gin at her right elbow and is holding a roll of swabbing to her ear. She is wearing Pemble's nightshirt. Pemble averts his eyes from the angry stitches that traverse her décolleté.

The darkroom is a mess. The tin bath is full of gore and the sawdust is clotted in heaps on the floor. Surgical tools are bundled up in Lily's shroud and the linnet's wing is stuck to the wall.

Lily Wilt's eyes swivel to meet Pemble's. 'I want ice cream,' she says, with all the tearful peevishness of a toddler.

৽

Lily likes to sit near the window watching the people pass by in the street below.

Mostly, she is listless. She spends the day crunching nuts and spitting out the shells. Occasionally, she breaks into ribald song.

Pemble is run ragged, bringing Lily everything she asks for: books, ribbons, a spinning top, a bird in a cage and a mandolin.

'I want to go out dancing,' she whines.

'You must recuperate, dear.'

'I am feeling worse, not better! What have you even done to me?'

Pemble asks himself the same question.

Lily has changed, she is changing daily. She has lost the alabaster complexion she had in death. Her skin sags and her teeth wobble, her eyes sink and her golden hair dulls.

୭

Pemble walks to the river and looks into it. More snow falls and turns to black sludge on London's busy carriageways. At the newspaper stands news is shouted of Lily Wilt's disappearance. The grief of her doting parents is heartbreaking. The reward for her return astonishing. Pemble staggers past, pulling down his hat brim. It is too cold to sit in the park so Pemble seeks refuge in the taverns. He takes to strong liquor. He dreads sleeping, waking and above all, going home.

୭

Lily has the bed dragged to the window so that she can look out during her recuperation. She carves patterns in the ice inside the window with her fingernails. She likes the sound.

With Lily's recuperation come cravings. Lamb cutlets give way to calves' livers. Calves' livers give way to cats' meat. Cats' meat gives way to cat meat. Pemble roams the streets at night in search of felines. He shudders as he hands over the wriggling sack. Lily smirks and draws the bed curtains. In a while Pemble hears the abhorrent sounds of crunching and slurping. Shortly thereafter he picks up the discarded pelts and tosses them in the fire. The rooms smell of singed fur. One day Pemble's feet stray towards Camden Town. Down a dark lane, down a dark passageway, to a dark recess. He stands before the façade of an abandoned bookshop. The sign above the door is too faded to be read. The empty shelves ascend dustily from floor to ceiling.

The cats grow cannier, Pemble must hunt far and wide. He returns late to the lodging-house. He climbs the stairs wearily, a hissing sack over his shoulder. The door to his attic rooms lies open. Mrs Peach stands, eyes wide, talking gibberish, by the side of Pemble's bed.

Pemble has no need to introduce his landlady to Lily Wilt, the bed curtains have already been opened.

Fortunately, he still has the tin bath and surgical tools.

ॐ

Nan Hooley haunts the street outside Mrs Peach's Guest House. Taking shelter under a shop canopy opposite, clutching her market basket and frowning up at the attic windows. The crossing-sweeper has been taking note of Mr Pemble's comings and goings. Nan presses a coin into the boy's hand and he reports a curious state of affairs. Sometimes Mr Pemble is abroad to buy goods. A music box, a pineapple, a caged canary. Other times Mr Pemble stays out half the night and returns with a wriggling sack.

And now here is Mr Pemble himself. With a furtive glance he steps out onto the street, pulls up the collar of his greatcoat and continues at a good pace.

Nan is shocked by the change in the young man. His eyes glazed and bloodshot, his beard tatty, his clothes stained, his boots filthy.

She makes haste to follow him.

ॐ

At a disreputable tavern in Seven Dials, Nan watches Pemble order a drink, sit down at a booth and stare into his glass. His face wears the countenance of the damned.

Nan takes the chair opposite and puts down her basket.

Pemble looks up at her and frowns. He knows her face but he doesn't know where from.

'Mr Pemble, would you happen to know the whereabouts of Miss Wilt?'

Recognition kindles in his eyes. 'You are the housemaid.'

'Yes, sir.'

Pemble removes, from the pocket of his greatcoat, a photograph. He sets it down on the table.

'I took this likeness of Lily yesterday. Please, tell me exactly what you see.'

ॐ

Nan offers Pemble her arm on the way back to his lodging-house. Initially he stumbles but the cold air and Nan's strong quiet presence seem to revive him. At the door he smiles sadly.

'You know what you have to do now, sir?' whispers Nan.

Pemble nods.

'Fortify yourself then.'

Pemble goes inside with a heavy tread.

For a while Nan stands looking up at the attic window, then she tightens the knot of her shawl and makes her way homewards.

ℒ

The day of Lily Wilt's funeral is one of bitter cold and blue skies. The gravediggers have worked long hours hacking into the frozen ground. The hearse moves sedately. Through the carriage windows a casket can be glimpsed, topped with a carpet of flowers. Six fine black horses clop through the rolling clouds of their own hot breath. Mourners follow, muffled in black bombazine and crepe and heavy lace.

The hearse picks up followers as it moves through London so that by the time the cortege reaches the cemetery the numbers have swelled. Lily Wilt continues to intrigue. In the story of this Sleeping Beauty there is one final mystery. Her body reappeared in the drawing room in Hanover Square as bafflingly as it vanished. The public were relieved. Until they discovered that Lily Wilt would no longer be on display.

Dark rumours abounded. She had been in the hands of one depraved. She had been modified in some unearthly way. The constabulary were not at liberty to say. The family made no comment.

In the cemetery, a waiting stranger listens to the sound of the funeral carriage approaching. His heart beats faster as he sees the leading horses, they nod their black feather plumes and pass him at a steady walk. Behind the carriage the crowds trail, sniffing and moaning. In the trees the crows, always irreverent, swear and heckle.

And so, Lily Wilt is committed to her final resting place, a conspicuous family plot on the main thoroughfare. In time a carved angel will be set there, it will rival even Lily's marble loveliness. The mourners depart, tipping down their hat brims, pulling their capes around them and huddling into their muffs, leaving the gravediggers to their job of work.

Nan Hooley stays until the last. Just to be sure.

Dusk falls and Walter Pemble kneels by the grave of his beloved.

He waits. Presently he hears her voice. A little irritated.

'This is not quite the ending I had planned, Walter.'

Pemble looks up, Lily Wilt stands before him, her glacial beauty restored.

'Darling Lily.'

She bestows upon him a sleety smile. 'I suppose there is one way we can be together.'

Pemble nods, dabbing his eyes. Pemble makes his way out

of the cemetery and turns himself in to the first constable of the law he comes across.

᳃

It is morning in the townhouse in Hanover Square. In the kitchen the butler reads the newspaper aloud and the housekeeper butters a slice of toast. Nan brings a pot of tea to the table.

'So, there it is,' says the butler.

'He was a fiend.' The housekeeper applies a dab of marmalade.

'A fiend indeed.'

Nan straightens the place settings and gathers crumbs.

'Walter Pemble, latterly employed as a photographer,' the butler reads aloud, 'is convicted of the theft of the earthly remains of Miss Lily Wilt "The Perpetually Sleeping Beauty" from her family's home in Hanover Square. Mr Pemble also pleaded guilty to the unlawful killing of his landlady who had discovered his crime.'

The housekeeper tuts.

The butler sips his tea. 'Depravity and dissolution.'

'All too commonplace,' says the housekeeper. 'Dissolution is.'

'The man lost his mind,' says the butler, in a tone that implies carelessness on the part of Mr Pemble.

The housekeeper frowns. 'Even so.'

'Quite.'

᳃

Crowds gather outside Newgate Prison. Not that the hanging is public but the weather is mild for January and it's a day out. Nan Hooley is among their number. When the time comes, she sheds a few tears for Mr Pemble.

Later that afternoon Nan takes out the old cigar box she keeps under her bed. Inside there's a silver thimble, a lock of grey hair, a few faded flowers and a photograph.

She looks at the photograph for the longest time. Then she strikes a match and applies it. The paper twists and bursts into flames and with it, Lily Wilt's grin. Nan drops it into the grate. She stands a while, deep in thought, about life and death and that awful thing in between. A little while later she manages half a rabbit pie.

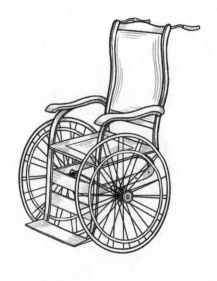

THE CHILLINGHAM CHAIR

Laura Purcell

The first sensation was a prickle upon her cheek. Then Evelyn became aware of her ears; ringing, stinging. Her limbs felt numb.

She seemed to be somewhere damp and bitterly cold. When she tried to move, pain shot through her leg and made her gasp. Her eyelids fluttered open, revealing . . . nothing. A great, colourless expanse.

Perhaps she had died. She was in purgatory, and the needles running down her spine were the payment for her sins.

No sooner had the thought crossed her mind, than the silence around her broke. An animal was panting, somewhere close by. Evelyn tensed, unable to raise her head and look. The creature breathed heavily, its paws crunching over the snow as it approached.

All she could do was whimper and shut her eyes. The animal was questing nearer, snuffling beside her ear. It tasted her forehead with its warm, slimy tongue.

'Go away,' she groaned.

But instead the hairy beast stretched across her ribcage; guarding her, claiming her for its own. All the breath was pressed out of her as the cold air echoed with a dreadful howl.

There were thuds and crunches in the distance. Someone called her name.

'Good girl!' said a man. 'Good dog.'

Slowly, Evelyn allowed her eyes to open and everything became clear. The expanse above her was not perdition but the sky, charged with snow, and no monster lay upon her chest; it was simply a beagle, summoning its master.

Faces crowded into her field of vision; gentlemen she vaguely recognised and the beloved features of her sister, Susan.

'Evelyn!' she cried. 'Evelyn, are you hurt?'

'I think . . . I am,' Evelyn croaked. 'I cannot recollect . . . what happened.'

'Snow fell off a branch and your horse spooked,' a handsome gentleman explained. 'He ran off towards the stables with the saddle hanging round his belly.'

That was right: they were hunting. Not at home but at another estate, Chillingham Grange. The man addressing her was Victor Chillingham himself. He leaned over her. Kind, solicitous eyes ran up and down her body, searching for injuries.

Evelyn could hardly breathe under the weight of her shame. Not only had she taken a tumble in public, she had fallen while staying as a guest at this gentleman's house.

The gentleman whose proposal of marriage she had firmly rebuffed.

'We must get you inside before you catch a cold,' Susan fretted. 'Do you think you can stand?'

Evelyn raised a hand to push the beagle away. Even that cost her pain.

'I am sorry to be troublesome, but ... I don't believe that I can.'

⁂

The doctor peered deep into her eyes. He smelled of laudanum and leeches. 'A nasty blow, to be sure. No injury to the skull, but there will be symptoms of concussion. Nausea, giddiness. I would not move her on any account.'

Mamma raised her handkerchief to her mouth. 'However did you manage it, Evelyn? You have never taken a fall in your life. Now on the *one* occasion we need everything to go perfectly ...'

Evelyn adjusted her position on the chaise longue. Her broken foot was elevated, wrapped in bandages and set with a splint. It itched like a flea-infested bed. 'I am sorry, Mamma. It was not my fault. Quicksilver bolted.'

The doctor opened his bag and began to write a script for the apothecary. 'Take this twice daily. I shall call again to check on your progress. In the meantime, my order is bed rest. Little movement and absolutely no excitement.'

'That is impossible!' Mamma burst out. 'Her sister is to be married on Twelfth Night and Evelyn is the bridesmaid.'

'I am sorry for that, madam, but it cannot be helped. Health must always come first. Preventing your daughter from contracting a brain-fever is my foremost concern.'

Clearly, it was not Mamma's. She shot Evelyn a look of utter fury.

'Shall I send my bill to Mr Chillingham, madam, or . . . ?'

'Good heavens, no!' Mamma cried. 'We have inconvenienced him *quite* enough for one day. Go to my husband. He is in the billiard room.'

The doctor bowed and withdrew, closing the door behind him.

Mamma inhaled a deep breath and patted her lace cap back into shape. 'I realise your situation is not easy, Evelyn,' she began tightly. 'Having your younger sister marry before you is a somewhat humiliating experience. But you had your chance to be the bride. It is too bad if you regret your decision now.'

'I beg your pardon?'

'You made a foolish mistake in refusing Mr Chillingham. I am not surprised if you have thought better of it. But begrudging your sister the match is beneath you. Consider that when Susan is Mrs Chillingham, and moving in higher society, she can find you another suitor. One you will have the good sense to accept.' She pursed her lips, eyeing the injured foot. 'If, indeed, you are ever able to dance at a ball again.'

It took all of Evelyn's restraint not to pick up the cushion and hurl it at her mother. 'What – you think that I did this on purpose? To spoil Susan's wedding? Mamma! How could you suspect me of such meanness?'

Snow drifted down the chimney. The fire spat in the grate.

'It does not matter, either way,' Mamma insisted. 'You

have not achieved your end. The wedding will go ahead, with or without you.'

There was a rap at the door. Evelyn flinched, sending hot arrows through her leg.

'Do come in,' Mamma called, in a far pleasanter voice.

It was Susan and Mr Chillingham. Evelyn blushed, hoping they had not overheard, but they were smiling in that eager and slightly unpleasant way people do when faced with an invalid.

'Poor Evie!' Susan crooned. 'What a disappointment, to be laid up like this! But never fear; we have a surprise for you. Or rather, Victor does. It was his idea.'

With much flourish, the couple parted to reveal the maid, Biddy, behind them, trundling a strange contraption across the threshold.

It was a large, cushioned chair, such as might be found in any drawing room, only the arms were impaled by vertical rods of brass. Three wheels propelled it; two at the front and one at the back. They moaned like an animal in pain.

'This belonged to my father,' Mr Chillingham told them, as Biddy manoeuvred the chair to the side of the chaise longue. She let the footboard down with a *snap* that made Evelyn jump. 'Did I tell you how severely he suffered in his health towards the end of his life?'

Evelyn viewed the piece of furniture with distaste. No one in the county needed to be *told* about the incorrigible old man; stories circulated freely. His bad temper and mean ways had given 'Old Chillingham' a reputation. There was a portrait of him hanging in the gallery; an oily-looking man with small, cruel eyes.

But his son Victor was gazing at her tenderly, the complete opposite of his father.

'You did,' Evelyn replied. 'I think you said that your father was rendered mute and could not use his legs?'

'Precisely. So I bought him this chair.'

'Not just *any* chair, Evie.' Susan came forward and turned one of the handles protruding from the arm. It made a clank and the wheels rotated. 'Look, you can steer it. And the whole machine is self-propelled!'

'They call it "Mr Merlin's Mechanical Chair",' Mr Chillingham informed them. 'The very latest invention. I spared no expense.'

'What a comfort it must have been,' Mamma sighed, 'for your father to have such a *dutiful* child.'

'I hope you know, Miss Lennox,' Mr Chillingham went on, 'that I will do everything in my power to assist you in your illness, too. You are a member of my family as much as my father was. Unfortunately, his chair will be of no use to you out of doors, but it should help you to navigate the house.'

'So you will not have to miss out on *everything* after all!' Susan beamed.

Evelyn tried to return their smiles, but the idea of sitting in the contraption was abhorrent. Even from this distance, she detected the stale, sour scent of the upholstery and glimpsed a dark patch on the seat.

Fortunately, Mamma's gratification knew no bounds.

'How infinitely kind! My daughter is greatly indebted to you, Mr Chillingham. You see she is struck dumb by the honour. She has been so careless. She must learn to ride with more restraint in future.'

'Please do not upbraid her, madam. The fault was not with Miss Lennox, but my grooms. That side-saddle had not been kept in good order, and the girth was not fastened correctly. Such mistakes are unacceptable. Rest assured that the man responsible shall be dismissed immediately.'

Mamma and Susan nodded their agreement. Only Biddy flinched behind the chair.

Naturally, the maid would feel for a fellow servant. It *did* seem rather cruel to send a groom away for a single error, especially while the mantelpiece was still decked with holly, ivy and mistletoe.

'Oh, please do not deprive him of his position, sir,' Evelyn said. 'Not on my account. I could not sleep if a man were to lose his employment at this time of the year. Let us forgive him, in the spirit of the season.'

Mr Chillingham bowed his head. 'Your tender heart does you credit, Miss Lennox. You are almost as benevolent as your sister.' He reached for Susan's hand. 'Very well. It shall be just as you wish.'

Susan rewarded him with a honeyed smile. They looked like the perfect, domesticated couple. Evelyn felt her stomach hollowing out. It should have been her.

She should not have listened to the gossip about Mr Chillingham. This docile lord of the manor bore no resemblance to the addict of dice and cards her friends whispered about. The rumours were clearly groundless: Victor Chillingham was a good man and she had spurned him.

'This excellent chair will not get you up and down the staircase,' Mamma pointed out. 'Really, Evelyn, it would be less of a bother to everyone if you slept down here instead. Biddy can fetch your trunks, and stay with you on a truckle bed should you need her. Does this sound like a reasonable plan, Mr Chillingham? I should not like my daughter to be causing any inconvenience . . .'

'Not at all,' he agreed easily. 'I have no objections. This little parlour is rarely used – I hope Miss Lennox will consider it her own for the duration of her stay.'

It could *all* have been hers: Chillingham Grange. The deer-park and the woods, a glassy lake, kitchen gardens for herbs of every kind. She might have been mistress of this imposing manor house with its sweeping staircases up to the main entrance, but now it would fall to her younger sister instead.

Susan came forward eagerly. 'Now do let us try the chair! I long to see it in action.'

Evelyn could not refuse. Biddy manhandled her off the chaise longue and into the device. The cushions received her with a sigh. Her thigh found a hollow in the seat; Old Chillingham must have left an imprint from the days he had spent enthroned there.

'Turn the levers out to go forward,' Susan urged.

Warily, Evelyn pushed both of the tarnished brass handles.

A *clank* trembled through the structure; she felt it in the base of her spine. With a high-pitched squeal, the chair crept into motion.

Susan clapped, delighted. 'Look at you go!'

It rolled at the pace of a snail. All the same, Evelyn worried that she didn't know how to stop. Slowly but surely, she was inching towards the flames in the fireplace.

She tried not to panic, but she could already feel the heat upon her skin. 'How do I—' she bleated. By blind luck, her hand hit a lever on the right arm and a rod dropped, grinding the wheels to a halt. The noise they made set her teeth on edge.

Her bandaged foot throbbed, mere fingerbreadths from the grate.

The others applauded.

'So kind! So useful.' Mamma simpered at their host. 'Well, Evelyn, what do you say?'

Evelyn's jaw clenched in a rictus of a smile. She had disappointed him enough; the least she could do was appear grateful now. 'Thank you, Mr Chillingham,' she forced out.

ॐ

That night Evelyn writhed upon the chaise longue, unable to sleep. The ache in her foot pulsed as steadily as a heartbeat.

It was not only her discomfort that kept her awake; down here, the world outside sounded louder. She heard the wind whooping around the house, testing the windows, and the steady drip of icicles melting in the eaves.

There was nothing to do but lie awake and nurse her regrets.

Had she taken leave of her senses, to refuse Victor Chillingham? Her friends had said he was a gambler, yet now it occurred to her how unlikely that was to be true. He had been entertaining the wedding guests in a lavish style throughout the twelve days of Christmas. He must be receiving a steady income from *somewhere*.

Not that her rejection of him had been entirely mercenary. There were family concerns, too. She had worried that he might change with age to become cruel as his father had been. And then there was the elder brother, whom she had never met. People said that he was deformed, degraded, and had been written out of the will entirely. But she should not have judged Victor for his relatives' faults. After all, she would not wish for people to evaluate *her* by the behaviour of Mamma.

The only consolation was that dear Susan would be happy. Her sister would own a fine house and have a charming husband to call her own. Still, Mamma was not exaggerating when she said it looked odd, for the younger daughter to marry first. It would make Evelyn appear strange, undesirable – especially if she was now condemned to walk with a limp.

She turned her head on the pillow, disconsolate. The horrible chair lurked by her side as a reminder of her lameness.

She needed to use the chamber pot, but the only way to do so would be to call Biddy for assistance, and she would rather hold it in. There had been *quite* enough humiliation for one day.

Strangely, Biddy did not make any sound in her sleep, nor were there movements from the guests upstairs. While the wind ravened outside, the atmosphere indoors hung oppressively still.

Evelyn tried to drift off with everyone else. Disjointed images rose behind her eyelids; trees outlined in white, hooves beating up powdered snow, dogs on the scent with their tails held aloft. She remembered odd snippets of the day. How the lake had frozen solid like a slab of marchpane. Susan telling her there was a poison garden somewhere out there in the grounds. She imagined all those toxic plants, buried in a snowy shroud, when she heard a sudden creak.

The sound made her flinch, sending agony down her leg. It was foolish; the noise could only have been Biddy, rolling over on her truckle bed. She dismissed it and attempted to move her foot back into a comfortable position, but then the creak repeated, louder, close beside her ear.

It was a settling, an exhalation; the noise furniture made as it bore someone's weight. Yet she realised it could not have come from Biddy's bed, on the other side of the room; it was nearer than that.

The noise was coming from the chair.

Inching her eyelids open, Evelyn peered across the short

distance between her pillow and the shadowy bulk of the contraption. Nothing appeared to have changed. Firelight flickered on the brass fittings. Even in the gloom, she could see indents in the cushions; the grooves worn by long occupation.

Well, it was a decrepit old device, bound to moan and settle. She tried to hold on to that thought as the upholstery squeaked, sounding for all the world like someone adjusting their position in the seat.

It was no good; she pulled the covers over her head and hid. 'Biddy,' she whispered. 'Biddy, are you asleep?'

No answer came.

Something whined, high-pitched like the beagle earlier, except this was no animal; it was the raw grind of wheels. Surely, surely, Biddy would hear them? This noise was bound to wake her up.

It took every ounce of courage Evelyn possessed to pull down the cover and peep out across the parlour, to where the maid had set up her truckle bed.

It was flat. There was no one lying beneath the sheets and she was all alone.

Or perhaps not.

Another creak came from the mechanical chair. Choking on terror, Evelyn let her gaze drift towards it. The contraption was still to her left, beside the chaise longue, but it was no longer turned to the side.

Now it was facing her.

'No,' she breathed. 'No, that is not possible.'

She glared at the arms, as if she might force them back into their proper place. Somehow, without any human intervention, the contraption had turned a full ninety degrees.

Panic noosed about her throat. She must not give into it. Clearly, this was a dream. The doctor had given her laudanum and that medicine always caused nightmares.

But this one was unusually vivid. She could feel the twinges from her broken foot and see the play of the fire. When she pushed at a bruise on her arm, it stung.

'Wake up,' she ordered herself.

The chair responded. Evelyn stared in horror as the crank on the right arm slowly began to rotate.

'No,' she cried. 'No, I will not have this.'

Desperately, she cast about for something, anything to end the dream. There was only one remedy to hand. Bracing herself, she swung her legs off the chaise longue and stood on her injured feet.

The agony was worse than she'd expected; shrieking inside her head until it drowned out the *clank* of the chair. If such pain did not wake her, surely nothing would.

But her consciousness wasn't rising to the surface; in fact, it started to retreat. The parlour, the fire and even the chair were all drifting further away . . .

Everything tunnelled into black.

෨

Evelyn awoke to a frantic thump.

'Let me in!' It was Biddy's voice, hushed but panicked. 'Please, miss. Open the door.'

Disorientated, Evelyn raised her head. Pale light washed across the parlour. The fire had long since burnt to ashes, but the curtains were open to another picturesque, icy day. She lay where she had fallen, crumpled at the foot of the chaise longue.

The chair stood by the door.

It was positioned so that no one could pass either in or out of the room. Although Biddy worked the door handle, it stuck on the chair's thick mechanical arm.

'Miss Lennox!'

Most of the pain had gone. Actually, Evelyn could hardly feel her feet; that was not encouraging. She gritted her teeth and dragged herself across the carpet, clawing with her hands, until she reached the chair.

She had never felt such powerful loathing for an object before. From this angle she could see the wheels, scuffed and worn. How could they possibly have rolled of their own accord, all the way across the parlour? She propped herself up on one arm and pushed at the wretched contraption with all her might. It rolled backwards.

Biddy half-fell into the room. 'Miss! How did you . . . Are you hurt?'

Evelyn did not have an answer. To speak of last night's events would be absurd.

Silently, she let the maid help her off the floor and into

the chair. She would rather have sat on the chaise longue, but it was too far away, and perhaps this was better after all. If Evelyn occupied the seat, at least no one else – or *nothing* else – could.

'Where were you?' she demanded of her maid, remembering the empty bed in the middle of the night. 'How did you come to be outside?'

Biddy's cheeks flushed. 'I was at the servants' breakfast, miss.' She began to busy herself with the trunks that the footmen had brought down. 'And now it's time we dressed you for your own.'

Evelyn was not convinced. 'No. I meant, where were you *before*? I awoke during the night and there was no sign of you! I tried to stand . . . The pain must have made me faint.'

Biddy opened her mouth. 'I . . . I'm sorry, miss. '

While the maid floundered, Evelyn spied a wisp of straw in her cap; remembered how she had flinched yesterday when Mr Chillingham threatened to dismiss someone from the stables. It did not take a great mind to put the two together.

'Why Biddy!' Evelyn gasped. 'Have you got yourself a sweetheart?'

Biddy blushed deeply. 'Lord, miss!' she chided, bending her head over the trunk. 'You know I'm not allowed followers, in my position.'

Which was not strictly a denial.

Well, let Biddy keep her secrets; Evelyn had her own. All through the long ordeal of dressing, she considered telling her maid what had really happened during the night, but she could not find the words. Hadn't the doctor said she'd taken a nasty blow to the head? Maybe confusion had made her see things. Such an explanation was not satisfying, but it was preferable to the alternative: that Old Chillingham was not ready to let go of his chair.

Finally, Biddy crouched to adjust the footboard. Evelyn's injured ankle had swollen to almost twice the size.

'I will not scold you, Biddy. And I will not tell anybody that I had an accident in your absence. But you must stay with me tonight.' Biddy nodded. 'Swear it,' Evelyn ordered, her voice pinched with fear. 'Whatever happens, do not leave me alone after dark.'

Biddy's eyes widened. 'I promise, miss.'

All of the guests were gathered for breakfast in a large, airy hall hung with tapestries. Arched windows looked out across the grounds, which sparkled under fresh snow. Evelyn saw the little walled gardens where the kitchen staff grew their herbs: some for cooking, some for medicine and some to poison vermin, like Susan had said.

'Miss Lennox!' Mr Chillingham broke off from his conversation and hurried to greet her. 'How do you feel today? Better? I trust you are well rested?'

Evelyn was startled into a vague and dishonest answer. She had not realised the gentleman truly cared about her, but he must. He pushed her chair and assisted her to an empty place at the table, while her own family had failed to notice her entirely.

There was a little difficulty fitting the mechanised arms of her chair beneath the dining table. Mr Chillingham began to fret. 'I can have a tray carried to your room instead,' he offered. 'Shall I wheel you back to the parlour?'

'Oh, no! There is no need for that. I will manage perfectly, thank you, sir.' She glanced down at the setting, the plate and its cutlery, to hide her blushes. Mr Chillingham was speaking rather *too* earnestly for a man destined to marry her sister in a few days.

At last, Papa dawdled over to check upon her. 'Well, Evelyn my dear, it is fortunate you managed to break only your foot and not your neck,' he said in his jocose way. 'We would have been forced to postpone the wedding. Your mother would never have forgiven you.'

She tried to laugh back, but her head was swimming and it was not entirely from her concussion. Why was Mr Chillingham looking at her like that?

'Susan would have remembered you more kindly, though,' Papa added with a wink. 'She'd lose a bridesmaid, but I daresay she wouldn't mind her dowry doubling in size.'

The jest was in poor taste, but she hoisted up a smile. Her father did not mean any harm – it was just his manner. However, she noticed Mr Chillingham's countenance darken with displeasure before he returned to his other guests.

The party planned to go skating on the lake once breakfast was finished. Of course Evelyn could not take part. In truth, she was glad; her ordeal from the night before had left her exhausted.

Susan fussed, stroking her hair. 'I do not like to leave you,

Evie. However shall I manage to balance on the ice, without you to hold my hand?'

'Mr Chillingham must hold it for you now.'

But Mr Chillingham seemed more concerned about Evelyn. He squatted down to the level of her chair. 'I will have the servants bring out all our collections to amuse you. There are medals and shells – a fine book of engravings too. I shall fetch that myself. Everything at the Grange is at your disposal, Miss Lennox. If you require anything further, you have only to ask.'

Evelyn sat dumbstruck. After the manner in which she had refused him, this kindness felt almost oppressive. Did he perhaps sense that she harboured regrets? She fervently hoped not. It was too late; they must think of Susan now.

Poor Susan was still smiling, oblivious to the *frisson* between her sister and her fiancé, but she was the only one. Mamma's eyes were pinning them both with a deadly glare.

ॐ

Fires blazed merrily in every hearth. Delicious scents of cinnamon and roast meat drifted up from the kitchens, and all the windows were laced with frost. It seemed impossible to believe that this house, this very chair, had appeared so menacing by night.

'I think I shall take some Peruvian bark for my head,' Evelyn told Biddy as they played backgammon in the library.

'There is a dull ache at my temples. It gave me the strangest dreams – I do not want to repeat them tonight.'

Perhaps the impact really *had* disordered her thoughts. That was why she had seen the chair moving, and it explained why she was feeling differently towards Mr Chillingham. It was simply a temporary malady, like a cold.

Biddy rose from her chair. 'I'll go and fetch the powder now, miss. The others should be back from their skating soon.'

As Biddy left the room, Evelyn noticed a portrait framed in gold on the far wall that she had not seen before. It was a painting of a young man with hooded, doleful eyes. The colours on the canvas were dark, and looked darker still due to the bad position in which the picture had been hung.

She trundled closer and dropped the rod to lock her wheels in place and inspect the picture. The artist had softened, but still included a decided lift to one of the sitter's shoulders. There was an inscription on the frame: *Alfred Chillingham.*

Biddy returned with the Peruvian bark. 'Ah,' she said, 'you've found him, have you miss? The Prodigal Son. Let's hope for Miss Susan's sake that he never comes back.'

'So it *is* him! The elder brother who absconded all those years ago. I did not realise that he was afflicted with . . . '

'He was a hunchback,' Biddy finished baldly. 'Like evil King Richard.'

Evelyn shook her head at the unkind words. Alfred was certainly not handsome like Victor Chillingham, but it had nothing to do with his misshapen back. 'I wonder why he disappeared so suddenly. What could have become of him?'

Biddy stole up behind her and peered at the portrait. 'I reckon it's true, what they say, miss. Just look at him. He's no good. You can see it in the eyes.'

'What do they say, Biddy?'

'Why, that he attacked Old Chillingham. As revenge, for all his mistreatment over the years.'

'*What*? I have heard nothing of this. Who tells you such wild rumours?'

'It's not just a rumour,' Biddy returned hotly. 'Look where you're sitting, miss. Why do you think they had to get the old man that chair? His collapse came on very quick. One week he was as right as rain and the next he could barely move.'

Evelyn curled into herself. Suddenly she did not want her spine to touch the back of the chair. 'Nonsense. The elder Mr Chillingham had an apoplectic fit.'

'But then why did his heir run off, just days afterwards? It makes no sense. The fit's just a story the family give out for appearances. But really, the hunchback attacked his father and pegged it. That's what the servants say.'

Evelyn narrowed her eyes. 'A member of staff has told you this? But surely they would not confide the family's secrets to a relative stranger!' Biddy shrugged and turned towards the backgammon board. 'Come now, Biddy. Admit it. You *do* have a sweetheart – and he works here in the stables, does he not?'

'I'm sure I don't know what you mean, miss.'

Evelyn glanced at her hand, resting on the arm of the chair.

She should not heed mere servant's gossip, but she could not help remembering last night, and the sickening way in which the lever had started to turn. If Old Chillingham *had* been killed by his eldest son . . . he would not be lying at rest.

They said the murdered wandered, wraith-like, until justice was finally granted. Yet since this gentleman had not been able to use his legs, perhaps the rules of the underworld had been altered, for him.

Perhaps Old Chillingham's spirit *rolled.*

❦

With Biddy beside her in the parlour, Evelyn finally managed to drift into sleep around one o'clock in the morning. Even then, her aching mind would not relax. She dreamed.

She dreamed of Old Chillingham with his small, beady eyes, counting the coins that his sons would inherit. One pile of money shrank while the other grew larger, making a steady *chink, chink.*

Then she dreamed of Alfred, the villain, fleeing in the dead of night. He carried no baggage, he wore no coat; there was not even a horse to bear him. His movements were those of a mad man. He tore through the woods where she had fallen, releasing wet green scents from the undergrowth. His hands scrabbled and clawed, torn to pieces by the brambles. If she had not known better, she would say he was running for his life.

Gradually, the aromas of the forest cloyed into something

sweet, almost sickening, All the while the trees echoed with an incessant *chink, chink.*

'Miss? Miss!' Biddy's voice wavered in the distance. Evelyn latched on to it – tried to wrench her mind away from the wild motions of Alfred. 'Miss, don't move!'

A breeze rippled past, lifting the short curls from her forehead. Or was it Alfred's bleeding hands, stroking her face?

'Stop. No!' She writhed in her sleep. Her broken foot sent up a flare of pain and she snapped suddenly awake.

She was outside, facing a bed of frosted twigs. Slender, pointed leaves sparkled here and there; they did not belong to any flowers she knew. Beyond them rose a stone wall, topped with black iron rails and it appeared – or perhaps it was her frightened imagination – that the spires were capped with small metal skulls.

'Miss Lennox!' Relief flooded her as Biddy appeared and hurtled down a path towards her, red in the face. 'What are you *doing*?'

'I . . .' Evelyn began. Looking down, she saw her slender figure was clad in a nightgown, crumpled between the arms of the mechanical chair.

Memory came to her hazily; the scents of outdoors from her dream and the regular metallic click of coins – only they had not been coins at all. What she had heard was the wheels, struggling over the path.

She shuddered. People *walked* in their sleep, but surely she could not have put herself in a chair, piloted it down corridors and through doors without being aware? If she had done this . . . she must have hit her head much harder than she thought.

Biddy examined her hands. 'Did you touch anything, miss?' she asked urgently. 'Anything at all?'

'I do not believe so. Why?'

'Don't you know what that is?' Biddy jerked a thumb at the tangled beds. 'Monkshood. It'll damage your nerves, make you numb and frozen. And *that* looks like hemlock – paralyses you from the bottom up. Whatever possessed you to come out here? You're not even dressed!'

'I . . . I didn't, Biddy. I don't know how . . .'

The maid looked as afraid as Evelyn felt. 'We've got to get you back inside before the other guests wake up.'

As Mr Chillingham had warned them, the chair was not designed for the outdoors. The wheels jammed and refused to turn on the icy paths. How had they managed to carry her from the house, across the grounds? Only the full force of Biddy's strength jolted them into motion now.

Jerkily, the chair rumbled past an open gate. The padlock that had secured it lay discarded on the grass. Evelyn read a sign and finally understood where it was that Biddy had rescued her from.

The chair had taken her inside the Poison Garden.

၅

Evelyn was in no humour to join in with the games, even as a spectator. She wheeled herself off alone to the conservatory, where a stove heated the delicate palms, ferns and succulents. It could not thaw the frigidity that had settled deep within her bones.

There were only two explanations for this morning's event: either the fall had caused her mind to fracture, or the murdered spirit of Old Chillingham was still here, controlling her chair.

He had been a horrible man in general, but what could he hold against *her*? Why play these terrifying tricks and wheel her towards toxic herbs?

Evelyn inspected the rods and levers, tapped at the scratched wooden arms. 'Where are you hiding?' she muttered. 'What do you want from me?' Leaning back, she began to wiggle in her seat, trying to mould it to her form, rather than the old man's. It was of no use. All she succeeded in doing was tangling her skirts in the wheels.

As she bent painfully to free them, she caught sight of a loose thread poking from the upholstered seat. Cautiously, she ran a hand beneath the frame. There was something there. A bulge.

Her fingers probed, finding a tear in the fabric. It was perhaps an inch long and perfectly straight. When she slipped her thumb inside, she realised it was not an accidental rip but a cut, made on purpose for concealment.

She withdrew a yellowed fold of paper that emitted a rank odour, like a nest of mice. With infinite care, she prised it apart and found dried flowers.

There was a purple, bell-shaped bloom and a sort of frothy

spray, each from a different plant. Along with them, ground into the creases in the paper were what looked like herbs, scooped from a bowl of soup.

Evelyn frowned, glancing from one husk to the other. Why had this been hidden? In wobbling pencil, Old Chillingham had scrawled a single word upon the paper: *Proof.*

It had clearly been an effort for him to write. He'd used all his strength to proclaim that this was evidence – but what of?

Biddy's words came back to her: '*numb and frozen . . . paralyses you from the bottom up.*' Old Chillingham *had* been palsied. Yet surely that did not mean . . .

She looked at the plants again. The leaves were pointed, just like the ones she had seen inside the Poison Garden.

'You were showing me,' she gasped. 'Alfred didn't attack you before he ran away – he poisoned you!'

'Miss Lennox?' Mr Chillingham's voice scattered her thoughts. He stood at the door to the conservatory, peering in with solicitude. 'Are you unwell?'

She gaped at him. It was too late to hide the flowers: they were spread upon her lap. 'I am . . . a little unsettled,' she admitted.

Mr Chillingham came slowly inside, shutting the door behind him to conserve the heat. Once again, he walked over and squatted beside her chair. His face was a picture of concern. 'Your mother is looking for you, Miss Lennox. My gardener said you were wandering the grounds this morning, half-delirious. Can it possibly be true?'

Evelyn faltered. The last thing she wanted to do was upset Mr Chillingham on the day before his wedding, but she could not conceal what she had just discovered. 'I *was* in the garden, sir. But it was not in a delirium ... I do not know how to explain it to you. The truth is that another person *took* me there, on purpose, to show me something.'

He frowned. 'Who would—'

She passed him the little bundle of herbs and paper. 'I could not believe it either, at first. But then I found this, tucked inside your father's chair.' She wet her lips. 'I saw these plants, Mr Chillingham. Outside, this morning, in the Poison Garden.'

He viewed the parcel as if she had passed him a dead bird. By the light of the stove his eyes looked deeper set, sunk within their sockets. 'Poison?' he repeated without understanding. 'The Poison Garden is kept locked at all times. For safety.'

'Yes, I am sure it is, but it was not locked today. I found—'

'Good God!' he cried. 'Do I understand you correctly? Are you trying to tell me that someone wheeled you outside on purpose and tried to *poison* you, Miss Lennox?'

'Oh, no! I am not speaking of myself. You see ...' It was coming out all wrong, but just how *did* you tell a gentleman that you had been visited by his father's ghost? 'It is difficult to explain, but I am trying to talk about Mr Chillingham senior. This was your father's chair, was it not? Well, I found those herbs hidden inside and you see that he has written *proof* upon the paper ... Do not think that I am prying into your family's affairs. I will tell no one of this. But I thought it right that *you* should see what I have discovered. You must take the evidence, and do with it what you choose.'

'You are confused, Miss Lennox.'

She was. She had a loose, boneless feeling; the only solid object was the chair beneath her legs. 'Yes. I am not expressing myself properly. All I meant to say was that your father hid those plants inside his chair. *He* may have believed he was being poisoned.' He stared at her. Quickly, she added, 'But elderly people take such strange fancies into their heads. Their minds can wander, towards the end . . . '

Mr Chillingham screwed up the parcel and threw it into the stove.

'Poor Miss Lennox,' he said softly. 'You must have injured your head a great deal worse than we originally thought.'

❧

'This is ridiculous, Mamma! At least let me *see* Susan! We should not be separated today!'

Mamma stood before the door with a key in her hand. She wore her best gown and had orange blossom tucked in the rim of her bonnet. 'Susan is upset enough as it is. I have consulted with your father and Mr Chillingham on how to proceed, and we all agreed it was better for you to stay here.'

'It is my sister's wedding day!'

'Yes!' Mamma cried, a catch of tears in her voice. 'Heaven knows we did not picture it would turn out like this! But attending the ceremony will excite you too much. This is for your own good, Evelyn. I cannot risk you taking a fever to your brain.'

Evelyn trembled. The shaking hurt her foot and made the chair creak. She wished with all her heart that she had kept her mouth shut. Why had she told Mr Chillingham? The old man was dead and Alfred had long gone; it did not matter what wrongs had been committed in the past.

'Please, Mamma! I am begging you. I will behave myself.'

'I am sorry, dear. This is the only course I can take. I must keep you well and protect Susan from scandal . . . There will be plenty to amuse you here in the library. A servant will stay with you, and let the physician in when he arrives.'

'Mamma . . . At least help me over to that seat. I do not want to be stuck in this wretched mechanical chair! '

Mamma would not meet her eye. 'Goodbye, Evelyn. Feel better, dear.' With that she left and shut the door behind her.

Evelyn stifled a sob. She could not believe this was happening. Everything had gone so awfully, so horribly wrong.

She was about to vent her grief when she realised that Mamma had not turned the key in the lock. Someone had stopped her, outside the door.

'Biddy! Get dressed for the ceremony at once! The guests are already at the church . . . Good heaven, you stink of horses, girl!'

'I've something important to tell you, madam.' Biddy sounded strained. 'Please listen.'

'Do not *pester* me, on today of all days . . .'

'It's about Miss Evelyn's accident, madam. Her side-saddle. One of the grooms took a look at it for me and he thinks it's been tampered with, broken on purpose!'

'Yes, Mr Chillingham *told* us the saddle should never have been used. Now, move along. The carriage will be ready for Susan any moment.'

'But madam – wait!'

Their voices faded away. Evelyn was left ringing with confusion and alarm. What had Biddy discovered?

She would have been able to go and ask her maid, if she had not spent her time trying to appease Old Chillingham's ghost. She would not be alone in a room, about to miss her sister's wedding. And why? All because the old man wanted to tell his tale!

She thumped the arm of her chair. 'I hate you,' she hissed. 'You have ruined everything. Why did you trouble me? I do not *care* how you died!'

The rod that locked her wheels disengaged. Evelyn only had time to gasp before she started to roll backwards. She tried to depress the rod again, but it jammed. Her hands tugged at the levers to no avail. They felt slack and weightless, as if the wires had been cut.

'No!' she gabbled. 'I apologise. I should not have said that. Please stop!'

The chair didn't stop. If anything it gained speed, reversing until she felt a bookcase connect with the back of her head. There was a moment of tension, of gathering; like a horse preparing to jump. Then she shot forward.

Evelyn shrieked, gripping the arms for dear life. Just before she reached the portrait of Alfred, there was a click and the wheels swerved to the left. The chair smacked into the door, propelled itself out of the library and kept going.

This was worse than when Quicksilver had bolted. At least a horse could be talked to, soothed, but the chair was relentless. Its wheels spun quicker than they were ever intended to go. She heard creaks and snaps, as though the whole thing might rattle itself apart.

Faster and faster it went, building momentum. As the house flashed past her eyes, Evelyn realised where they were headed. The chair was barrelling straight towards the parlour where she slept. She remembered how the chair had crept in the direction of that fireplace on the very first day and a terrible premonition took hold of her.

'Stop! I'm sorry!'

The door stood open. The wheels nearly left the floor as they bumped over the threshold, but they showed no signs of slowing. Her first fear had been right: Old Chillingham was aiming straight for the hearth.

Suddenly, the seat seemed to buck. Evelyn was pitched on to the floor, landing painfully and releasing the scream that had been building inside of her all day.

There was a thunderous crash. The chair shivered into pieces, wood and metal flying in all directions. It had hit the dado on the wall beside the fireplace, leaving a hole the size of a plate.

Biddy flew into the room. 'Miss!' She dashed to kneel

beside Evelyn and pull her head onto her lap. 'What has happened to you? Was it *him*?'

Black patches flitted across Evelyn's vision. She made out Biddy's snow-crusted boots and a smear of muck upon the maid's cheek. 'What . . . *Him*? Who do you mean?'

Biddy nipped her lips together. 'Miss, someone is trying to hurt you. I've been telling your mother all day, but she won't listen. Your saddle's girth was cut, and the snow drift that spooked your horse didn't happen by accident. A boy in the stables was paid to frighten the beast!'

Her head reeled. She had an excuse to be delusional – but surely Biddy did not? 'That cannot be true! Who on earth would want *me* dead?'

Biddy raised her eyebrows. 'Who do you think? Who would Mr Lennox's money go to, if he only had one child?'

Fingers of ice crept up Evelyn's back. She remembered her father's joke about the dowry. If she had died in the accident, it would have been Susan's husband who grew rich.

Rumours of Victor Chillingham's gaming habits came roaring back. Gamblers could be desperate . . .

She fought to sit up. 'No,' she declared. 'No, he would not do that to me. He cares about us. We are family.' Something behind them cracked. Awkwardly, Evelyn turned her head to see mortar crumbling from the hole the chair had made.

'Ugh!' cried Biddy. 'What's that smell?'

All at once, something gave way. Plaster broke, there came a rattle, and debris rushed out of the hole like an afterbirth. Borne on the tide of dust and rubble was a collection of human bones.

Biddy shrieked.

The longest, grizzliest piece was a spine curving gently in a scythe.

'It's Alfred,' Evelyn breathed.

But how could that be?

If Alfred was dead ... then he had not hurt Old Chillingham at all. He had not even run away. His body had been concealed and there was only one person who could profit from his disappearance: the same man who had hurled the evidence of poison into the stove.

Now she realised why Old Chillingham's ghost had been so insistent to be heard. Victor Chillingham was a murderer – and he was marrying an innocent young woman.

'God above! Where is Susan?'

'She was already in the carriage,' Biddy wailed. 'Your family must all be outside, or they would have come running, like I did, when you screamed.'

Evelyn couldn't stop shaking. There would be time enough to absorb the shock and the horror later – all that mattered now was Susan. She tried to move her leg, but knew she would never be able to stand. 'Biddy, you must stop that carriage! She cannot marry him. Run, Biddy, run!'

With a sob, the maid tore from the room.

Evelyn sat trembling, staring at the remains of Alfred and the chair. She had wronged them both. The dead Chillinghams had not been working in hatred, as she had thought, but in kindness. Trying to warn her.

She heard the front door bang open. Biddy's strangled

shout carried across the courtyard, but there was no voice raised in answer.

Instead there came the crack of a whip passing through frigid air. Leather creaked, hooves made a hollow *clop* and Evelyn realised the carriage had already started to move, pulling her sister farther and farther away.

THE HANGING OF
THE GREENS

Andrew Michael Hurley

This year, the spruce and holly appeared in people's windows much earlier than usual, and by the start of December every house in the village had been decked with evergreens, apart from mine.

Most of my neighbours have known me for a long time, but they must still think it odd that I don't put up a tree. They perhaps assume that I'm staging some puritan protest against the commercialisation of the season. I'm not. I just can't wait for it all to be over.

For weeks now I've been avoiding the shops that sell garlands of mistletoe and I've turned down every invitation I've had to a coffee or an evening sherry in case I'm forced to admire someone's Christmas tree.

It's the smell of the greenery I can't stand. Or, rather, what the smell reminds me of, even now, years later, when I'm miles away from Salter Farm.

⊱

David wasn't to know any of this when he came around last night a little drunk from the office party, with a wreath for the living room and a handful of holly that he'd taken from the park. It was a sweet gesture and I tried not to react too strongly, but he knew that he'd done something to upset me. And then I'd had a night of him trying to pry the lid off it all.

Even though I didn't give much away, I think he eventually realised that he'd dredged up an old, unpleasant memory and after that he'd had the kindness to leave it alone, but I know he'll ask about it again.

I can't just spill my past like David does with his. There are certain things it doesn't do me much good to revisit. Like what happened at Salter Farm.

The problem is that the more I dissemble, the more he'll want to know what I'm hiding; he'll think that he's touched upon the very thing that makes me the way I am: diffident and distant; haunted sometimes, he says.

He'll try to convince me that by talking it all out there'll be a kind of release from whatever hold the memory has on me. And that I shouldn't worry what anyone thinks, including him.

Just lay the story bare, Ed, he'll say.

Well then.

༄

It happened more than half my life ago, when I was twenty-seven and still trying to please a God whose existence was as indisputable to me then as the existence of air. I was unbearably ambitious, as earnest as a missionary, pretending that the things that made me unhappy had been shrewd decisions or deliberate sacrifices.

Oh yes, I'd chosen not to moon about after a girlfriend (or *any* friend come to that), I'd chosen not to socialise with people my own age, I'd chosen to carry on living with my parents – because it meant that I could make myself indispensable to the parish, as God had intended me to do.

Back then, I'd considered it an act of devotion to fill my days to the brim. And as if there hadn't been enough to do on a Friday afternoon – between one committee meeting or another and setting out the chairs for the folk club in the parish hall – I'd started a counselling group called 'Talk to Me', which met in the side chapel by the font.

A dedicated half dozen came for a while and I prided myself on helping them make good progress with their difficulties through discussion and prayer. So much so that by the summer they had no need to attend any more.

It had been a victim of its own success, as Reverend Alistair had put it. Kindly, I can see now; to avoid the truth that I'd driven them away with my determination to give them all the answers. A sympathetic hand on my arm, he'd suggested that I restart the group closer to Advent when a person was more likely to have the year's disappointments on their mind.

I'd taken him at his word (well, why would he have said it if he hadn't meant it?) and for several Fridays I waited in the cold church for the full hour on the off chance that someone might turn up. But it was almost halfway through December before anyone appeared.

His name was Joe Gull, a small, watery-eyed man who came endearingly well dressed that first afternoon, thinking it only respectful when, by his own admission, he hadn't set foot in a church for decades. By the way that he seemed to constantly seek permission to be there, I got the impression he thought himself an unusual case. But it wasn't uncommon at all for the sick to come back to God.

And he was sick. I could see that straightaway. He moved with a pain that he couldn't quite disguise and had the pallor of someone who'd been ill for a long time, someone who wasn't going to get any better. What was wrong with him, he didn't say – I suspected it was cancer – but it was clear that he didn't think he had long left. Which was why he asked if we could meet again sooner.

With him being the only taker for the group in months and wanting to make the most of his enthusiasm, I'd been only too glad to say yes. And he'd come a couple of days later and again two days after that in a pattern that quickly became a routine.

It had been a struggle when I had so many other commitments and it was getting closer to Christmas, but I made time for him anyway because I felt (so deeply, so unquestioningly) that God had brought Joe to me and that I had a part to play in his preparations for the end.

There was no better confirmation of this than when he began to disclose certain anxieties to me that he said he couldn't share with anyone else.

He'd always been a weak man, he said. Always riddled with bad spirits. He hadn't always done enough to keep them away. Sometimes, in fact, he'd invited them in.

And because of that, he'd come to accept that he'd been handed a well-deserved sentence, as he put it. Yet, why make it so short, he said, that it would give him little time to repair the damage he'd done in his life?

I pointed to the fact that he was still here, and that meant God *was* giving him the chance to make amends. Though he'd been less than convinced.

It hadn't helped that he thought in terms of retribution all the time. It wasn't that, I told him. God never reprimanded anyone during their earthly life. He only gave them opportunities to know themselves as mortal and fallible and correct the faults that both things caused before they came to bear in the final judgement. And it was never too late to know God's grace, I said. Think of the two thieves crucified next to Jesus.

That had pacified him, but only a little, and only in the moment. I'd seen it before in people like Joe who'd been wandering the wilderness for years. Because they'd never sought God's forgiveness, their sins became manifold and magnified far beyond what was true.

He'd been a drinker, yes, and although I knew about the corrosive effects of the habit from a pamphlet I'd happened to pick up in the doctor's and from what Joe had told me himself, it was hard to imagine that it had led him to do anything so bad as his remorse suggested. And as for evil spirits, I was sure that the only ones he'd ever had inside him were the ones that came in a bottle.

That he'd lived a hard life was evident enough. The first time he'd come to St Peter's, I'd noticed immediately that his hands were covered in welts. His face, too, was chipped at here and there. His left ear nicked like a stray cat's.

He was like many of the men I'd come to know during those Friday afternoon discussion sessions. Men always balancing on the edge of another defeat.

However, as Christmas approached, it was good to see Joe's despair turn into determination to make the best use of however long he had left. I brought in paper and envelopes, helping him word the letters he wanted to write to friends he felt he'd betrayed and relatives he'd apparently wronged.

And because I'd been vain enough then to believe that God was moving through me and I had indeed become *essential*, I agreed without question when Joe asked me to go and see the Oxbarrows.

His friendship with them had ended unpleasantly some time ago, he said, and the guilt of it was excruciating. Even after everything they'd done to help him stay off the booze, he'd started drinking again, which had done more damage to them than him. He'd hurt Helen badly and had made Murray even more unwell than he already was.

None of it had been intentional of course, he said, but they had every right to despise him, nonetheless. They'd been so kind and yet he'd been unable to appreciate it, unable to think of it as kindness at all because of the malignant *thing* inside him at the time. If he could make his peace with anyone before it was all over, he wanted it to be with them.

Though it had to be done properly, he said. A letter wouldn't be enough. It would only be possible to make things right by going to Salter Farm itself. And only if I went without him. Because he knew that I would be able to explain how he felt to Helen and Murray far better than he could. It wouldn't seem so blunt an apology.

I said yes, of course.

৯

The Oxbarrows lived over in Blakeley Cross under the Bowland fells — one of those places that couldn't really be considered a village as such, more a scattering of buildings among the sheep fields. On the map, the lanes followed the ancient boundaries of these pastures and even though Joe had circled the Oxbarrows' house for me, I still managed to get lost in the maze. The snow only added to the confusion, making every junction look the same.

It was by mere chance that I found the cottage at all: a sandstone lump of a place set back from the road down a track lined with beech trees. The way was thick with leaves that, until I drove up to the house, looked to have been undisturbed since the autumn.

Worn down and peeling, Salter Farm had been built at a strange angle to the lane, making it appear as if it had its shoulder permanently to the weather. It seemed even more cowed now that the snow was catching the corners of the roof slates and the lightless windows; laying a fleece over the yard and the bare field in front of the house; falling on the van parked by the woodshed, each tyre flat, the front end dismantled.

If not for the smoke spilling from the chimney, the place would have felt abandoned.

The weather had thickened into a near blizzard as I got out of the car and went over to the porchway of the front door. From a length of rope hung a large bell, like something a Tyrolean cow might wear, and keeping my hands in my pockets I set it going with my elbow.

It was three o'clock in the afternoon a few days before Christmas and it was snowing hard, but I suspected that here it was as desolate as this all year round. There were no other houses in sight – I hadn't passed any since crossing the river – and Salter Farm was a farm in name only. There were no cattle sheds or paddocks or chicken coops. Only the cottage remained, and what I guessed was Murray's workshop, and behind it an empty field that climbed to an old plantation on the fellside. A straggling acreage of pines that had been invaded by holly, cypress and yew. Because it was so still, I could hear voices coming from the trees. Voices and the sound of vegetation being hacked down. Foresters, I assumed, cutting spruces to keep up with demand in town.

I didn't want to make a nuisance of myself, but I was certain that if I could just sit down with the Oxbarrows, even for a few minutes, I'd be able to plead Joe's case and start to bring them round.

After rattling the bell again there was no response, and I tried tapping on the curtained window of the front room instead, calling for Helen, imagining her more likely to come to the door than Murray if he was as poorly as Joe had said, with his delicate heart and his watery blood.

But neither of them answered, and I thought that they were probably ignoring me. I didn't blame them, living out here. It was the advice I gave all the time to the elderly folk I visited. Unless you're expecting someone, don't answer the door.

The last thing I wanted to do was trespass, but then again I didn't want to leave without at least one more attempt to speak to the Oxbarrows, and so I went through the wicket gate at the side of the house, thinking that I'd try them at the back.

The voices in the plantation came again, echoing enough to send a pair of woodpigeons flapping out of the pines. Whoever was there had set off from Salter Farm, it seemed. A chain of footprints ran away from an open gate and up through the snow to the treeline.

I wondered if the plantation belonged to the Oxbarrows. It made sense. Joe had told me that Murray earned a living from making and restoring furniture and to have had his raw materials so close at hand must have been good for business. Perhaps now that he wasn't well enough to work, he had to make his money by selling off the timber – or the fir trees at this time of year.

Perhaps he charged for the use of his workshop, too, the doors of which were open as I went past. Inside, a few small birds fluttered around the huge circular saw and landed on the pieces of furniture that Murray had evidently been in the process of repairing before his health took a turn. A large bedframe, a Welsh dresser, an oak table, a grandfather clock and, leaning against it, a bicycle with a twisted front wheel – the one that Joe had mentioned, the one he'd been riding the night Murray found him.

It was still unfixed, even now.

He'd gone crashing off the road, he told me, coming away from the John Barleycorn – a pub way out in the sticks where he could drink in peace.

It had been a foul December night and he'd had no headlamps or enough tread on his brakes and he'd put away a skinful of scotch and brandy, and all that had sent him careering into a ditch on a sharp downhill corner.

How long he'd lain there for he didn't know – it might have been five minutes or five hours – but by the time he felt himself being shaken back to consciousness he was saturated from the rain.

He'd been dimly aware, he said, of bright lights and an engine shuddering, and then of being dragged out onto the road. Supposing it to be the police, and being in no fit state to resist, he'd allowed himself to be led to the van and strapped in tight, while the man who'd rescued him retrieved the bicycle, and a shoe.

Murray hadn't said anything much at first other than

to introduce himself, and hand Joe the towel he used for cleaning the windscreen so that he could press it to his head. Now thinking him a medic and that he was aboard an ambulance, Joe had asked if they were going to hospital. But Murray had suggested somewhere closer, if he didn't want to bleed to death.

It had been inevitable, said Joe, that he'd end up injuring himself like that sooner or later. He'd been drinking with more intent since they'd turfed him out of the hostel a month or two before and he'd been forced to call on the charity of friends and relatives. The ones he'd then written to with my help. Those who'd put him up only for him to let them down – by coming in steaming at all hours, by helping himself to their food and pocketing their money, by stealing a bicycle.

It hadn't taken long for him to run out of favours and last chances and before Murray had picked him up a few weeks before Christmas he'd spent two nights sleeping in an old pig shed he'd found a short cycle ride from the pub.

Given that, and the fact that he'd been insentient in mud and rain for God knows how long, he must have stunk out the kitchen, he said, that night at Salter Farm. But Helen hadn't said anything while she cleaned up the gashes on his forehead, and Murray had merely run him a bath and presented him with a dry set of clothes, taking his old ones away and burning them while Joe scrubbed himself clean.

Just like the doctor who'd come the next day to examine him, the Oxbarrows hadn't chastised Joe for the way he lived or for the state he'd been in when Murray had discovered him. But at the same time, they hadn't simply turned a blind eye to his problems.

Knowing far better than he that he stood more chance of recovery if he remained at Salter Farm, they coerced him to stay by giving him what they knew he needed most: a roof over his head, food on the table, attention and tenderness. But not pity, said Joe. Murray and Helen, they'd been canny enough to know that men like him – men playing host to such a devious spirit – took advantage of pity. They'd been smart enough to make him work for his bed and board. Smart enough to make the only job on offer that of delivery driver, meaning that there was no way they'd let Joe behind the wheel unless he was sober.

So, just as Murray sometimes had to net the birds that flew into his workshop and got too close to the machinery, he'd been trapped too, said Joe, for his own good and in the gentlest of ways.

It was clear that the Oxbarrows had once had a great deal of compassion for him and despite what had happened I didn't think that it had run completely dry. It was possible that they weren't really angry with Joe at all but blamed themselves in some way for his relapse. It was a ludicrous thought – they'd been perfect Samaritans – but if it were a genuine *feeling* nonetheless, it might mean that they were looking for a way to lay the ghost of guilt. In turn, they'd be more receptive to Joe's willingness to take the blame and that, perhaps, would be the first step to accepting his apology.

All of this I'd be able to detect as soon as I got them talking, I thought, and stopped under the windows in the gable end of the house, hoping that Helen or Murray might look out at me from curiosity if nothing else. But no one appeared and I went on into the long wreck of a garden at the rear.

In the snow, amongst the brambles and the rimy husks of hogweed, was a cracked sundial and several wooden sheds all folding in on themselves. Beyond them was a rotting arbour and at the very end, a kennel.

Expecting a dog to emerge – something brawny and hostile at an isolated house like this – I waited a moment before going up the steps to the back door and knocking on the glass.

Inside, a woodstove blazed and I could see that the kitchen had been festooned with masses of evergreens, and three or four fir trees had been left leaning against the wall.

When no one materialised, I moved along the pathway at the back of the house, rapping on the window of another room and then the next, both with their curtains drawn.

In case one or other of the Oxbarrows was inside, I leant closer to the glass and said, 'I'm from St Peter's. In the town. Could I speak to you? I wouldn't keep you long.'

That was true enough. I would have to set off sooner rather than later. Retracing the route I'd taken through that web of narrow lanes was going to be difficult enough since I had no idea how I'd got here. In the dark, it would be harder still.

I knocked again, and when there was no reply, I began to resign myself to the fact that I would have to go back to Joe without having made much progress.

He would be disappointed – even anxious that he wouldn't live to see another chance for reconciliation – but I'd felt more than capable of convincing him that if patching things up with the Oxbarrows was important, then God would grant time for it to happen. It just couldn't be rushed. If it was God's will that Joe had to be patient in winning their trust, then that was that. And he could be assured that it would be all the more precious when it came to him.

Returning to the kitchen door and tapping on the glass one last time, I looked through the room to the hallway, hoping to catch Helen or Murray moving about the house.

In the brownish light that came in through the window above the front door, I saw a stepladder lying on its side and the floor littered with evergreens.

I rapped on the glass again harder, lifted my voice, and then, given that it seemed likely that Murray or Helen had taken a fall, it only felt right, as I was there, to make sure they weren't hurt.

Fortunately (or at least I thought so then), the door wasn't locked and, once inside, I could see the full extent of the decorations the Oxbarrows had put up. The low beams had been trimmed with masses of holly and pine branches, the windows framed with ivy, into which dozens of little candles had been entwined. The trees that I'd seen through the window stood bunched together, their tips bent against the ceiling, their syrupy citrus smell overpowering and sickly in the heat of the stove.

I said hello and, getting no answer, I went into the hall, stepping over the fallen ladder and picking up some of the greenery. The whole of the corridor was strewn with mistletoe and spruce, and the broken wreaths of yew and fir that had been seemingly torn down from the walls. The ivy that had been wound around the spindles of the stairwell now hung in tatters, and the candles that had been tied into the stems lay broken on the floor.

The door of the front room was ajar but given that it was cold and dark inside I looked in without expecting Murray or Helen to be there. From the smell I could tell that it had been dressed like the kitchen and, switching on the light, I saw heaps of fir and cypress covering the hearth, the mantelpiece, the closed-up piano against the wall. The photographs of Helen and Murray on the dresser were almost hidden in thickets of holly.

Coming back out, I stood at the bottom of the stairs and called up to the next floor.

'I didn't mean to just walk in,' I said. 'Are you both all right? I'm from St Peter's. In the town. I'm Edward Clarke.'

Hearing nothing, I climbed the wooden steps, still talking so that they might hear me coming and I'd be less likely to alarm them.

'Joe Gull asked me to stop by,' I said, looking in the rooms I came to on the landing – one a bathroom, the second giving onto the stairs that led to the top floor. 'And I happened to be in the area,' I said, trying the door of the third room and finding that there was a light on inside.

'Can I come in?' I said. 'Is that all right? I'm from St Peter's.'

∾

Murray was lying belly down on the double bed, one hand twisted around to rest on the small of his back, his other arm hanging off the edge of the mattress, his knuckles touching the floor. The curtains were drawn and the light from the lamp on the table next to him caught in a glass of water, the bottom of which was thick with the sediment of dissolved tablets; beside it, a cigarette lay as a dowel of ash in a saucer.

It was cold in the room, and that might have accounted for it, but there was nothing of the smell that I thought a body was supposed to give off. Murray couldn't have been dead for long. And I had no doubt that he was. My grandfather had looked just the same in his bed at the home; he'd undergone the same thorough evaporation of colour.

I guessed that Murray must have been hanging up the evergreens and had fallen from the stepladder, dragging down what he'd nailed to the picture rail as he grasped at something to hold onto. Then he'd come upstairs to collect his nerves with his pills and a cigarette and had been taken by some kind of seizure, or a heart attack perhaps.

He looked just as ill as Joe had described him. Like

someone who'd lost a great deal of weight quickly and recently. His clothes were far too big for him and the excess skin of his jowls made it seem as if his face was gradually slipping off onto the pillow.

Whatever had happened to poor Murray, he'd endured it alone. Helen wasn't here. And now she'd come home to the worst possible news.

It being close to Christmas, the odds were that she had gone out visiting family (though by what means, I didn't know; surely not on foot?) and there was no telling how long she'd be. I thought about calling the police station over in Clitheroe but worried that it would only add to Helen's distress to find a panda car and an ambulance in the yard when she returned. And, naturally, they'd want to know why I'd gone into the house uninvited.

Of course, at some point I'd have to admit that I'd let myself in but reckoned that Helen, if not the police, would be able to see that there'd been reasonable justification for it. She might even thank me in the end for my decisiveness, I thought, and so I went downstairs to look through the address book by the telephone in the hallway. If I could get hold of a brother or a sister, perhaps, then even if she wasn't with them, they'd at least be able to put the word out.

Though what I'd say, I didn't know, and as I dialled the first number in the book I tried phrasing my opening lines in the way that seemed the least likely to create confusion or panic.

But nothing felt right, even the truth sounded

compromising, and I was relieved when someone started clanging the cow bell in the porch and I could put the receiver down.

I took so long undoing the bolts that whoever had been outside had given up by the time I opened the door. Footprints led around the side of the house to the wicket gate and from there I called out, before going as far as the workshop and calling again, only for the bell to sound once more.

But when I went back to the front door, whoever had rung it a second time hadn't waited. There was no one there.

And my car was gone.

It wasn't possible for it to have been stolen; I would have heard the engine turning over for one thing, and it couldn't have been removed so completely from sight so quickly. Anyway, there was no one around, not for miles, apart from the people up in the wood. Unless they'd been the ones who'd come ringing the bell, I thought, wanting me to move the car for some reason and had done it themselves when I hadn't answered. But I'd only been gone a minute and I hadn't parked in anybody's way; there was no other vehicle to be in the way *of*, apart from Murray's battered delivery van. The car simply couldn't have been taken. There were no tyre tracks leading out of the yard.

And yet there was no trace, either, of the ones I'd carved into the snow when I arrived.

I wondered if whoever had rung the bell had gone into the house and, looking over, I saw that someone must have done as the curtains in the Oxbarrows' bedroom had been opened. And going in through the front door, I heard voices in the kitchen and found the stepladder back on its feet, the evergreens rehung on the walls, more fulsome and fragrant than they had been before.

They drooped from the lintel of the kitchen door in such heavy bunches that I had to rake aside the vegetation to get through, taking far longer than I ought to have done to cross the threshold – as though I was pushing my way through some especially overgrown part of the plantation.

I put it down to the thickness of the foliage but when I tried to make myself known, when I asked about the car, my voice only sounded inside my head, as though I was thinking rather than speaking. And it was as though I was a spectator rather than a participant when, coming out scratched from the holly and the pine needles, I found myself unnoticed by the three people there in the room.

None of them looked at me. Not Murray or Helen or Joe, who sat close to the woodstove, wrapped in a blanket with a mug of coffee by his feet. The dog that I'd expected to come and see me off, a sharp-looking Dobermann, lay in the apron of heat, attentive to the bursts of heavy rain on the windows and Helen's quiet monologue of comfort as she dabbed at the cuts on Joe's forehead.

'Thank God you found him,' she said.

Murray looked over and went back to the soup he had simmering on the range.

'He was lucky I almost ran over his bike,' he said. 'Otherwise, I'd have driven straight past him.'

Helen pulled another tuft of cotton wool from the bag and dipped it into the bowl of water on her lap.

'Do you think anyone at the Barleycorn knows him?' she said.

'I'm sure they know him,' said Murray. 'Whether they care about him is another thing.'

'Why did they let him get so pissed?'

'It's not up to them to tell him when to stop, is it?'

'I know, but look at the state of him, Murray. It's clear enough he hasn't got the money to waste on drink. It's fucking immoral taking it off him.'

She dropped the bloodied lump into the bin and caught Joe's head as it wilted.

'You'll have to hold him,' she said, and Murray came over, steadying Joe's head in his hands as a tremor set in.

'He's still not thawed out, the poor bastard,' said Helen and she took another blanket off one of the chairs near the fire and flapped it open.

Only, it unfolded into a much larger piece of cloth, white and freshly laundered, that settled on the kitchen table where Helen smoothed it out.

Somehow, it was morning time now. The room was filled with brilliant winter sunlight. A small pot of snowdrops sat on the windowsill.

Joe appeared at the kitchen door, ruddy-faced in his overcoat, and stood there uncertainly until Helen noticed and called him in.

'Don't worry, we won't keep you long,' she said, pulling out a chair for him to sit on. He took off his work gloves, paired them neatly on his lap, and stroked the dog when it came sniffing at his legs. He looked healthier than I'd ever known him to be, smiling in a way that I hadn't seen before. There was something else different about him too, something that evaded me for a moment before I realised what it was. He had no scars.

'He's ready,' said Helen, standing behind Joe with her hands over his eyes as Murray came in, taking great care to be secretive, and set down a sponge cake iced with the words 'One Month Dry'.

The surprise revealed, Joe accepted Murray's handshake and Helen's kiss and then blew out the candle, sending the room into darkness – a granular darkness, heavy to breathe in and suddenly ferocious with sound. And as the noise died away and the dust with it, I found that I was now in the workshop.

I wasn't dreaming. There wasn't quite that kind of absurdity to it. There was more direction. As if I were being shown things that I had no choice but to watch.

I don't remember feeling frightened – that came later – only numb. It was a sort of paralysis, maybe. I don't know what to call it. The best I can do is to compare it to how I'd imagine someone waking up under anaesthetic to feel: conscious but immobile; a mute onlooker.

I watched Joe and Murray pick up the length of timber they'd cut and load it onto a trolley stacked with other planks of pinewood. The disc of the saw came to a standstill, smoking lightly. Murray opened the doors wide, taking off his mask to light a cigarette. The trees outside were dripping with rainwater and blossom in the sun. It was the middle of the springtime now, teeming and bright-wet. The dog appeared, as polished as an otter, shook its coat, and then accompanied Joe and Murray as they manoeuvred the trolley out towards the van.

When they'd gone, little birds flew in, settling on the pieces of furniture or on the teeth of the saw wheel.

More arrived, more still, finches and warblers, turning the place into an aviary, until a darting of swifts across the face of the open doors seemed to draw the birds out, as if they were answering a call.

I followed them – no, I was *taken* – out of the workshop and into the embers of a late summer evening. The swifts jubilant in the sundown, they scudded low over the field in front of the house, the grass luxuriant as fur, the ancient ridge and furrow of the earth beneath it found by the long shadows of the beech trees. Ripe and full, they shaded the van completely as it came up the track from the road.

Joe was driving shirtless and unhurried, an elbow hanging out of the window. In the yard, he circled the steering wheel with his hand and then backed up to the workshop, where Murray was sweeping.

The months of labour, the sobriety and kindness, had transformed Joe. When he jumped down from the cab, he looked lean and summer-baked. He was much younger than I'd thought him to be.

Making Murray laugh at something I couldn't quite hear over the birdsong, Joe picked up another broom and together they hefted the sawdust into a pile by the door.

In the warmth of the evening it rose and spread as dense as mist. Mist that cooled to drizzle. Drizzle that turned to rain on a day in autumn.

Now, almost all the leaves from the beech trees had fallen in a sodden carpet across the yard, where Murray squatted by the van to inspect the damage that had been done to the front end. The left-hand corner had been crushed in, the headlight shattered, the bonnet rucked as if it had been punched hard from the inside.

Murray's head dropped and then, standing and shaking the wetness off his hands, he went to the window of the front room.

Now I saw him from inside the house, mouthing through the glass at Helen who knelt next to the sofa where Joe was lying cadaverous with drink, a bucket close to his head.

And then it was a different day, and I watched him lying in the same position, the bucket full.

Another day.

Another day.

Now here he was, going through the cupboards in the kitchen, through Helen's purse.

There he was wheeling his broken bicycle down the track under the beech trees.

Now returning, furtively, the pockets of his overcoat weighed down.

Here was Helen pouring a bottle of cheap gin down the sink.

Joe trying to take the U-bend apart.

The dog barking at him.

Baring its teeth.

Joe swapping the wrench for a hammer.

The dog limping away down the garden to its kennel.

Murray wrestling the hammer off Joe.

Joe fleeing up the stairs to his room.

The house filled with his cries.

I willed myself to go to him, but time lurched on, removing me to the workshop again. Murray was there alone planing curls of pinewood off a door, his eye blackened by a bruise. The injury aside, he looked markedly unwell now. He was grey in the cheeks, thin and drained; just as he'd been when I'd found him lying on his bed.

The door opened and Helen came in, rubbing her arms against the cold.

'He's here,' she said. 'Crawland.'

'Already?' said Murray. 'I didn't think it would be today.'

'You did tell him to come as soon as he could.'

Murray put down the plane and dusted off his hands on his overalls.

'Don't look at me like that, Helen,' he said. 'He knows what he's doing. I told you. He helped that friend of Tommy Bell's, and Sandy Huggan's daughter.'

'What was wrong with her?'

'She wouldn't eat.'

Helen put her hands in her pockets. 'What is he, a priest? He looks like one.'

'He has a church of some kind, I think,' said Murray. 'People go and listen to him speak anyway.'

'Which people?'

'I don't know,' said Murray. 'I've just heard, that's all.'

'So, what will he do?' said Helen. 'Say a prayer? I think Joe needs more than that. And so do you.'

She helped him on with his coat, zipping it to the top and turning up the collar.

'He's here now,' said Murray. 'Let's at least listen to what he has to say.'

ی

Outside, it was a winter's afternoon, with freezing fog hanging over the yard and the field. Helen and Murray went back to the house and I went with them through the front door and down to the kitchen where a tall, gaunt man – this Crawland Murray had invited – sat at the table. He shook hands with them both and then, putting on his glasses, inspected the bruise around Murray's eye.

'That looks sore,' he said.

'It would have been worse if Joe had meant it,' Helen replied.

'Oh, it was intentional,' said Crawland. 'No question of that.'

'I keep thinking that it must be something we've done,' said Murray. 'Or not done.'

Crawland shook his head and let Murray sit down.

'No,' he said. 'As I told you on the phone, the only mistake you've made is to try and reason with it, that's all.'

'It?' said Helen.

'The spirit Joe has inside him,' said Crawland.

Helen scoffed and Murray looked at her.

'Please, Helen, hear him out,' he said.

Crawland glanced over at the Dobermann lying miserably by the fire, its back leg bandaged.

'Do you think it was Joe who did that to your dog, Helen?' he said. 'Do you think he was capable?'

'Not the Joe I know.'

'That's precisely my point,' Crawland said.

'But that doesn't mean there's something inside him,' said Helen. 'It means he's ill.'

Crawland smiled without hiding his condescension.

'If you choose not to believe me and you'd rather try to find some other explanation,' he said, 'then that's your privilege, of course. But you'll just be complicating matters for Joe and it's Joe we're trying to help. The truth will make far more sense to him than anything you come up with, I can assure you.'

'He was doing so well,' said Murray, lighting a cigarette. 'It's been almost a year. I can't believe he'd go backwards after so long.'

'Why, because of all the cakes you've baked him for being good?' said Crawland.

'Because he was always telling us how much better he felt without the drink,' Helen said. 'Why would he suddenly want to go back to it?'

'It's what the spirit wants, not him,' said Crawland. 'Because Joe's been ignoring it, it's fighting to be heard.'

'But why would he even listen to it?' Murray said.

Crawland took off his glasses and put them on the table. I could see that, like the Joe who'd come to me at St Peter's, his hands and face were freckled with old scars too.

'We have to think of Joe as a child,' he said. 'A child under a bad influence. He's not going to take any notice of you any more, he won't try and please you, no matter how many rewards you promise him.'

'So what do we do?' said Helen.

'It's quite simple,' Crawland replied. 'We remove the influence.'

'Remove it how?' said Murray.

Crawland contemplated them both.

'There are certain things growing in the woods that will be unpalatable at this time of year to the sprit that's tormenting Joe,' he said. 'We can bring them into the house and drive it out.'

'We?' said Helen.

'There are people I can call on to help,' said Crawland. 'People who understand what you're dealing with.'

Upstairs, Joe cried out, in pain or in the throes of a nightmare.

'Call them,' said Murray. 'If it's the best thing to do.'

'It is,' Crawland said, standing and squeezing his shoulder.

He went out and Murray and Helen argued.

Argued again as they made breakfast on a dark, wet morning, so at odds with each other that Murray shut himself away in the workshop for the rest of the day and Helen in the kitchen.

Time shifted and now Joe was sitting at the table as Helen brought him a bowl of soup.

But he wouldn't eat.

He refused it like the child Crawland considered him to be.

Now the soup was on the floor. The bowl shattered.

The back door opened.

There was Joe climbing the fence, escaping.

Joe, sometime later, out cold in the yard.

Helen picking him up.

Murray holding his head under the gushing kitchen tap.

Joe forced into his room.

The Dobermann barking outside his door, louder and louder.

Then whining.

Here was Helen screaming for Murray.

The Dobermann with its throat cut.

Joe flashing the knife as Helen tried to take it off him.

Helen wrapping what was left of her hand in a towel.

Murray holding Joe's door tight. Joe wanting to be let out, desperate to say sorry.

Murray nailing Joe in.

Helen's arm sleeved with blood.

Murray driving her off to the hospital. The van rolling along the track, its one working headlight bounding among the trees.

I watched them turn off onto the road as the last of the daylight was swept aside by snow that came down heavy and ash-like, clotting where it fell, swiftly burying everything it touched.

Upstairs, Joe called out for Murray and rattled the handle of his door before he began overturning the furniture in frustration. Rage, repentance, deference, he lurched from one to the other until exhaustion must have put him to sleep. He didn't stir when Murray came back alone, closed the door quietly, lit a cigarette and telephoned Crawland.

ℰ

The next day: snowdrifts and silence. A sky the colour of paper.

The doors of the workshop were open and after a moment, I saw Murray come out carrying a stepladder. On his way back to the house he stopped to wait for the three men who were coming down the fellside from the plantation. Crawland and two others who looked as if they might be his sons.

I realised that it had been their voices I'd heard when I first arrived at Salter Farm. And when they came in through the gate, I could see that each of them held a huge bunch of holly.

Voices came from another direction now too and I watched

a dozen people coming off the road and up the track towards the house. They were dressed as I was, buried inside hats and scarves, their coats encrusted with snow like the sheep I'd passed on the way here. They too held armfuls of greenery which they carried in through the front door. Things that they'd picked from the hedgerows and the woodlands round about, from their own gardens perhaps. Garlands that they'd made themselves. Faces and animals fashioned out of the interlaced stems.

Murray stopped Crawland as they went in through the front door.

'Does it really have to be today?' he said.

'We can't keep Joe nailed into his room,' Crawland replied. 'He's suffered enough.'

'Of course,' said Murray. 'But can't we at least wait for Helen to be discharged? She'd want to be here.'

'I think it better for Joe if she stays where she is,' Crawland said. 'If there's anyone here with any doubt about what we're doing then the spirit will only take strength from that. Do you have any doubts, Murray?'

After a moment, Murray shook his head and then set up the stepladder in the hall.

From the top floor, Joe beat on his door and sent down alternate vows of violence and contrition. None of Crawland's people took any notice but went in and out of the house with a quiet diligence, climbing up to the plantation and returning with more shrubbery. For the younger ones, it seemed as enjoyable as any other Christmas tradition and although they got in the way, the grown-ups let them help drag in the spruce trees for the kitchen.

It was only Murray who seemed distracted by Joe's threats, looking up at the ceiling as he climbed the ladder.

'He'll see it as kindness in time,' said Crawland, holding another wreath for Murray to hang. 'It was what I needed in the end – to have the spirit removed. I was a slave, just like Joe.'

He looked to his two sons, who were winding ivy through the balusters of the stairs, and they nodded in agreement.

Above them, Joe yelled and cursed.

Crawland touched Murray's arm.

'It can't stay,' he said. 'Look at what it did to Helen. It'll hurt you too and kill Joe before long. It'll empty this house. That's what it wants.'

Murray took the wreath from Crawland and hung it on the wall. All around him Salter Farm gradually filled with the smell of sweet, cloying resin that seemed to coat the insides of my mouth and nose with every breath.

ॐ

When the house had been dressed, when Joe had given up shouting and had taken to bargaining instead, Crawland and the rest went about slotting little candles between the stems and branches and lighting them. The soft glow brought out the gloss of the leaves and the berries and the eyes of the children, who were as enraptured as they might have been in a Christmas grotto. A little boy in a red woollen hat was lifted up by his father so that he could light some of the candles wound into the ivy on the stairs.

As the work came to an end, everyone waited expectantly as though in church, Murray trying to ignore Joe's pleas by watching the snow filling in the window above the front door.

Somewhere, a clock rang and Crawland moved from one person to the next, placing a hand on each head, murmuring what sounded like a short prayer and handing out boughs of holly, five or six apiece. His sons followed him, distributing lengths of string so that everyone could wind a handle around their branches and make them into a sheaf.

Once they were done, Crawland nodded to the person closest to the front door and they opened it wide, letting in the cold. It was almost full dark outside and the snow fell in goose-feathers on the yard and on the field.

One of Crawland's sons handed Murray the hammer he'd been using to nail up the evergreens and invited him to go first up the stairs. He was reluctant to do so and Crawland held his head gently and spoke close to him, in words that were for him alone, until Murray began to nod and concede. And then, wiping his eyes, he headed up with Crawland and his sons, each carrying their bunch of holly.

Hearing them coming, Joe raised his voice, thanking Murray over and over as he jemmied out the nails from the doorframe, thinking that he was about to be released.

I wanted now more than anything to will myself away

from Salter Farm. But I seemed compelled to stand with the others as they waited and listened to the sound of shouts and footsteps coming closer — from the top floor to the landing, from the landing to the head of the stairs, where there was some kind of tussle, Murray pleading with Crawland to stop.

Then the banister juddered as Joe fell into it, half-sliding, half-tumbling down the stairs, trying to find something to hold onto and pulling the ivy loose. The candles scattered and went out, prompting the children to scrabble about after them as their parents stepped forward with their holly and thrashed Joe where he lay.

One of them tried to haul him in the direction of the open front door but he twisted free and made for the kitchen instead, sending the children scampering into the arms of their parents and knocking aside the man who tried to stop him. Holding his jaw, the elderly gentleman blundered into the stepladder, which fell hard to the floor, sweeping down the wreaths and mistletoe that Murray had nailed to the wall.

Led by Crawland, those who were bold enough pursued Joe and I was caught up in their wake, it seemed, drawn through the boughs of pine and spruce hanging across the kitchen doorway.

Now Joe was trying to get out into the garden, yanking at the handle as Crawland and his sons whipped his back. When the others joined, Joe lost his grip and wrapped himself up in his arms on the floor, crying out for Murray, who did his best to drag them off, but he could do nothing more than grasp at shoulders and collars and elbows. There were too many of them and he was easily shoved aside, beaten with holly himself until Crawland took him away and the others strong-armed Joe back into the hall, knocking down more of the greens in the process.

I don't think I'd ever seen anyone so truly terrified before as Joe cowered under the green faces leering at him from the walls, and threw himself to the floor in a ball as someone thrust at him with a stag's head made from the branches of a thorn tree.

They took hold of him again, but yanking an arm loose, Joe managed to get himself into a stooped half-run and was harried out of the house by those who'd been waiting at the front door. He made some ground across the yard, but eventually floundered in the deep snow and couldn't get up quick enough before those who'd given chase caught him. Crawland and his sons galvanised the rest now and the parents carried their children on their shoulders so that they could get through the snow quicker.

At the edge of the crowd of flailing arms, the little boy in the red hat was set down and then ushered forward, hesitant at first and then flogging Joe's head more viciously than the others, tearing a chunk out of his ear, trying to jab the stalks of holly between Joe's fingers and into his eyes.

Finally, at some word from Crawland, Joe was lifted to his feet and they clapped and whistled him to the track under the beech trees, lashing at him with the holly when he stumbled.

Murray went after them, begging them to stop and calling for Joe. I went too, but by the time I'd made it to the end of the path, there was no one in sight, there were only voices somewhere down the road.

They were singing now.

A chorus of joy and triumph rising over cries that didn't sound human any more. They were more like those the dog had made under the blows of the kitchen knife.

Although the voices petered out, I was sent after them. For a while I followed their footprints, the trail of discarded holly branches, the strings of blood, until the snow covered their tracks and I wandered on blindly. Or at least it seemed so to me. But of course I was being guided at each junction, steered around every corner, unable to turn back or avoid the conclusion.

Here was a track off the lane. Here was a bridge across a frozen stream. An open gate. A dark field. Three shabby horses nervous by the wall. Afraid of the thing at the edge of the white, abraded pond. A dead man, already half buried by the falling snow.

❧

There it is. That's everything. It happened so long ago now that it ought to be easy to mistrust the memories of that afternoon, but they come to me more vividly than any others – especially at Christmastime.

If I do tell David, he'll simply attack it with logic, I know, and rather enjoy the process of sifting out my sentiment and conjecture from the facts.

He'll be straight on the internet and he'll learn that there was indeed a place called Salter Farm, that a man called Murray Oxbarrow was found dead there by his wife; that they couldn't decide whether he'd meant to take quite so many pills. He'll read about the rumours that connect Murray to the death of a Joe Gull whose body was discovered nearby, but he'll find that they are only rumours.

David won't disagree that I went to Salter Farm, but he'll say that my memory of it is false, that it's been built solely out of what I've read about the place. It's the only rational conclusion, he'll say. But what about Crawland? There's no mention of him anywhere. Helen must have kept quiet about him, for her sake. How do I know about Crawland?

David will say that I've plucked him out of another story I've heard. The mind is a magpie, Ed.

But the problem is that I know that none of it is fabricated. All the details that David discards as unlikely and implausible will still be there as bare facts to me. The chief one being that Joe Gull was dead, and had been for several years, when he turned up in his best suit at St Peter's and asked for my help.

In the days after I'd come home from Salter Farm, not knowing what was real, afraid that I was losing my mind, the only thing that made any sense to me was to think of it all as some grand parable of humility. Or honesty. Because if I were being truthful with myself, then I'd wanted Joe to trust me, rather than God. In which case, I'd never had a calling; I'd only ever been listening to my own voice. And so, I'd been sent to Salter Farm in order to learn my place, to know that I was nothing more than an eyewitness to God's design.

Then at other times I wondered if, drifting in some sort of purgatory, Joe had seen me as his emissary, his chance for deliverance. Perhaps his regret had been so strong as to bring him back to seek out one last brief opportunity to beg forgiveness of the Oxbarrows, not knowing that Murray was dead and Helen was no longer living at Salter Farm.

Or was it that he just wanted someone to know what had happened to him, that Crawland and the others had killed him, whether they meant to or not?

Every year at this time, I'm forced to try to understand it all and I get nowhere. I only know that it happened.

It happened. And that's all there is to say. But it's not enough, I know. To say *it happened* lays nothing to rest.

Can you imagine what it's like to never be certain of anything any more? I'll say.

But David won't understand what I mean.

And God's no help. He never was. He only ever made me a silly little boy trying to fit the sky into a matchbox.

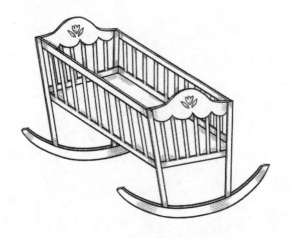

CONFINEMENT

Kiran Millwood Hargrave

I write this record as though it is testimony given before God, a prayer poured straight into the ears of angels, for there is none now I can trust but myself: my own heart, my own pen. I am not in the habit of keeping a diary, so I confess all that follows is recollection: but I swear on my soul this is just as it happened. As it is happening.

It must be understood in the clearest possible terms that I, Catherine Elizabeth Mary Blake, on this day, the twenty-fourth of December eighteen-ninety-eight, am of sound mind, whatever they may say.

I know I am the daughter of Sophie Mary Winsome and John Albert Winsome, now deceased, and the year-long wife of Richard Arthur Charles Blake. I know I live at Blake Manor, a stone's throw from Tenbury Wells, in the county of Shropshire. I can name our queen, our prime minister, our colonies, the extent of our empire. I know my commandments. I will write everything in such detail as to try to conjure you straight into my memory, of how each thing happened.

I tell you all this to demonstrate what you must believe is the truth: that though my body is weak, and my mind much assailed, I am not mad. Though when you hear what follows, you will understand why I might wish to be.

§

I was confined in the carmine room. It was made ready the moment my bloods were missed. A plain place it was, quite out of fashion, with yellow silk wallpaper ravaged by moths, and heavy green velvet curtains lined with their eggs, which made me sneeze whenever I threw them back. I loved it anyway, that room, because of the vista.

Blake Manor sits at the intersection of forest and river, atop a hill that gives a gentle and lovely view of both. If you stand at this window and close one eye – or if like me you are unable to wink and must instead cover one eye with your palm – two quite different worlds become apparent. The first, familiar to me from my childhood visitations to the Mussoorie hills, of rolling, verdant green and the river cutting silver through their bases. When you swap to cover your other eye, the second is revealed. This is the valley of thick forest, wild and brown and shadowed, like something from a fairytale.

Despite the appeal of this aspect, the house is instead turned, like a churlish child, with its back to the valley. Its approach, fine gates and frontage look out instead on a rather ordinary stretch of ornamental garden, laid out like an unplayed chessboard in squares of roses in the summer, and more roses in the autumn. This fragrant if soulless arrangement is jealously tended to by Noakes, who Richard told me came with the house. As is the way with old houses, he and his wife, the housekeeper Mrs Noakes, are as much a part of Blake Manor as the grand piano or the Blake family itself.

Perhaps this is why the wildness at the rear of the house was looked-over in favour of Noakes' ordered flowers. That land is not the Blakes', though they have tried many times to buy it. Rather it belongs to a farmer by the name of Bright, a widower, who will neither cultivate nor sell it. Their ownership goes back to the Domesday Book. But this is not the place to speak further on the Brights. All that matters for now is the room, and the view that brought me here, and my insistence that it should be painted red.

Dr Harman was quite against it from the first moment. His teachings told him a delivery room must be white, or at the least a pale colour: blue as meltwater, or green as moss. But it had to be red, I told Richard, because that was the colour of my mother's delivery room in Bombay, where I was born. I became rather upset, as Mother died not two years ago, and it felt important to have her somehow there. Richard kissed my forehead in his way that always soothes me, and only asked if it should be reading-room red, or carmine. I said the latter, because it tasted better on my lips, like the waxy cylinder of my favourite lip stain.

They sent a great vat of it across from Hull, the pigments from beetle wings brought not from India, but Peru, and mixed with acid on the docks. When the house-boy levered the vat open, Richard asked me again if I was sure.

In truth, I was not. The colour was nothing like Mother

had described, something warming and spicy and soothing, like supping cardamom milk. But Mrs Noakes was nearby with her pinched disapproval clear on her grey face, and so I smiled widely and said I was certain.

I did a lot of things differently under Mrs Noakes' gaze. I was all exhaustion the first five months, my ankles swelling and my stays seeming to shrink by the moment as I wore them, but I did not let her see how I longed to sleep, how uncomfortable I was. It was a kind of competition between us, for she is not the sort of woman who likes a fuss, and I am. But I was stupidly proud about it all and wished to impress her. Why is that? A housekeeper, with a long, blunt face like a trowel, or a terrier. I could laugh thinking about it if I did not so dearly need to scream.

I should have said no, the day they split open the vat and showed me a colour that could only have been formed under the Devil's watch. A colour that made me think of wounds, of the split open insides of pigs. I thought it would be all right, that at least I would have the view. Even when they came with new drapes, deepest purple velvet and heavier even than the green, I did not understand, truly, what lay before me. Not when they fixed the button connecting to a bell in the kitchen. Not even when the lock, brass and thicker than my thumb, was installed into the heavy oak door, and the key, solid and intricate and without copy, appeared on the ring at Mrs Noakes' narrow waist.

༄

Anyone with any knowledge of such things will understand why I am loathe to share the details of the birth, or rather, what I can recall. But the circumstances in which it started are, I believe, significant.

It is the custom in these parts to attend church for each of the days of Latter Advent. It is also the custom in these parts for it to snow most of winter. I had heard of snow, of course, even seen it on postcards Father sent from his mission station in Ladakh, the mountains white and enormous as clouds. But it is one thing to know what snow is, and quite another to understand it. To see it blanket the entirety of the world overnight, to feel it pillowing your steps, creeping up over your boots and flooding your stockings with its icy bite. The ways it plays with sound, batting it about like a cat with a mouse, and the fearful crunch like tiny bones beneath your feet.

I was already unsteady, my belly too large to wrap about with my arms, hindering my sleeping and waking hours both. But it was tradition to walk the mile to church no matter the weather, Mrs Noakes informed me, and as the almost-new Mrs Blake, I was compelled to keep up with it.

We had completed the journey the previous days without much ado, but this day was different. Noakes had shovelled the path as usual, which takes us down the long and manicured drive and out onto the country road that snakes around Blake Manor's exterior wall. But it was so cold, our breath instant smoke from our lips as we peered out of the front door, that ice had already made a rink of that approach. Richard insisted we must take the shorter route from the back of the house, through the fresh snow. Mrs Noakes argued briefly, but was cowed by a curt word from my husband. I felt a thrill at her anger as I was appropriately bundled into several layers of wool stockings and a most unbecoming scarf that smelt of mothballs.

We stepped from the conservatory doors into snow calf-deep. The wool about my legs served only to drink in the freezing slush, but Mrs Noakes was close behind and so I did not complain. Richard gave me his arm and I clung to him, enjoying his warmth, his solidity, as my legs grew heavy and more cumbersome even than they already were. Before us stretched the view I had so come to love, seen at eye level: the forest coloured in black and white by the bright cold air, the river glinting as a blade and just audible beneath its layer of crystalline ice. The snow gristled beneath our boots as we walked the gentle slope that would take us to the public thoroughfare eked from Bright's farm, running between their boundary and ours all the way to the church.

Now I wonder if I imagined my husband's hesitation at the gate that bounded Widower Bright's land. Certainly something happened: a sharp inhale, or else a tremble in Richard's taut forearm. It was enough to make me pause my fierce attention on my sodden feet, and look up into his face. It is a fine face, if a little weak chinned, but he hides it well enough with his whiskers. His eyes, normally round and cherubically gay, were hooded. His whiskers quivered. He looked like a fox, scenting a hunt. He looked afraid.

But then he sensed me looking, and opened the gate, stepping through without further ado, and holding it open for first me, then the Noakeses following behind. What I am certain I did not imagine is that, before either Noakes stepped through the gate, they crossed themselves.

Richard allowed them to walk ahead, both of them hunched, even poker-backed Mrs Noakes, and hurrying faster than I would have imagined possible for people of their advanced years.

'Whatever is the matter with them?' I asked Richard.

He chuckled, a little too loudly. 'You know how superstitious these country folk are.'

Richard fancies himself suburban, you see.

'Superstitious of what?' I asked, focusing on neither stumbling on my numb legs, nor allowing my teeth to chatter.

Richard gestured with his free arm. I followed its path, to the trees in their glitter, the river enfolded in white hills. 'The Bright witch.'

'Witch?' I blinked up at him. 'The widower?'

'His wife.'

'But she is dead.'

'That is how you make a widower.'

'So why are they afraid of her?'

'It is not the best idea to divulge such information to a woman in your condition. Indeed, there is never a good time.'

'In which case,' I insisted, 'you had better tell me anyway.'

'If you wish,' he shrugged, but his pace increased slightly so I had to all-but-skip to keep up. 'There are many stories about her. But it is widely accepted that her husband was a strong man, a virile man by all accounts, who upon marrying her found himself diminished.'

'Is that not a common complaint?' I teased, but Richard did not so much as smile at my cleverness.

'I mean that quite literally. I did not see him myself, but Mrs Noakes tells me that when last she saw him he was . . . ' He wrinkled his nose. 'It is not a pleasant image.'

'I do not mind,' I said.

'Shrivelled,' he said. 'I believe that was the word. His whole body shrunken, and his cheeks sucked in, his legs wasted. He remains so to this day.'

'It sounds like polio. We saw many cases in Bombay.'

'It is not polio, nor any such earthly concern.'

I would have teased him about how he sounded rather superstitious himself, but I was quite out of breath by now, and happy for him to talk us all the way to church.

'One of the worse effects was that his decline left him unable to have children. My father himself offered the family doctor to help, but he refused.'

I confess I am not surprised. Dr Harman is a brisk man, with very cold hands.

'Or rather,' said Richard, dropping his voice though the Noakeses were far ahead and there was no one to hear us but the trees, 'Mrs Bright made him. We – they believe . . . he was taken over by her. Not by love, or infatuation. Body and soul, taken and commanded by her. Possessed.'

I snorted, a most unladylike sound, and Richard flinched.

I found enough breath for an apology, and he patted my glove. 'It is all right, my dear. Dr Harman warned your humours would be inflamed. Whatever the case, they partook in baby farming.'

An image of little chubby heads lining a furrowed field like turnips sprang fully formed into my mind.

'You know,' continued Richard, 'buying babies from unsavouries who cannot even find a place in a workhouse. At first no one noticed, the farm is so isolated, but soon it came to the constabulary's attention that around a dozen babies had been bought by the Brights.'

'It's kind of them,' I said, rubbing my belly gently.

He shuddered. 'Except when a detective started looking into it, they found not a trace of a child in the house.'

Instantly nausea filled my throat. I did not want him to continue, but as though I were in the grip of a nightmare, I could not prevent it.

'She had been killing them,' said Richard briskly. 'Burying them in the forest. They found most of them. She was hanged as a murderess, but many believe her a witch, too, for Mr Bright had no knowledge of the babies, being bedridden. Seeing her picture in the paper, I believe it. Black eyes she had, to match her heart.'

I looked once more out to the woods, bustling close on my right side. I noticed for the first time that Richard had placed me between himself and the Bright land. The snow on the path before us was a dazzlement, but the branches of the wood were so thick the snowfall stopped abruptly at the treeline, as though an edge had been drawn and the colours parted between black and white.

I have always loved the smell of forests. On our travels in India they were sweet, sharp scents of gum and flowers, all of it smoked through heat, stalked by tigers. I knew English forests smelt different, and that the pregnancy had done something with my nose, turning apples into rot and coal into muffins fresh baked.

But this forest, over the mothballed wool wrapped about my throat, smelt of something deep and opaque. Earth, yes, but also air, the night air turning thin over mountain peaks, something metallic, fresh pulled from clouds or rock. It smelt, and I am ashamed to say it, like myself, that place where I bled and would soon birth from, where Richard entered me and our baby would leave. A familiar and animal scent that sent something thrilling through my blood.

The shadows seemed soupy and textured beneath the trees. My vision flickered, unable to land on anything in particular, the darkness making near and far tunnel against each other and my eyes, snow-strained, ached. I closed them briefly, turned back to the house. There it sat in its perfect pocket astride the hill. There was the conservatory sifted through snow, there the frost glittered on the roof tiles. And there, in window of the carmine room, the heavy purple curtains twitched.

'Are you all right?'

I squinted. It had been a small movement, as if someone was just opening them a moment to check the weather. A usual movement. But there was no one in the carmine room. I knew this because Mrs Noakes kept it locked as a prevention against dirt and dust, so that all she will need to do when the delivery comes is throw back the cover sheet. She also kept the window cracked open, to allow the fresh air to sweep it clean. It must have been a breeze, stirring the fabric.

This sensible conclusion cheered me enough that I ignored its quieter cousin. Those curtains had required two men apiece to hang them, and new iron railings bracketed to the wall. They were so heavy I had to use both hands to pull them aside. I squinted up at the trees. Not a whisper of wind stirred the dusting of snow atop their uppermost branches. Then, below them, in the shadows directly to my right, something moved.

I stopped, and Richard turned to me, impatience in his tone.

'I should not have told you about the Brights. Are you upset?'

I had not the breath to answer him. Dread had clamped itself hard about my throat.

There was someone in the forest, someone watching us.

The white of two eyes. The glint of a mouth opened and closed. The wet snick of a swallow.

My nostrils flooded suddenly with the animal smell, and it took on something else, a warmth like breath, though there was no one standing close and level with me, breathing upon my face.

'Catherine?'

Richard's voice was far away, and so was his arm in mine. My whole body seemed to have faded from me, so I was only eyes fixed on the shadowed forest, only a heart beating loud enough to make my vision tremble. In the forest, the mouth opened again, and now I saw the face around the mouth as though it were lit from within, bones showing dark against the skin, and from the back of the throat came, sudden and keening, a sound like a trapped fox. It was my voice, my face.

Richard was shaking me now, and I felt something come loose. I snapped back into my body, and my body was aflame, my belly cramped in a vice.

'Mrs Noakes!' I heard him call. 'It is begun! Mrs Noakes!'

As I sank back into the snow, and as Richard bent over me, the animal smell filled my nose, my throat. The twisting in my belly worsened, and I let it carry me down. I could not even warn Richard, could not even tell him to turn around to see her, standing at his shoulder. A woman, with black eyes.

THE FIRST DAY

I rose on a tide of agony, gasping and crying. My jaw was clamped between two cold fingers, and metal filled my mouth, then the white sour taste of amla, which I knew was not amla at all but laudanum, and I knew if I swallowed I would sink again and not be able to tell them. But the cold hand, Dr Harman's hand, now held my lips closed, and I was choking on it, and I could not fight any longer.

The laudanum seared my throat, and my whole body fell heavy as purple velvet, buffeted by invisible waves of pain, so far off I could only feel it in snatches. There were fingers crawling inside my skull, probing the underside of my mind. In that dizzying moment of confusion, she was inside, black-eyed, black-hearted. I felt her, smelt her. And in another moment the fingers pushed through and around, over my skull, yanking my hair tight. I tried to pull away, but the fingers were insistent.

'Now, Mrs Blake. We must keep this neat or else the knots will never come out.'

Mrs Noakes, her hands at work on my delivery coiffure. It was a style I picked myself, two thick braids looping my skull. But it was squeezing, the pins sharp enough to stab my skin. My head was heavy as an anchor on the useless chain of my neck, but I managed to turn towards her voice. *No*, I thought, the horror enormous and crushing as a boulder. *No.*

Mrs Noakes' eyes were two black holes.

I struggled like a drowning man who is more water than breath. Again, amla bitter on my tongue, and the second dose of laudanum sank me deeper.

In Bombay, the heat was a coat, the lick of a warm tongue. The sound of dogs woke us each morning, the *tuk-tuk* of the fans put us asleep. My ayah warmed milk and sweetened it with sugar. She even put sugar on my amla, making everything sweet. When I was sick she sang to me though Mother and Father said I was too old for such things. When

I had pox she bathed me in yoghurt. I wanted her softness now, her warmth, her milk and dahi remedies.

The skin of my head was tearing, and between my legs I tore too. Dr Harman's hands were cold as snow. I was screaming without a sound, on and on, and at last the scream escaped, shrill and piercing. An unbroken cry. But it was not from my mouth.

༄

THE THIRD DAY

The room was red and dark as the inside of my eyelids. I lay very still, and all was very quiet. For a good while I was not sure if I was awake or asleep. The laudanum was slowly releasing my limbs, my tongue, all of which ached as I stirred. And then the pain between my legs, and more, tight at my skull, arrived and I knew I was not dreaming, and the world was changed. I was a mother.

'Awake, ma'am?' Mrs Noakes sat in the armchair beside the bed, illuminated by the gas lamp. Her eyes were her own, and in her arms was a bundle of crisp, white cloth. 'You have slept a whole two days. Dr Harman thought it best to let you.'

'My baby?' My throat was dry enough my voice scratched.

'A girl.'

'A girl?' I felt tears start in my eyes, and I held my arms out for her.

Mrs Noakes stood and placed the bundle into my arms. A pink face, a snub nose, mother-of-pearl eyelids, lips neat and pink as a rosebud, a smell like fresh bread and lavender. And love, so sharp and hot it burnt. My daughter. The joy and shock of it made me gasp.

'There, ma'am,' said Mrs Noakes, and her voice was softer than usual, its terrier yap mellowed. 'We must not let you get excited.'

She took my daughter from my arms, and I grasped after her. 'But—'

'Plenty of time for that,' she said. 'It was a difficult birth, as you know better than any. Dr Harman has advised complete bedrest for the duration of your confinement.' Mrs Noakes clucked her tongue at my confused expression. 'It is the custom, and Dr Harman agrees it is for the best.'

'I have never—'

'You coming from foreign parts, you would not. But it is a common enough practice,' said Mrs Noakes, bending and placing my baby into the crib Richard had ordered from town. 'Nine days of rest.'

'Nine?'

'You must drink this.' She lifted a steaming cup from the bedside table. I swallowed the broth, lukewarm. 'Good. There must be no excitement, no conversation. Perfect quiet.'

'Richard—'

'Not for a few days. You and the baby both must rest until the doctor says you are healed.'

She pulled a fresh nightdress from the chest of drawers. I raised my arms, obedient as a child, and she hauled off my stale, sweat- and blood-soaked one and slipped clean cotton over my head.

'The braids have held nicely,' she said approvingly. 'We shall keep them in for the duration. Until then, you must press the bell if you wish to feed her, or use the chamber pot.'

She pointed at the call button that we had repaired during the redecorating.

'Chamber pot?' I repeated faintly.

'And there is laudanum to manage the pain.' She tapped a glass bottle placed on the chest of drawers. 'You must have some now.'

'Please, might I hold—'

'She is asleep,' said Mrs Noakes briskly. 'And if she is sleeping, you certainly must. Lie back.'

I shook my head. 'Please, may I speak with Richard?'

'No, ma'am,' says Mrs Noakes. 'Doctor's orders. I can bring him in to explain to you directly?'

With no desire to see anyone but my baby or Richard, and Mrs Noakes resolute, I sank back on the pillows. Mrs Noakes unscrewed the glass bottle, and poured the medicine onto a shallow-bowled spoon. I swallowed it without complaint, welcoming the tiredness, the instant unravelling the laudanum brought to my body. My baby was born, and I was alive. It was better than many women got.

Mrs Noakes adjusted the heavy curtains, and the sound was like leaves rustling. A trill of fear crept up my neck, but it was too late. The laudanum had too firm a hold. The key scraped in the lock. As I fell into muffled oblivion, I remembered the curtains, twitching in a non-existent breeze, warm breath upon my face. Black eyes in black shadows. The wet click of a mouth, opening.

☙

THE FOURTH DAY

I heaved myself upright, my belly and legs feeling loose as frayed knots. At the foot of the bed, something crouched over the crib. My breath hitched. The shape was curved and low, as if it kneeled, and I searched for a sharp object that I could bring down on it, pierce the hunch of its back. Her back.

Moving slow, I reached up to my hair, and slid a pin from its place in Mrs Noakes' tight plaits. The tautness between my legs told me the stitches Dr Harman had feared had come to pass, and I had to crawl like a child to the edge. I brought the pin up, up, over the crouching woman.

Eyes snapped open in her back, either side of the arch of her spine.

I reeled back, crying out, and all at once the room filled with light so bright it seemed to vibrate around me.

'Catherine!' Arms wrapped around me, lifting me back to the centre of the bed. Richard. 'Catherine, you must lie still.'

'Sir, you cannot be in here.' Dr Harman replaced my husband, his cold hands on my shoulders, lifting my eyelids. His whiskered face came close to mine, and behind him I saw Richard pacing. 'Mrs Blake, calm yourself. Is it the pain?'

'No!' I cried, pointing at the foot of the bed. 'There!'

The two men looked, and Richard began to laugh. He moved to my other side, sat on the bed in the candid manner I loved him for, and caught up my trembling hand. 'That is our baby, Catherine. Surely you remember that?'

'Not the baby,' I snapped. My eyes are stinging from the light, as they had caught between snow and shadows. 'She's there!'

'Mrs Noakes is downstairs. You only need use the bell—'

'There!' I insisted, but I did not need Richard to interrupt me this time. I could see for myself, in the bright light issuing from the open door, see clearly. There was no woman, crouched over our baby's crib. Only the fan shade, brought over to shield the child's face. Mrs Noakes must have pulled it up to better aid her sleeping. The eyes then – our baby's eyes. I shuddered at what had nearly occurred, and let the pin slip from my fingers.

A thin wail came from the crib, and Richard stood and lifted our daughter, bringing her to me.

'Sir, that is not—'

'Only a moment,' says Richard impatiently. 'She's distressed, can't you see?'

'Exactly why the room must be kept dark, sir,' said Dr Harman. They sniped at each other, but I did not care, because she was in my arms, and I felt dizzy with love. She settled immediately, the little shells of her eyelids barely twitching.

Richard huffed, evidently having lost the argument. 'Come then, Catherine.' He pressed a whiskery kiss to my forehead, and gently prised the baby from my grip. 'Only another week, and it shall be Christmas, and you shall be well.'

'Can you bring her closer?'

Richard looked to Dr Harman, who narrowed his eyes. 'If it will prevent you from getting up to look at her?'

'Of course,' I said. 'I only wish to have her close by.'

Dr Harman nodded disapprovingly. Richard lifted the whole crib, and placed it gently down beside the bed. I lowered myself back down with a sigh, and Dr Harman approached with his fearful spoon, and I swallowed, summoning my ayah to me, and amla berries, my baby's cheek just visible, the soft rise and fall of her chest, as the door is once again closed and the room plunged into red-black darkness.

༄

THE FIFTH DAY

In the carmine room, there was no sense of what was night, and what was day. The purple curtains were lined with some impenetrable cloth, and it was not until the fifth day, woken by my full bladder, that I summoned the strength to move to the window.

I rolled carefully to my side, to look at her. She was sleeping, as she always seemed to, swaddled tight so only her head showed, perfectly round, her lashes grazing her cheek. I resisted the urge to bring her to my breast, and manoeuvred myself upright. It had been necessary to summon Mrs Noakes by the bell button for every little thing, but today the pain had receded somewhat, and I didn't want to sink back into a laudanum haze just yet.

I positioned myself over the chamber pot, braced against the bed frame, hissing as the stitches pulled and my skin burned. It was too dark to see the contents of the pot, but lately my passings had been tinged with blood, which Dr Harman assured me was normal.

Nudging the pot out of sight under the bed once more, I pushed myself fully upright. It was the first time I had stood in days, and I nearly swooned, my head made light with laudanum and broth. It is a side effect of such a thing to reduce appetite, and it was another reason to miss my ayah, whose cures meant paratha fried in ghee, dahl stirred thick enough to stick in your throat and laced with garlic. Here, it was almost as if I were being punished, near-starved and drugged, with no company, no light. At least that I could remedy.

My legs felt swollen and stiff, and I walked as though I moved through the snow that brought on my labour, feeling my way forward in the murky dark like a blind man, until at last I felt the soft give of the curtains in my palms. I grasped them, bringing my body close to press against their length, panting slightly with the effort my short traversal had wrought.

Behind me, my daughter sighed and sucked in her sleep. I sighed in answer, the sharp lance of love piercing my chest as I heaved one heavy curtain aside, the iron ring grating slightly on the railing. An uncertain light broke through the gap, dim and unmistakably with the quality of early morning, and I sidled into the space between window and curtain so as not to let the light leak over my daughter's face.

Keeping my half-eyes closed to allow them time to adjust, I reached out and placed my palms on the glass. Immediately came the pull of cold from the thin panes, the fresh-painted frames no defence against an English winter.

I cracked my lids a little wider, and found grey fog pressing itself hard against the glass. The night lingered on the break of day, and I brought my forehead to the frigid surface so my breath made its own mist. In the mirror made of glass and fog, my own face looked back at me. I could see no further than the window, and tried to conjure the much-loved view: the river, the hills, the forest—

My face blurred. I brought my hand up to once again wipe the pane clear of my breath, but then the reflection came apart from itself, splitting. I placed my hand back on the window to steady myself, fearing I was about to swoon, but my body held steady, still and caught as though tied by the hands and forehead. Before me, my face drew back, back, but my forehead was still pressed close to the glass.

It was no longer my own.

My hair was loose and knotted, though I could feel the scrape of Mrs Noakes' braids holding strong. My eyes were wide and without whites. Beneath my hands, sudden through the thin pane, leeched a fierce warmth.

There was another hand, pressing the glass from the outside. Slowly, impossibly, it began to push. I could feel the glass creaking, and the loose-haired, black-eyed face that split from mine broke into a wide smile. Her teeth were white and even, and it was an expression of such malevolence my heart seemed to stop cold in my chest. She was here to hurt me, to hurt my child.

I pressed my palms back, and her smile split wider. She brought her forehead to match mine, and it was hot as fever. I smelt the animal smell of the forest, the metal and the mulch, and beneath my hands the glass began to crack, hairline fractures that splintered into spiderwebs spanning the pane.

She was going to get in. She was going to take my child.

I was weak from the birth and bedrest, and in the grip of a terror so entire I could barely breathe, but I pushed back, matching her for force. Her smile grew impossibly wide, as though she would swallow me whole, her eyes two deep pits, her stench smothering, and I pushed and pushed, yelling with the effort. I met her gaze, and heaved my whole weight behind my hands.

The window shattered, and she ricocheted backwards, vanishing into grey. The fog flooded in and I stumbled back, feet tangling in the curtains, the iron railing tearing down off the wall and cracking the wooden boards beside me. But I heeded none of it, intent only on reaching my daughter, now wailing in her crib.

I barely registered the door opening, Mrs Noakes' cry of alarm, barely felt the room fill with freezing cold, barely noticed my palms were sliced and speckled with glass. I brought my daughter to my chest, ripping aside my night-gown so I could feel her skin against mine, and it took Dr Harman and Richard both to prise her from my grip.

ও

THE SIXTH DAY

'It is impossible,' said Dr Harman, his voice rising in response to Richard's hiss. 'It is at best foolhardy, and at worst unsafe for baby and mother both.'

'I will not allow them to be separated,' said Richard, his tone matching the doctor's. 'Over what? An accident?'

'You believe it an accident, sir?'

'She says it is so, and I believe her.'

'You are experiencing this for the first time, sir. All of it. Marriage, children. Me, I have seen it a hundred times. It changes a woman. Their mental make up is altered irreparably. Your wife is exhibiting signs of serious disturbance.'

'And what is your answer for that?' said Richard, all but

shouting so I could prise my ear from the wall. 'More laudanum? More darkness?'

'It is backed by science,' said Dr Harman. 'As well as by
tradition. Your own mother—'

'And separating mother and baby, is that science?'

Dr Harman's voice dropped to an inaudible level once
more. I twisted to lie back on my pillows again. My hands
rested in my lap, bandaged beyond recognition, the iodine
Dr Harman treated them with staining the fabric yellow and
stinging worse than the cuts.

Guilt throttled me, to hear Richard defend me so. But
there was no question of telling him the truth. I knew how
it sounded, knew that they would take the baby from me
and fill me with laudanum and worse, perhaps even send me
away, like Mother.

But I also knew what I had seen, had felt, had smelt. And
the fact was, however improbable, the witch Bright had come
for my daughter, and I was all that had prevented her. I was
engaged in a struggle for my daughter's very soul. I looked at
her, lying milk-drunk in her crib, and promised her for the
hundredth time she was safe beside me. It was imperative
we should not be parted.

So I offered Richard an explanation that was as close to
sense as I could make it. That I had woken confused from the
laudanum, and tried to open the window, stumbling against
it with enough force to break the glass.

Mrs Noakes swept up the shards that had fallen to the
floor, the tinkling sound making my teeth ache, and Noakes

boarded the whole thing over with thick planks. There was talk of moving us from the carmine room, but it was agreed that would only inflame my distress further. And now dear Richard had argued for us staying together, and against any more laudanum. It was just as well. I could stand the pain if I must, and I needed all my wits collected close to me if the witch Bright came again to my window.

Dr Harman was sent in disgrace from the house, but Mrs Noakes and Richard himself agreed the confinement must remain in place. Richard allowed me another gas lamp, and agreed to bring me paper and pen when I claimed boredom, so I could record what was happening in the clearest possible terms.

The only change I did not request was that the door should be kept unlocked. In my terror, I did not think straight. I believed the lock was as good a protection as any against the witch Bright's advances. Now I know that this was my fatal error. There is no defence against evil but good. None that can withstand the Devil but God.

෴

THE SEVENTH DAY

To keep myself from sleeping, I placed myself on the edge of pain. Rediscovering the hairpin I had discarded in the sheets, I took to placing it at the small of my back, so if I began to sink back against the pillows, it would needle and so wake me. I kept the gas lamps turned high, and never pressed the bell button, preferring to cause myself discomfort when feeding my daughter or using the chamber pot rather than have Mrs Noakes open the door.

I do not know if you have ever gone a day and night without sleep, but it is as close to torture as I can imagine. My head soon took on a feverish aspect, and my piss continued to come out hot, stinging and bloody. I discovered some old, stale smelling salts in the dresser, and took to sniffing them to the point my nose bled, dappling my bandages so Mrs Noakes, bringing more broth, thought I had bled through and replaced them with fresh. I was learning a woman was a creature of blood, from the monthly curses to birth and on and on. My ayah had told me as much, but until now I'd had no cause to believe her.

But the encounter with the witch Bright had strengthened me in ways too. I had beaten her back. I was now into the seventh day of my confinement, and if I could only stay awake another two days, then my baby and myself both should be churched and saved and safe.

Of course, to only stay awake is not so simple. Especially when you are weak from loss of blood, from surviving on broth and in darkness – one is wont to wilt like a starved flower. Hence the hairpin, the smelling salts, the resolve and knowledge to record all that is happening, to remind myself it is not some fearful dream, but my own fearful reality.

❦

THE EIGHTH DAY

It was approaching six o'clock, and Richard had lately explained through the locked door that he and Mr Noakes were to attend church, having missed several Advent services. I asked, again, if I might join him, but he told me it was out of the question, and that Mrs Noakes was only in the kitchen if I needed her. I lent slightly against the hairpin, and said in my steadiest voice that I would be quite all right. Our daughter was watching the light of the gas lamp flicker across the ceiling, and I was watching her, the wet gleam of her eyes, the length of her lashes, when quite suddenly the lamps extinguished.

Between the late hour, the locked door and the boarded-up window, the darkness was absolute. My daughter whimpered and I grasped gently for her, finding with relief her soft cheek, the lavender scent of her swaddling. I lifted her onto the soft slump of my belly, rocking her gently in one arm as my other fumbled for the lamp.

I became aware of a hissing sound, and instantly my dread returned. A long exhale, unbroken and loud, pushed from clenched teeth.

I wheeled around blindly.

'Who's there?'

There was no answer. Only that awful, unnatural hiss.

I felt in the sheets for the hairpin, but could not find it. I opened my eyes as wide as I could, searching for a crumb of light, certain I would see the witch Bright's terrible face, her lank hair, her black eyes – and then a smell arrived. But it was not the forest smell, not my own sharp sweat nor my baby's fresh skin. It was bitter and familiar. Gas, released from the blown lamps.

I almost wept in relief, still holding my daughter tight to my chest, and inched my way around the bed to the bedside table where the lamps stood. I could feel their residual heat even through the bandages, the glass sending warmth through the air. It brought back her palms on mine through the window, and I withdrew my hand with a gasp, clutching my baby with both arms. The smell of gas was growing stronger by the moment, and I knew I must turn the lamps off to prevent it entering our lungs.

Still half-blind, I placed my daughter down onto the bed, and with my clumsy hands fumbled for the metal screws. I found one, and turned it with relief, the hissing diminishing. My head was starting to spin now, and I forced myself not to panic. Feeling for the other lamp, my exposed fingertips met hot glass. The skin sizzled but I felt my mind clouding, and searched on for the screw.

Finding it, I twisted sharply, and the hissing ceased.

'There,' I said, to quiet my racing heart. 'There.'

As I turned to lift the baby again, I heard another sound. Breath. It was issuing from the far corner of the room, beside the boarded window, but even as I froze, bent over my child, it came closer.

My teeth began to chatter. The smell of dirt forced aside the gas, and the breath advanced still closer. There were no footsteps, no sound except that breath, heavy and deliberate, unmistakable, dreadful.

Then I felt warmth across my neck, and my baby whimpered, and I recovered myself. I lifted my daughter and clasped her tight to me.

'Get away,' I shouted. 'Get away!'

With my other hand I hit the bell button, over and over, and as the sound of breath, the stench of things long buried filled my ears and mouth, I began to kick out, backing up to the door. I hammered on the locked door with my back, and my feet, yelling and crying, and the witch Bright was before me, invisible in the darkness, standing forehead to forehead against me, my baby crushed between us.

The door opened and I tumbled through. Mrs Noakes cried out and righted me, but I backed away from her.

'Ma'am?'

Mrs Noakes looked as terrified as I felt, eyes wide, mouth hanging open in shock. She reached out for the baby, but behind her, in the half-lit carmine room, the curtains stirred. The witch Bright was coming.

I shoved Mrs Noakes out of the way and slammed the door.

'Lock it!' I shouted over the sound of the baby's cries. 'Lock it!'

'Give me the child,' she said, her voice shaking.

I held her tighter. 'For God's sake lock the door!'

I lunged at the key at Mrs Noakes' waist, and she screamed and stumbled away from me, into the door. The hinge had caught, and the door rebounded off its frame, opening wide and dark as a mouth.

The witch Bright was out.

I ran.

My breasts were heavy and ached with milk. Between my legs stung and pulled. My feet were swollen, numb with disuse, but I ran with my baby in my arms because our lives depended on it, our souls, hers and mine both.

'Mrs Blake!'

Behind me, Mrs Noakes was clambering to her feet, but she was bent and bruised, and I was still young though I was weak. I was wild with my fear and my fury, and no one would hurt my child while I had breath in my lungs.

I plunged down the stairs, bare feet jarring on the wood, and tore through the house to the conservatory. I could see Noakes and Richard had come this way – their tracks were imprinted on the fresh fallen snow.

There was no time for a coat. Upstairs I heard footsteps, too deliberate and quick to be Mrs Noakes'. My mind wheeled. What if she had been possessed? What if at this moment she was in the grip of the witch Bright? There was only one place we would be safe from her.

I tumbled into the white cold night. My feet burned as though I walked through fire, and I pelted across the short stretch to the gate.

'Mrs Blake, stop!'

Mrs Noakes was silhouetted in the doorway. She seemed enormous, her hair hanging loose around her face, and with impossible swiftness she followed me out into the night. I threw myself through the gate. My husband's footsteps shone in the bright starlight, a path to salvation.

I stumbled on, no breath to hush my child, no way to make her understand that it was for her I ran through the freezing night, and so I had to withstand her cries, her mewls, each a wrench on my heart.

'Stop!'

The witch Bright did not even disguise her voice now. It was deep and awful, a bellow. But I would not obey, I would not stop, I would save my daughter's soul, even it meant wrecking my body. I chanced a look behind, and she was impossibly close. To my right, the forest rippled with malice, the shadows filled with buried souls, lost and wandering.

'You will not have her,' I cried. 'You will not take her!'

Ahead, the final approach to the church was lined with candles. A Christmas tree loaded with snow and topped with a silver star dwarfed the stone structure. But there it was: the cross. Safety. Sanctuary.

The service was over, and the doorway thrown open, leaking gold light onto the snow. Shadows lined the steps, and I forced them aside, sending them sprawling, and threw myself across the threshold.

Panting, I dropped to my knees before the altar. I saw the priest's face frozen in shock, heard Richard's voice say my name, felt strong, warm hands appallingly hot on my frigid skin, trying to take the child.

'Please,' I said, holding with what strength I had left. 'Bless her. Please.'

The priest knelt before me, his lined face kind. My whole body shook with relief and cold. He placed his hand on my baby's head, and murmured a blessing.

Her cries faded, and her screwed-up face relaxed. I brushed the tears from her soft cheeks, and kissed her nose.

'Safe now,' I whispered. 'Safe.'

Her perfect, pink eyelids opened. And in the hallowed light, my baby's eyes shone black.

This record is held in the archives of the Shropshire and Wenlock Borough Lunatic Asylum.

AUTHOR'S NOTE

Mrs Bright is based on the real case of Mrs Amelia Dyer, the Victorian baby murderess. Catherine Blake's audio-hallucinatory symptoms are influenced by my own experiences of psychotic depression, and by research into postpartum psychosis, a condition that is to this day much mistreated, misunderstood and maligned. For further reading on this illness please see *What Have I Done?* by Laura Lee Dockrill.

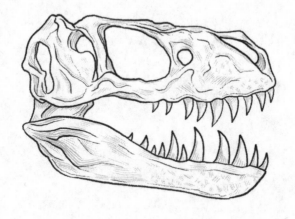

MONSTER

Elizabeth Macneal

Lyme Regis, September 1838

All of Britain, Victor thinks, is being exhumed. Back in London, his brother's fingernails are clagged with soil, his hothouses filled with tiny shoots that will form the arboretum of a new cemetery in Stoke Newington. Their father oversaw the digging of the new waterways – straight, surgical lines bisecting the city – making, as he so often said, *enough money to fill the whole of Regent's Canal with gold sovereigns*. And here is Victor, the once-brilliant son, in this wretched Dorset town, shivering in his oilskin coat, as a small red-headed boy leaps across the beach and tries to point out *serpent stones* and *devil's toenails*. Above them, the cliffs are as tall as mountains, ragged-edged.

'There's one,' the boy says, prodding at a pile of yellowed sand.

Victor peers closer. He can discern nothing but stones and an old screw. Perhaps this is women's work after all – their small, darting eyes can spy the fossils, while men like him can dig them out and categorise them.

The child repeats, 'There, *there*,' and a hot rage comes

over Victor, and he swings his cane and smashes it into the small nest.

'There's nothing *there*,' he bellows, and the boy scuttles back, frightened.

They hurry on, the rain almost horizontal, the clouds so low and black it might be dusk. He could be at the inn with his wife, tucking into a thick scone topped with cream, his socks steaming by the fire. He could be at home, in civilised London. He hates this infernal sore of a town, its houses hunched like a row of drunks, its hills steep enough to drive the breath from the lithest of men. The rain has driven down in thick sheets each day, leaving even his underclothes damp and humid.

Lyme Regis was his idea, a whispered promise in the early days of their courtship when Mabel said she longed to see the ocean. He remembered a paper he had recently come across in White's, about Gideon Mantell and his Iguanodon. There was a stretch of coast, he recalled, where all sorts of curious creatures had been unearthed. He straightened his cravat. 'Well, my dear, you shall have your wish. One day, I shall take you to this little village on the Dorset coast.' He added, with thespian affectation, 'And there, while you admire the sea, I will make my name, unearthing a peculiar beast. And I shall name it *Prodigium Mabelius*.'

Mabel smiled, coyly without showing her teeth, and it had

convinced him that she was the proper specimen of wom-
anhood, a person he might easily impress. Here, he realised,
was a girl who believed in him, and with that encourage-
ment – why, he might achieve anything!

And then she looked at him, her eyes so big and pale. 'I
read that your brother had recently discovered a new type
of orchid. This monster shall make you just as impressive.'

She had not meant to wound him, Victor told himself,
but he touched his forehead as though she had struck him.

As a child he had been brilliant. As a child, he was gilded,
puffed up with promise, excelling at anything he turned his
hand to. Cricket, Latin, mathematics – he was revered and
feared by teachers and pupils alike. Beside him, his brother
was as pale as a wilted shrub, and could think of nothing
but damned *flowers*. He pressed them, catalogued them, grew
them from tiny bulbs. Victor called him 'Daisy', and picked
his rare orchids for buttonholes. 'They're only *flowers*,' he
protested when his brother wept. But then the years ticked
past and Victor, the all-round marvel, the *dux* of the year,
had found his mind was a bird in a cage, never satisfied. It
flitted against the bars of finance, of politics, of trade, never
settling long enough to establish himself.

One day, he had looked up, and realised that his brother
had spent the decades chipping away at his one passion, and
had transformed himself into a renowned horticulturist.
Daisy was being consulted on planting plans everywhere
from Buckingham Palace to the new rash of cemeteries.
Daisy had a townhouse in Mayfair, and a country house in

Richmond with his own hothouse. *Daisy* was the talk of the town. A cold certainty had lodged in Victor's chest, that a grave mistake had been made, and the world was celebrating the wrong brother.

And then he and Mabel were married, and they set out for Lyme Regis in a storm of trunks and bonnet-boxes, Mabel clutching her collage book of spaniels, her sharp silver scissors. The rasp of Mabel's blades irritated him only a little, the lick of the paste-pot. He smiled at her and said nothing. It was a new beginning, he told himself, as they whisked past villages and turnpikes, the countryside already browning with early autumn. Five days of travelling, of nights in tumbledown inns. Four nights until he had summoned the courage to touch her at last, to subdue her body beneath his.

As the coach jolted forwards, he tried to read the books he had acquired on the topic of plesiosaurs and iguanodons. The words danced and rearranged themselves, but one phrase shone out, on page after page. *Royal Society*. A grand institution, gilding all that came into its orbit. Benjamin Franklin's kite experiment. James Cook's journey to Tahiti to track the transit of Venus. Isaac Newton's *Principia Mathematica*. All of these reports had been published within its walls, all of these illustrious men passing under its great stone arch. Soon, he thought, he'd be tripping over fossilised creatures, the beaches littered with ribs and spines and long, smooth skulls. He pictured the applause that might greet his own discovery, the realisation that at last he, Victor Crisp, was a man of science, of renown, of utter greatness—

He fell forwards as they took a steep hill, his book splayed on the floor.

'Quite all right,' he said, gathering himself, though Mabel had said nothing. He cursed, dusting his hands against his trousers. 'Quite all right,' he repeated.

Snip, snip, snip. A poodle with a pink bow was being slowly excised from a child's picture book.

He looked out the window. 'There's the sea, just as you wanted. We must be almost there.'

Mabel did not look up. There was a tremor in her wrists. He wondered, briefly, if she was afraid of him. The memory of the night before – her milk-white thighs, her body clammed shut and barely yielding beneath him, that surprising nest of dark hair (he had persevered regardless) – brought a small pang of remorse. He tried to smile. 'Ah, here we are,' he said.

Even then, the rains were beginning. Fat drops that landed on the pavement like grease-stains. Clouds as thick as wool. Gulls screamed. Victor stepped out of the coach and looked around him. The inn was a cheaper establishment than he'd been led to believe – a thin, crooked spine running up the middle of the building where it was slowly subsiding – and he checked Mabel's expression for any displeasure. 'Let's hope the ceiling doesn't fall in on us in the night,' he said, hoping at least to make her smile, but she kept her gaze on the pavement.

The innkeeper greeted them, two red-haired children playing at his feet. The boy rolled fossils across the threshold.

The girl clutched a beef shin wrapped up like a doll and shushed it. 'Don't cry,' she whispered.

'Welcome,' the man said, ushering them into the hotel. Tallow candles wept down the walls, the air dense with the reek of raw meat. Ornamental man-traps and scythes hung from the ceiling, their jaws rusted. He turned to Victor with a strange, narrowed look. 'I should warn you now before it's too late.'

'Oh?'

'They say the inn is haunted.'

Victor laughed, and Mabel said, 'Ooh.'

'Just like in those novels you read,' Victor said. 'I'm sure it's all the same here. Yawning graves, monks in chains, and all that nonsense.'

'No,' the man said, leading them through a narrow corridor to their chamber. Victor ducked beneath a low, blunt blade. 'Things have a habit of being different from how they appear. Transforming themselves. Scottish selkies, you know the story?'

Victor shook his head.

'Seals who turn into women. Women who turn into seals. We're often visited by the ghost of a seal who was netted off these shores and clubbed to death by a group of sailors. The next day, they found a battered woman's body where the sea creature had been laid to rest.'

The man brushed his fingers against Mabel's wrist. Victor noticed how close the innkeeper stood to her, his head bent to her neck. Mabel, he noted, did not move away. He chuckled; a haunted inn, a lascivious proprietor. What was next? A host of carolling urchins?

'The candles extinguish themselves at night,' the man continued. 'It's little seal breaths, blowing them out.'

Victor smirked again.

'There's often a pattering of footsteps after midnight,' the boy added, following them into their chamber.

The room was small, its floorboards at a slant, the window as small as a narrowed eye. Victor would have preferred to share a bed, but he saw that Mabel would have her own little chamber just off his own, entered through a communicating door.

'Listen out for the slap of flippers,' the boy continued. He made a high *ark, ark* sound, curiously close to a whine of female pleasure. 'Slime found on the sheets.'

'Groaning beds.'

Very good, Victor thought. Even Mabel knew what they were about, her cheeks pink.

In that moment, the bed seemed to grow monstrous, to fill the room. Glossy purple hangings like cuts of offal. A dimpling in the pillows, as though already dented by a stranger's skull. All the ghosts of those who had *fucked* here before them. Victor fiddled with his pipe, hoping the man and boy would leave.

'Here she is,' the man said, pointing to a small painting hanging above the dresser. 'Not as fair as you, of course,' he said, and Victor saw how he placed a hand on Mabel's shoulder. He coughed and pretended to inspect the picture.

The art was crude, little more than the work of a child.

But in truth, the image disturbed him. A seal's body with the passive face of a girl, skin peeling from her shoulders as neatly as a half-pared clementine. So much *flesh*. It reminded him of the woodcuts he kept pressed between the pages of his Bible – the women with tight breasts, their pudenda as smooth and featureless as marble.

'Heavens,' Mabel said. 'She's quite frightening.'

'It's all nonsense, dear,' Victor said, leading her away.

But Mabel did not follow him. She bent to the child's height. 'Are those fossils?' she asked him. 'My husband's going to find a fantastical creature and make us both rich. He's going to name it *Prodigium Mabelius*.'

The innkeeper exhaled with what sounded suspiciously like laughter. Mortification drew Victor's eyes to the floor. If anybody but Mabel had said it, he would have thought they were mocking him. But from his wife – he wished only that she knew what to keep quiet and what to share.

'My nephew can take you out on the Black Ven cliffs,' the man said, gesturing at the red-headed child. 'He has a nose for it, like a pig for cherries. Not that there've been any spectacular finds for years.'

'When the rain stops, I'd be delighted,' Victor said.

'It's easier to see the fossils when it's wet. They shine black from the mud,' the boy lisped. He was missing his two front teeth, and he wobbled his bottom incisor with his tongue.

Mabel tilted her head at Victor. 'You aren't afraid of a little rain, dear?' she said. 'I'm certain you'll find me a marvellous beast if you venture out each day.'

'But—'

'I think,' she said, twirling her little silver scissors in her hand, 'of all your qualities, I most admire your dedication. I *know* you can do it.'

She smiled at him, and added that she couldn't possibly join him, not when her lungs were so weak after a bout of influenza three years before.

ॐ

Gone are his dreams of glory, of unearthing a mythical creature. Gone are his dreams of anything at all except a dinner of cold mackerel, washed down with hock, and even then he dreads Mabel's disappointment when he tells her – yet again – that he has found nothing. Eight days, and nothing but rain! Too exhausted even to attend the dances at the assembly rooms. A droplet of water snakes down his back. His teeth are beginning to chatter, his trousers are soaked to the knee. The boy is so far ahead that Victor can barely see him in the mists. Victor pauses to see what three gulls are fighting over, their sharp beaks pecking at the meat of something soft. A beached jellyfish, bleeding into the sand.

And then he hears it. The sound of a cleared throat, and then the long, low rupturing of something fundamental splitting in two. He sees it dimly, as though through a fogged window; the cliffs giving way, tonnes of black earth crashing down.

'Please,' he cries, as if he is trying to reckon with

someone – with what? The rocks themselves, with God? He could not have known how liquid his legs could feel, how shapeless his vision. He is aware of little except a pain in his chest, the sharp taste of pennies. He tries to run but he slips, falls back into something soft and wet. It is the jelly-fish, he realises, its slime coating his hands, soft and cold. He is paralysed, gummed to the ground, his legs as heavy as girders, waiting for the earth to eat him up. It is strange, he thinks, how he does not think of anything particularly important – just Mabel, last night, sitting opposite him at dinner. The comfort of it. She was dissecting a sardine with a silver knife, pulling loose the hair-thin ribs. *She is mine*, he'd thought. *We are each other's.*

What will she say when she hears the news? He imagines the gentle fall of tears, then years of steady devotion to his grave. But who else will mourn him? His funeral can only be quiet, modest, not the great procession he once imagined it to be. Thirty years on this earth and he has nothing to show for it. None of the wealth and fame that his masters tipped him for. It has been years since anybody said, 'If anyone can do it, Victor can!' His name, once a source of pride, has begun to feel like a taunt.

The stench of the lime kilns above the town, of cordite, of newly turned earth. He is vaguely aware that somebody is shouting, though he cannot discern the words. Just a long, low keening, the sound a hinge might make when it needs oiling. And then, the sound begins to subside. He taps his legs, his side, his arms. No pain, nothing. He stands, shakily, dusting the sand from his coat, wiping his hands on his trousers. He feels absurd, foolish. The landslide has stopped. A thick slug of earth inches into the sea. The cliffs are crumpled. He should leave, run. More might fall. The whole coast might be turned to nothing but rubble. But he finds himself walking towards it. The sky is as silvery as the inside of a shell, the rain a faint spritz. It feels as if it is only him in the world—

The boy, he thinks. The boy with the two missing teeth whose name he cannot remember. He was ahead, his red hair disappearing into the fog, just when the landslide came down.

'Child,' he calls, but he knows there is little point. The boy is certainly dead.

And then he sees it, black and glossy. Shining in the grey afternoon light, high up on the mound of soil. A shape almost skull-like. Victor blinks, takes a step forward, and another. He is running towards it, the pain in his ankle almost gone. Elation sings within him. He observes this moment as if already preparing it for anecdote, for history. The moment of discovery, the shock of epiphany. A tall, drenched man, clambering over the landslide, hurtling towards scientific advancement. The mud, so viscous! It clings to his thighs, squelches under each footfall.

I knew the second I saw it. That is what he will say when addressing a large audience at the Royal Society. *An instinct for discovery, I'd call it.*

His fingers claw the rock. How triumphant he must look!

His hands aching with cold, earth-blackened to the elbow. Thunder rumbles like applause. A fork of lightning brightens the afternoon. A ribcage. A fin. A pristine monster. For thousands of years it has been asleep, just waiting for him to discover it.

Everyone is digging, he thinks again, his joy coming in short, delighted yelps. His father with his canals. His brother with his plants and cemeteries. And he, Victor, for a magnificent creature which is sure to make his name.

৯

It is almost dark when the carthorses arrive. He smells them almost before he hears them, the rotten-fish reek of whale oil lamps. He gestures wildly. There is the innkeeper and the little girl with her bone doll, racing along the beach. The tide is creeping in, gasping as it rolls itself over the stones.

'Here!' he calls, from his place on the mound. 'Here! I need ropes. Shovels. Hammers. We need to work fast to save it.'

'Thank heavens,' the innkeeper shouts, and they clamber over the earth towards him. The man looks about him, squinting in the gloom. 'But where is he?'

'There,' Victor says. 'Look at it!' The long-snouted skull. The black paddles. He waits for their wonder, their envy.

The man looks about him wildly. 'But Wilbur. Where's Wilbur?'

Victor bites his lip. He had forgotten all about the boy; forgotten that somewhere beneath this stinking mass of earth lay the body of a small child. 'I'm sorry—' Victor stammers. 'He didn't have a chance – you should have seen it! It came down so fast—'

The innkeeper takes a step forward. For a second, Victor thinks that the man is about to hit him. But his hands are limp at his sides, his jaw slack, and there is pain written on his face. Victor steps to the side and watches them, the man and the girl, as they crawl over the earth, calling the child's name, nudging the soil, pawing at it, driving in sticks. He wants to tell them it's useless, that the boy is certainly dead. He looks about him, watching the creep of the tide. How long does he have? If nobody helps him, his discovery will be plucked away by the sea, lost forever. A small cry breaks from his throat. His one chance at fame and glory is already dimming.

He scrabbles in his pocket for pen and a paper, waves the promise of ten, twenty pounds before two thick-armed men. They shift from foot-to-foot, but they nod at last, and follow where he leads them. Hammers chip at stone, ropes creak and pull. As the rain washes away the dirt, Victor sees that the creature is perfect, more pristine than he ever could have imagined: ribs, spine, paddles. They dig in stakes, attach more ropes, though Victor flits about, fretting they will split it in two. The horses kick fat clods of clay, veins straining, heads hideously shadowed in the lamplight. A moaning, whether human or animal, he could not say. Waves thundering, beating.

'We have to turn in. The tides,' the men shout, and

already the waters swill around their ankles. The inn-keeper and his daughter turn back to the town, their hands empty, their heads bowed. He watches their lamps recede to pinpricks.

But Victor will not leave, and he collars one of the men when he tries to yoke the horses. He takes out his pocket-book once more, scrawls hideous sums, and the men drive their whips against the drays, until at last – at last, with a ferocious crack, the creature loosens. Victor dances from foot-to-foot as they strap it to the cart, wood heaving under the weight. 'Hurry,' he whispers. Then louder, 'Hurry!' The tides reach Victor's thighs, current almost tugging him sideways. Spume thunders against his waist.

'I'll tie it down,' he tells the men, and it is only now that he sees how frightened they are, how the horses are restless, the whites of their eyes gleaming.

They plough through crashing waves, and Victor sits on the cart, the water bubbling up against the boards. The night is so black and cold. He is shaking, his whole body convulsed with the sea's chill. There is mud in his hair, in his ears. He bows his head and cradles his creature like a mother might clasp a child.

୭

Cutlery grinds on porcelain. The fish pie is lukewarm, spiked with bones. Victor picks a tiny translucent spear from his gums and lays it on the side of his plate. Mabel does not look at him, does not speak. She has barely spoken since he came in, drenched to the bone, dripping mud. He hoped she would join him to watch the beast being unloaded at a shopkeeper's house just off the parade, but she drew herself away from him, shook her head. It was he who stood in the wet streets, who bartered with the owner, who instructed ten men to carry it down the mouldy steps to the cellar. If he could have, he'd have had it ferried to his chamber, or slept in the vault beside it.

His knee hops up and down. 'Can you believe it?' he whispers. 'My monster! Wait until you see it. It's magnificent. It might be the greatest find since William Conybeare's *Plesiosaurus*.'

'Mary Anning's,' she says.

'Pardon?'

'Mary Anning found that *Plesiosaurus*.'

'A quibble,' he says. 'Conybeare catalogued it, didn't he?' He clasps her hand. 'In a few days, perhaps tomorrow, the press will be here. The men of science! The palaeontologists.' He breathes deeply. 'The Royal Society! Oh, when they hear!'

'Cabbage?' the innkeeper asks, clasping a tureen of limp yellow vegetables.

Victor strikes his forehead. 'What if it isn't safe in that cellar? What if they sell it?'

'Cabbage?' the innkeeper repeats. His eyes are red, a gauntness to his cheeks.

'Thank you, James,' Mabel says, and she looks at the man with an expression close to affection. When he moves to place the cabbage on her plate, his fingers brush hers. He is surprisingly handsome, Victor notes with some surprise.

'I couldn't possibly, *James*,' Victor says, patting his belly. 'That'll be all.'

With a bow, the man turns and is gone. Victor notes how Mabel's eyes track his movement across the room. She is a soft-hearted creature, he tells himself; she merely pities him for the death of his nephew.

'I believe it is a new species in the *Plesiosaurus* family. If I'm correct, I've decided to name it *Plesiosaurus V. Crispus*.'

Victor waits. His wife continues to saw her food. Nothing, not even a flinch.

'I know I promised that I'd name it—'

'Why do men always have to dig?' she interrupts.

He has never heard this tone from her before.

'Sorry, dearest?'

'Why can't men just leave things where they are? Why do they always have to be picking things up and—'

He dabs at his lip. 'This is about the boy, isn't it?'

She slams down her cutlery. He is surprised to see tears in the corners of her eyes.

'It's an unpleasant business, I grant you that. I've decided to pay for a magnificent funeral, fit for a gentleman. Mutes, a black carriage—'

'And that will bring him back?'

He pulls at his cravat. 'The landslide was hardly my fault. You're looking at me like I'm some kind of *murderer*.' He shudders. 'It was unfortunate that the boy had to be tangled up in it. But when you've spent a little time in the world, you'll realise that human beings are often the collateral of progress. Men die when constructing great bridges, when colonising new lands. It happens.'

Her mouth is tight, blood gathering at the corner of her lips.

A thought strikes him, and he suppresses a sudden urge to laugh. 'Isn't it fitting,' he says, disguising his amusement as a cough, 'that the fossil-hunter has become a fossil? There he is, buried under all that earth.' The world swims, that bizarre ceiling of scythes and pint pots and traps, and he feels apart from it, overcome by the guffaws that break from him. 'The boy has,' he gasps, flapping for a glass of water, 'he has – fossilised – himself! – Will – they – dig – him – up – and—'

Cold water explodes across him. 'What on earth—' he begins, and then he sees the empty glass in Mabel's hand. Her eyes are so narrowed and cold that it frightens him.

కా

Victor attends the assembly rooms alone that evening. Mabel says she has a headache, and he leaves her at her scrapbook, her scissors cutting in sharp, fast snips.

By the time he has walked up the hill, he finds himself out of breath, his vision misting, a sharp pain in his side. The streets are unlit and he stumbles on debris – an old net, an oyster shell – wishing he had brought a lantern. It is still clouded, moonless, an owl floating low over the town.

Hurrying, quicker, the sound of violins drifting through the streets.

There, ahead of him, the hall blazes. Civilisation, he thinks, almost running, wondering why he hasn't attended before. The room will be filled with holiday-makers, people of fashion and taste. There, in the light of a thousand candles, tortoiseshells will gleam as hairpieces. Whalebones will tighten waists. Ammonites will glint on ears and throats, bearing no trace of the black, acrid soil they were once plucked from.

At first, nobody notices him enter. And then, a man takes his hand and clasps it. A nudging begins, murmurs passing in the break between dances.

'It was you, wasn't it?' a gentleman asks him. 'Victor Crisp, isn't it? The man who discovered that magnificent creature.'

He bows his head, nods. Several glasses are raised towards him. A man hands him a brimming glass of punch. He accepts it, takes a sip.

'The Royal Society will be delighted to hear of this,' a gentleman says. 'The greatest find in years, I'd wager.'

Victor nods. 'The Royal Society,' he echoes, but his voice sounds curiously detached. He is cold, he realises, but hot too; so hot he dabs sweat from his forehead. 'The Royal Society,' he repeats, louder, with more emphasis.

The man stares at him.

Victor rocks forwards on his toes, trying to suppress the shivering that seizes him. Someone pats his back. He should smile, accept their thanks, perhaps even make a speech.

And yet, why does he feel so – so empty, so alone? His guts swirl as if he needs to empty his bowels. Outside, the wind keens, rattling the windows. He taps his ear. The howling grows louder, just like the sound he heard on the beach as the earth tipped down – the creature, he wonders, could it be the creature screaming, or worse – the boy?

But nobody else is looking around them. No one, in this refined ballroom, expresses any alarm. The sound, it seems, thunders only in Victor's ears. He tries to steady the tremble in his hands, nodding his appreciation to the room. A hundred teeth grin back at him. A low cheer, and the glass slips from Victor's hand and falls to the floor.

Through the parlour with its hanging scythes, up the stairs. Nobody has left a candle for him. His hand fumbles for the banister, his legs woolly and tripping on the wood. Up in his room he slams the door shut, breathing hard. The painting regards him, the half-seal girl, shucking her skin. Her eyes so round and blue. A foolish tale he thinks; one creature cannot transform itself into another. He seizes it and places it on the floor, facing the wall. He forces open the door of her little bedroom.

'My kitten,' he whispers, 'my darling.'

He coaxes at first, wheedles, begs, and yet he is pleased when she draws back, shame flushing her cheeks, her knees pulled in tight around her. He used to visit a girl on Jermyn

Street, often found himself wound into her seedy little nest by the force of his lust – how she excited him, horrified him! Babette; that was her name. A Parisian girl, from the Marais. He would bound into her chamber, find her legs spread in wanton pleasure, fingers stroking that small, hot *thing*, hips thrusting to meet his. How she braced herself for the weight of his pleasure – his need, giving way to hatred, until he began to imagine her in a pit, naked and writhing, her plaque-furred tongue begging to lick and suck and swallow.

What a relief, then, to discover that his wife might be a different species entirely. But how dry and tight she is, how he has to force his way in! He cannot look at her, convinced, against all logic, that he has wronged her. He has a sudden urge to stop, to tell her that he has never loved anybody as much as he loves her; to say, *let us start again*. But then he remembers his father, shaking him when he wept over a cut knee. *Once a man loses respect, he loses it forever.*

All night, his dreams are fitful and unsettled. Monsters turn to boys, boys to monsters. His bedclothes stick to him. The light from beneath his wife's door disturbs him, the snicker of her scissors, the slide of the glue against paper. Before dawn rises, he hears lanterns clanking, the townsfolk hurrying to the landslide now the tides are out.

When he can bear it no longer, he sits at his desk. He begins the letter he has already composed a hundred times in his head, trying to still the tremble in his fingers. He writes the address first, glorying over the looping *R*, the way he curls the *S* of *Society* over two lines.

Dear Sirs, I write with news of a magnificent discovery, of which I am certain your society will be most interested—

The letter written and sealed, he turns to the single piece of correspondence he has received in the last week. As ever, it is full of his brother's plantish nonsense – all talk of saplings and cuttings, and the arboretum in Abney Cemetery that will be planted in alphabetical order. *Daisy* has even listed all the trees as if Victor could possibly give two figs – *Zanthoxylum will be the final addition. Did you know its common name is American toothache tree?*

He takes a fresh sheet and longs to write the simple, gloating words, *I am now a great man, Daisy! The Royal Society will send a man to verify my discovery, and then it shall be written into all the history books. I shall be the Crisp brother whose name echoes through the centuries!* But he knows that his brother would not care; competition and resentment have only ever run in one direction. The only thing that matters to *Daisy* is his hothouse, his nursery of carefully-labelled saplings.

There is a knock at the door. Victor opens it, expecting, for a moment, the red-headed child. And then, as a black-haired girl scowls back at him, Victor remembers that the boy is dead. He blinks, steadies himself on the doorframe. His head feels clouded, as if there is a thin membrane separating him from the rest of the world.

'Ah, kippers again,' Victor says with false joviality, eyeing the chipped silver tray. The bodies are limp and the shade of gangrene, three milky eyes staring at him. He gestures at the desk. 'Place it there, please.'

The child is about to scuttle away when Victor holds out a hand. 'Wait,' he says, reaching for his pocketbook. He holds out a thick wedge. 'The boy who died—'

'Wilbur. My cousin. They found him this morning.' She bows her head.

'Marvellous!' He wonders where they have lain him. In that early morning light, they will have brought him in on the same cart, scraped the mud from his nose and ears.

Her eyes, already small and tight from weeping, seem to narrow even further.

'It can be a mercy,' he says, quickly, 'to have a body to bury.' He clears his throat, pressing the notes into her hand. 'I'd like to contribute to the costs. To have no expense spared. Hire mutes to stand at his door. A great funeral. Give him a farewell fit for a duke!'

The child is staring at him, shielding the money as she would a small and precious creature. She tightens her fingers into a fist, takes a step back. Victor hears her footsteps retreating steadily at first, and then quickening, hammering through the small inn.

৯

Victor dresses quickly and hurries down the street to visit his creature. It is a bright day, gulls tossed about like scraps of lace. There is a reek of decaying shellfish, seaweed raked into rotting, fly-buzzed piles. Girls rattle baskets of devil's fingers and verteberries. 'A penny a piece,' they cry, but

Victor pushes past them, scoffing at their mere trifles. He could not have imagined the monster he would unearth, the fame that would be his. *Plesiosaurus V. Crispus*. He lifts the doorknocker, raps three times. Silence. He has a sudden panic that somebody has stolen his beast – that they will sell it and pass it off as their own. He knocks harder, fist to the wood. A shuffling.

'Patience, my friend,' the man says. Then the man looks at him. 'Are you quite well, sir?'

Victor nods, almost running to the cellar. He cannot wait to be beside it, to touch its cool flank, to lay his head against its dark ribcage. In the gloom, he can make out little – the windows are shuttered, only a single candle burning from the corner. He stumbles down the stairs, his hands brushing against white crystals. Water plinks from the ceiling.

'There she is,' he breathes. The shopkeeper follows with a candle.

The man agreed to store the creature in his cellar until – until what? If this were high season, there'd be a host of scientific gentlemen who would tell Victor what to do, who could even verify his creature is genuine. But Victor does not know the steps he must follow – he can wait, only, for an answer from the Royal Society, for the gentleman they will inevitably send. And then, he is sure, they will arrange its transport to London where the real work can begin.

Victor calls for a bucket and a brush and, sitting in that chilled and airless cellar, he begins to clean his creature. To prise ancient silt from between its teeth, to wash grime from the broken edge of its skull. He takes a hammer to its spine, chips away useless pieces of stone. The scent of cordite fills the room, its skeleton exposed for the first time in thousands of years. The bones look dark and polished, but still he dips a cloth in oil and rubs them in slow, circular movements. He has never touched anybody so tenderly, so gently. He remembers how he lay beside Mabel on that first night, her sleeping breaths as steady as a ticking clock. He could not believe she was his, that they were forever yoked together. He hovered his hand over her shoulder, longing to pull her close to him, to breathe her in and embrace her. But brute lust was the only way he knew. In the morning, he had his way again, his body slamming into hers with the force of a piston. When he was finished, he sank back against the mattress and tried to still the shame that thrummed within him.

Throughout the day, gentlemen visit him in his cellar. Amateur men of science and a boy from the local broadsheet, and another from a society periodical. They bring callipers and rulers, measuring teeth and ribs and fins. One man agrees it is a type of plesiosaur, but a species never seen before. It is, they all agree, remarkably complete. 'Almost,' one says, 'as if it died just a year ago. As if it is newly skeletised.'

Victor nods. For the first time in his life, he finds himself at a loss for words.

'Heavens, are you cold?' the man asks. 'You're shaking.'

'She's warm enough,' Victor says, sweat dripping from the end of his nose.

A laugh. 'How droll.' Then, 'Sir? Mr Crisp? Your teeth. They're chattering.'

He jumps. He had not been jesting; he had thought the man was addressing his creature. It is only then that he realises that the clicking sound is his own teeth, that his throat is aching. He has an irresistible urge to crawl on to the table and curl up beside his beast.

'Sir?'

The voices fog. He stares again at it. At his *Plesiosaurus V. Crispus*. The name feels too cold. It needs something more personable, a pet name. *Wilbur* bursts on to his tongue, but he cannot remember where he heard the name before. And then Victor rears back, his hand over his mouth. How hadn't he noticed it before? The skull is small like a human child's, iron filaments scattered about it like reddened hair – it has hands, a boy's tiny fingers! Skin, pale pink and—

'Whatever's the matter?' The man touches his sleeve. 'Mr Crisp—'

'It has a skull,' he whispers, 'just like a child's . . .'

He sees the man edge away from him, smoothing his suit. He picks up his callipers and addresses Victor carefully. 'The skull,' he says, with surprising evenness in his voice, 'is shaped like a crocodile's. The anterior is bluntly triangular. The temporal fenestrae are narrower on this specimen than others we have discovered, and the palatal bones are thick. There is little about it—' he clears his throat – 'you might say, nothing, that bears any resemblance to the cranium of a juvenile *homo sapiens*.'

Victor nods. His breath catches in his lungs, and he tries to stop himself from toppling forwards. 'Yes, I see that now,' he gasps. 'I was mistaken.' He feels like a chastened schoolboy. He runs his finger over the scooped shape, trying to imagine away the two missing incisors, the adult teeth poised above, waiting to descend.

༈

'Will they be here soon?' Victor murmurs.

'Who?'

He does not recognise the voice.

'Royal – Society.' He is arrested by a coughing fit, shallow gasps dredged up from deep within him. He is trapped inside, weighed down by heavy covers and curtains the colour of meat. Vaguely, he remembers men carrying him back from the shop, arms sharp in his armpits. He feels as if he is trapped underwater, his limbs as leaden as those of a drowned sailor. Each lungful is an effort. His arms are as heavy as paddles.

'Rest.' The voice again. He opens his eyes. The black-haired girl stands and leaves.

'Wait—' he stammers, but it is too late.

He thinks of Mabel's voice over dinner, her eyes that could not meet his.

Why can't men just leave things where they are? Why do they always have to be picking things up—

This should be the moment he steps into the sunshine,

Mabel's arm in his. This should be the moment he is invited to grand houses, to dinners and luncheons and picnics along the coast. His eyes blur, and tears pool in his ears. 'Mabel,' he murmurs, but no warm hand finds his, no sponge dampens his forehead. Where is she? Why isn't she by his side? The door to her chamber is open. He longs even for the snipping of her scissors.

When the sun is bright and sharp, a great wailing wakes him, and he tries to pull himself upright. He cannot bear to be on life's periphery; he needs to see what is happening. The world rings. Instead, he concentrates on a metal jug glinting on the bedside table. It is smooth and cool to touch, a dead fly bobbing in the water. He grimaces, takes a long sip, then begins coughing again. Someone has placed the selkie painting back on the wall.

He thinks, at first, that he will faint when he stands, but he manages to stumble to his desk by the window. Below, a great carriage rolls through the town. Ostrich feathers bob on the heads of black horses. The coach is festooned with curling black crepe and ribbons. Peasants trail it. Fishwives with glittering scaled hands. Cooks, pink-cheeked and in their soup-stained pinnies. Butlers and footmen in their tatty livery. The whole town has turned up to mourn the child.

The mutes are there, just as he ordered, their mouths pulled into expressions of sombre sympathy, their clothes dark and neatly buttoned. Each holds a wand. They are an incongruous sight; at a grand house in Mayfair they would not look out of place. But here, in this crooked street – they do not fit at all.

How much time has passed, he wonders, since the boy was found? A day, two, three? He imagines a gentleman from the Royal Society rolling into town and glimpsing this procession. What would he think then? This spectacle – this *circus* – can only draw attention from his creature. Suspicion settles into cold certainty. They mean to entwine the boy with the monster, he thinks, until nobody can think of his great discovery without the discomforting reminder of a child's death, with the raw grief of a town in mourning. As he stands there, his angry snorts steaming the glass, he forgets that this funeral was his idea; he thinks only of his plesiosaur, sleeping in that damp cellar, finding itself slowly eclipsed.

❧

After that, Victor knows he and his creature must leave this town. He can wait no longer for a letter from the Royal Society and a gentleman who may or may not arrive. He will bring the monster to them; he will make arrangements for it to be transported on *The Unity* this very afternoon, wadded in the belly of the ship, held down by ropes. And if they try to stop him – if they want the creature buffed, polished, cast in clay before it is moved – well, it is *his* to do as he pleases.

In the street, sweat purls down his back, his cheeks. The world rolls like seasickness. Around him, he hears whisperings. A woman draws herself into a doorway. The girl selling fossils scampers away from him. He coughs thick spit into his handkerchief.

Nobody will look at him, their eyes averted, as if *he* is a murderer, a monster – as if he wanted the child dead! As he stumbles on a loose cobblestone and steadies himself, he thinks he sees a whisper of red hair behind him. He swivels. The girl with the beef-shin doll stares back at him with dark, empty eyes.

Tomorrow, he tells himself, hurrying a little, he will be gone. Tomorrow, he and Mabel will be sitting in the coach, reins clinking, horses whickering, distance opening up between him and this godforsaken town. While waiting for the shopkeeper to answer the door, he turns and watches the sea, the waves dancing with tiny pinpricks of light. Bathing machines are pulled in and out of the water. He notices the innkeeper, sculling in the shallows, coaxing a woman down the steps. He splashes her and she trips into the water and laughs. He pulls her towards him and kisses her, soft tender marks left on her shoulder. Victor smiles. For a moment, he was struck by the girl's similarity to his wife – that glossy brown hair, her easy way of moving.

'Yes?' the shopkeeper asks.

Victor turns. 'I need you to make urgent preparations. The creature will leave on today's *Unity*.'

'Today?'

'I'll pay you well,' he says.

In the cellar, he barks orders with an assurance he does

not feel. Other labourers are fetched, brute men who can lift and ferry. They shake their heads, trade glances, but they obey him. He watches it all, too exhausted to help, cursing them when they handle his creature roughly. He imagines bruises blooming where their fingers grasp and tighten, the monster's breath catching where its ribs fracture. Its shroud is new linen, its coffin a wooden crate. The boy will be buried in the churchyard by now.

In London, he will allow nobody to open it before he arrives. He will prise loose each nail, lever away the wooden boards. He will roll away the soft fabric. The room in which he works will be ornate and vaulted, gentlemen at his side. A chandelier will blaze overhead. They will be so far from this damp cellar; so far from this crooked little town, from the boy's death which nestles in every nook of the place. His monster will be unwilded. It will be catalogued, named, controlled. Everything will be tamed once more, like a wild bull sawn into pink cutlets.

ဪ

They say he is too weak to leave, that his fever is still too high. That it would be madness to set out on a long journey when he is still so sick. They say he needs a week of bedrest, perhaps more, that he sinks often into delirium, even if he is unaware of it in his lucid moments. He dismisses the physicians with a wave of his hand. All night, coughs rattle him. He curls up on the damp sheets like a prawn, like a child in prayer. Sleep is stealthy, creeping up on him, snatching itself away. When the village clock strikes two, he is certain he hears footsteps close by – bare feet slapping wooden floors. He puts it from his mind and tries to sleep. In the morning, he tells himself, he and Mabel will be in the carriage. They will be gone. London will be their new beginning.

A sudden smacking. Fast breathing. Creaking.

Victor sits up. Shivers rattle his teeth. He remembers the red-headed boy on the day they arrived, his face sombre as he talked about the hauntings.

Little seal breaths. The slap of flippers.

And there it is, the *ark ark* sound he was warned about. When Victor stares at the painting of the selkie, he is certain he can see her eyes flickering, the skin beginning to peel from her throat.

He hauls himself to his feet. The sound, it seems, is coming from the adjoining door. His nightgown whispers against his legs. The fire is still glowing, and he seizes the poker, edges towards Mabel's room. The hinges are oiled and the door does not creak.

In the narrow crack, he does not understand at first. A candle flickers. His wife's mouth is open, glistening, her eyes pinched shut. A small moan escapes her. And then he sees it – a creature moving at her waist. Her legs pulled apart. A mouth feasting on her, her fingers gripping its dark fur. It is the innkeeper, he realises, his head pressed to her *thing*, lapping at her. The devilish women cavorting on the woodcuts – writhing Babette with her silken body—

He remembers the first time he reached for Mabel's hand – so small and pale and childlike! – and she had let out a small gasp, as though shocked at such intimacy.

This cannot be his wife, he tells himself, but he knows that dimple in her chin, that soft puckered mouth. He knows what he is seeing, and he knows, too, what he saw earlier – his wife, in the sea, laughing with this – this *creature*. Another man would force his way into that chamber, would wrench the innkeeper by the throat, would hurl his wife into the street. But Victor feels only flattened, bereft. His throat is choked with the sudden urge to cry. His arms hang limp at his sides. He stumbles back, half-tripping. On his desk, he spies her scrapbook. How proudly she once showed it to him! Those little lapdogs and spaniels she liked to cut out! He sent her dozens of cards of terriers and wolfhounds, knowing how she would treasure them.

He lights a candle, turns its thick pages. Towards the back of the book, he sees hybrid creatures, animals snipped about. *Monsters*. He blinks, certain his eyes are deceiving him. A leg of a kitten, the beak of a chicken, a dog's tail, a duck's paddles. All collaged together. He slams it shut, breathing hard. How is it possible that she can be so different from what he believed her to be, so disturbed? Is it this damp and wretched town, working its way under her skin, sickening her?

The sounds grow louder, the unmistakable pounding of two bodies slammed together. Fucking, and not caring who hears! Her *ark ark* grows louder – a noise he never thought would fall from that slim throat. Victor takes the painting and throws it across the room, watching as the glass pane cracks, his foot bleeding where it strikes him. He falls back, starts to run. Out, down the stairs, through the scullery with its hanging scythes. His bare feet beat the pavement. For once, he is cool. His nightgown whisks against him. Nobody is on these streets. Above him, the moon sharpens itself. *Half-mad*, he thinks; and yet, this seems like the right thing, the *only* thing for him to do.

The church is small, the cemetery little bigger than a garden. He thinks of the great Valhallas that his brother will plant, Highgate and Abney Park and Brompton – their Egyptian Avenues, their vaults, their tombs hewn into the hillsides, their wide paths with carriage turning circles.

The soil, he sees, is fresh, heaped in a great pile. There is not yet a gravestone. He kneels like a dog, dirt flying out behind him, digging, digging, digging. Instinct drives him, a certainty that he needs to do this, that this is *right*. His hands are cut and sore, one nail half-torn. The minutes turn, the headstones around him like rows of rotten teeth. Just the sound of earth sifting.

And then his hands scrabble against it. No crate. A grimed linen covering. When he touches the boy's soft feet, he feels only a hard fin. In his wound state, the child's collarbone is a smooth clavicle. Victor starts to moan, to unwind and grapple. In the hull of the ship, as it carves around the foot of the country, he is sure there will be a boy's body. It will arrive in London with great pomp and fanfare; his crate will be opened and they will find a red-headed child inside. All of London will laugh at him. The Royal Society will ridicule him. He will be lampooned in *Punch*, his life turned into a joke—

The world blurs through his tears. His wife, turned into a devil. His great discovery, ruined. The only thing which has not been transformed is his pitiful, disappointing life. He gathers up his creature, clasps it in his hands. He kisses the boy's head (its long skull, he thinks), his fingers (its little paddles). It is so small in his arms, so damp and earth-covered; he cannot understand how stone could be so soft, how it could weigh so little. No other possibilities enter his mind. He staggers towards the cliffs, to the sound of slapping waves. His feet split open on brambles. Nettles score his legs. He limps forwards, knows only that he needs to return it to the sea, that only then will the last few days be undone.

Why can't men just leave things where they are?

Seals who turn into women. Women who turned into seals.

He has loved nobody like he loved Mabel. All his life, any affection has been cut off as soon as it has sprouted. His father, slapping him when he tried to embrace him at the age of four. His mother, turning from him with a tight, pursed mouth. Taunts and scoffing the only way he knew how to interact with his brother. Dear, flower-addled *Daisy*.

On the top of the cliffs, the wind is ferocious, biting at the skin of his cheeks, at his bare legs. Below him, the mouth of the ocean waits, its tongue clicking back and forth over the stones. Victor hurtles forward, slipping and sliding on the wet earth, his fingers gripping the creature's soft red hair, its cold blue lips. A stone tumbles from underneath him, and he is flying forwards, arms outspread. Legs pedalling air. In the moments before he hits the pebbled beach, he and the dead boy are flying, and Victor feels only exhilaration, a sense that this is how it was always supposed to end.

ABOUT THE AUTHORS

Bridget Collins is the award-winning author of numerous novels for teenagers and two for adults: *The Binding* and *The Betrayals*. *The Binding* was a *Sunday Times* bestseller, shortlisted for various awards including the Waterstones Book of the Year, and was the number one bestselling debut fiction hardback of 2019.

Kiran Millwood Hargrave is a poet, playwright, and the author of several award-winning books for children and young adults. Her debut novel for adults, *The Mercies*, was a *Sunday Times* bestseller and won a Betty Trask Award. Kiran lives in Oxford with her husband, the artist Tom de Freston, and their rescue cats, Luna and Marly.

Natasha Pulley is the *Sunday Times* bestselling author of four novels: *The Watchmaker of Filigree Steet*, *The Bedlam Stacks*,

The Lost Future of Pepperharrow and *The Kingdoms*. Her first novel won a Betty Trask Award and was an international bestseller. She lives in Bristol and teaches Creative Writing.

Jess Kidd was brought up in London as part of a large family from County Mayo, and is the author of three award-winning novels: *Himself*, *The Hoarder* and *Things in Jars*. In 2016 Jess won the Costa Short Story Award and published her first book for children, *Everyday Magic*, in 2021. Her fourth novel launches in 2022.

Laura Purcell is a former bookseller and the bestselling author of four award-winning Gothic novels. Her debut, *The Silent Companions*, was a Zoe Ball and Radio 2 Book Club pick and won the WHSmith Thumping Good Read Award. Laura lives in Colchester with her husband and pet guinea pigs.

Andrew Michael Hurley is the award-winning author of three novels: *The Loney*, *Devil's Day* and *Starve Acre*. *The Loney* won the Costa First Novel Award, Book of the Year at the 2016 British Book Awards and was hailed a modern classic by the *Sunday Telegraph*. Andrew lives and writes in Lancashire.

Imogen Hermes Gowar is the author of the *Sunday Times* bestselling *The Mermaid and Mrs Hancock*, which won a Betty Trask Award and was shortlisted for The Women's Prize and

the MsLexia First Novel Prize, amongst numerous other awards. Imogen lives and writes in Bristol.

Elizabeth Macneal is the author of two *Sunday Times* bestselling novels: *The Doll Factory*, which won the 2018 Caledonia Novel and has been translated into twenty-nine languages, and *Circus of Wonders*. Elizabeth is also a potter and lives in London with her family.